The Paul Bowles Reader

The Paul Bowles Reader

Selected and with an introduction by Peter Owen

PETER OWEN PUBLISHERS • LONDON

PETER OWEN PUBLISHERS
73 Kenway Road, London SW5 0RE

This collection first published in Great Britain 2000

ISBN 0 7206 1091 5

A catalogue record for this book is available from the British Library.

Printed and bound in Great Britain by MPG Books Ltd, Bodmin, Cornwall

Contents

Introducing Paul Bowles

by Peter Owen

PAUL BOWLES wrote his first novel, *The Sheltering Sky*, in 1949, and since its publication he has always had something of an 'underground' reputation. The book was an immediate bestseller on its US publication and has continued to be read and to be kept in print for the past fifty years. It was finally established as one of the great novels of the century when it was made into a film by Bernardo Bertolucci in 1990.

I, like many others, have always felt that Paul should have received the Nobel prize, but his choice of subject matter – violence, drug addiction, bisexuality – and his setting his stories outside Europe and North America ruled him out: the judges in Stockholm tend to vote for mainstream work and American writers are expected to depict 'the American experience'.

Paul spent most of his life in Morocco, but he travelled widely in Latin America, Sri Lanka, Thailand and throughout North Africa. An only child, he was born in 1910 into a middle-class New England family. His father – whom he did not get on with – was a dentist whose musical ambitions had been thwarted by his family, and his mother – whom he did like – was a former school teacher; his maternal grandfather owned a department store. In 1931 he abandoned his university education to study music with Aaron Copland in Paris. His parents did not wish him to leave, but he managed to raise the money for his passage. He told me that he did not borrow it, he never borrowed money. He was slim, fair-haired with blue eyes and of middle height. Once in Paris he was befriended by Gertrude Stein and met many writers, musicians and painters in the thriving expatriate community of the inter-war years.

Paul had excellent manners, integrity and considerable common sense; he was always impeccably dressed and had an almost pathological fear of dirt. Although he lived in Tangier for many years he remained an American abroad, maintaining a foreigner's mistrust of local hygiene and customs.

I have assembled this selection, with the assistance of Peter White, in order to make this great writer known to a new readership. It is not easy to extract from novels, and this is the reason we have chosen whole chapters that stand on their own. Everything Paul wrote was art. He once said to me, 'Writing is not difficult but finding subjects is.' His output was small over fifty years: *Let It Come Down* followed *The Sheltering Sky* and was first published in 1952; *The Spider's House* appeared in 1955; and his last major novel, *Up Above the World* – inspired by his visits to Latin America and the only one of the novels not set in North Africa – came out in 1966. A novella, *Too Far From Home*, appeared in 1991, but I have not included extracts from this, as it is short and can easily be read in its entirety.

After my last visit to see Paul in Morocco in 1998 I returned to *The Sheltering Sky* for the first time in many years and still found it riveting, discovering nuances I had previously missed. It is the test of a great writer that one can return to his or her books with the same amount of pleasure as when first reading them. Gore Vidal, who regards Paul as one of the great short-story writers of our time, wrote when he reread his favourite stories, 'Bowles' art is still as lovely as ever.'

The short stories in this volume are extracted from several volumes which my company has published: *Midnight Mass*,

Call at Corazón, *Points in Time*, *A Thousand Days for Mokhtar* and *Pages from Cold Point*. Some of these stories had appeared elsewhere before; others were published for the first time in these collections.

In 2000 Penguin Books published an anthology of Paul's stories, and I have refrained from duplicating their selection. This means that I have not included the story 'Pages from Cold Point', regarded by many as a masterpiece. Set in the West Indies, it is the story of a father who is seduced by his degenerate son. I asked Paul whether it was based on real people; he said it was not but *was* inspired by a visit to Jamaica. His stories were often sparked by people or places, but mostly they are the product of his imagination, art and, as he put it, 'the unconscious'.

I have included two pieces from *Their Heads Are Green* (1963), which has become a classic of travel writing. This was the first of Paul's books I published and which I acquired when I first met Paul in the early 1960s.

My wife and I were on a holiday in Morocco. Someone had reminded me that Paul lived in Tangier, which we were to visit. I telephoned and the phone was answered by an American voice which turned out to be that of Jane, Paul's wife. I explained to her that I was a visiting publisher and a great fan. He was out, but I was invited to telephone later. We met and at the end of my visit he gave me a bundle of manuscript pages and said, 'These are some travel pieces I have written. You might look at them and see if you like them enough to want to publish them.' This was typical of Paul's modesty.

I have taken the first chapter from Paul's autobiography *Without Stopping*. It is an account of his New England childhood, and in it his family is vividly brought to life.

Paul was a considerable linguist, and he translated a number of writers from various languages, including the Guatemalan

Rodrigo Rey Rosa, Moroccans Mohammed Mrabet (from the Moghrebi) and Mohamed Choukri (from the Arabic) and the Swiss-born Isabelle Eberhardt from the French. He told me he did this as an exercise to keep his hand in when he was not doing creative work. He said that he always wrote something every day, whether it was letters, journals or translations.

My first meeting with Jane, at the same time as I first met Paul, was significant. My initial impression was that she was not particularly friendly, but I later learned that she had recently been very ill and that she was protective of Paul's privacy. She was a major writer herself, and her novel *Two Serious Ladies*, which she started to write at the age of twenty-one in the late 1930s, had been published in 1943. On a later visit to Tangier Paul suggested that I publish it, as it had never appeared outside the USA. I did not then know the book, but, after much difficulty, managed to borrow a copy as the Bowleses no longer possessed one – in the 1960s it was very hard to track down. I published it to great critical acclaim in 1965. A year later I published her book of stories, *Plain Pleasures*, since when I have handled her overseas rights, selling editions of her books throughout the world. I got to know Jane well, and she became a good friend. She was a warm woman but suffered a recurring mental illness and increasingly bad health. She died in 1973. I once asked Paul if Jane would have been a writer if she had not married him in 1938. He said, 'It is the other way. Jane was first; I started writing afterwards. My first vocation was music.'

I met Paul often over the years, and he was always the same civilized and kind person. He continued to live in Tangier after Jane's death, from which he never really recovered. They had had two separate apartments, and he retained one of them. He smoked *kif* every night and did not rise until after midday. After Jane died, the telephone, which had been in her apartment, was disconnected. This made it difficult to contact him, but it also protected him to some extent from an invasion of fans. However, he never turned anyone away if they arrived on his doorstep. He was always courteous, offering his visitors tea. Paul drank very little alcohol – an occasional Dubonnet or a glass of wine.

His strict and isolated childhood made him reserved and self-sufficient, and this was sometimes mistaken for coldness or aloofness. He was a gentleman and among the most modest writers I have ever met. Some ten years ago I asked him if he thought his work would be read fifty years on. He replied, 'No, of course not. Why should anyone want to read me? Books are through and won't be read then.' I believe he underestimated his art and that there will always be people who will want to read his books. I asked him if he regarded himself a survivor of the old world or a bridge to the future. He replied that he saw himself as a survivor of the old.

Paul was reticent about his personal life and sexuality. He told me once that if you look 'it's all in the books'.

He was never malicious, and in his autobiography *Without Stopping* he never stooped to make use of salacious material about the many famous people he had known.

Paul might have regarded himself as traditionalist, but, like many major writers, he was ahead of his time and has wielded considerable influence on the authors who came after him.

Paul Bowles died in November 1999, two weeks before his eighty-ninth birthday.

PART I

NOVELS

The Sheltering Sky

The Sheltering Sky *(1949) has been acclaimed as one of the great novels of the twentieth century and was turned into a major film by Bernardo Bertolucci. Port and Kit travel into a remote part of the Sahara region of southern Morocco by bus, where they meet a variety of characters, both European and Moroccan. Port becomes ill with fever and dies, and Kit is befriended in the desert by a Moroccan who takes her into his harem with devastating consequences. Chapters 2–4 are reproduced here.*

2

ON the terrace of the Café d'Eckmühl-Noiseux a few Arabs sat drinking mineral water; only their fezzes of varying shades of red distinguished them from the rest of the population of the port. Their European clothes were worn and grey; it would have been hard to tell what the cut of any garment had been originally. The nearly naked shoe-shine boys squatted on their boxes looking down at the pavement, without the energy to wave away the flies that crawled over their faces. Inside the café the air was cooler but without movement, and it smelled of stale wine and urine.

At the table in the darkest corner sat three Americans: two young men and a girl. They conversed quietly, and in the manner of people who have all the time in the world for everything. One of the men, the thin one with a slightly wry, distraught face, was folding up some large multicoloured maps he had had spread out on the table a moment ago. His wife watched the meticulous movements he made with amusement and exasperation; maps bored her, and he was always consulting them. Even during the short periods when their lives were stationary, which had been few enough since their marriage, twelve years ago, he had only to see a map to begin studying it passionately, and then, often as not, he would begin to plan some new, impossible trip which sometimes eventually became a reality. He did not think of himself as a tourist; he was a traveller. The difference is partly one of time, he would explain. Whereas the tourist generally hurries back home at the end of a few weeks or months, the traveller, belonging no more to one place than to the next, moves slowly, over periods of years, from one part of the earth to another. Indeed, he would have found it difficult to tell, among the many places he had lived, precisely where it was he had felt most at home. Before the war it had been Europe and the Near East, during the war the West Indies and South America. And she had accompanied him without reiterating her complaints too often or too bitterly.

At this point they had just crossed the Atlantic for the first time since 1939, with a great deal of luggage and the intention of keeping as far as possible from the places which had been touched by the war. For, as he claimed, another important difference between tourist and traveller is that the former accepts his own civilization without question; not so the traveller, who compares it with the others, and rejects those elements he finds not to his liking. And the war was one facet of the mechanized age he wanted to forget.

In New York they had found that North Africa was one of the few places they could get boat passage to. From his earlier visits, made during his student days in Paris and Madrid, it seemed a likely place to spend a year or so; in any case it was near Spain and Italy, and they could always cross over if it failed to work out. Their little freighter had spewed them out from its comfortable maw the day before, on to the hot docks, sweating and scowling with anxiety, where for a long time no one had paid them the slightest attention. As he stood there in the burning sun, he had been tempted to go back aboard and see about taking passage for the continuing voyage to Istanbul, but it would have been difficult to do without losing face, since it was he who had cajoled them into coming to North Africa. So he had cast a matter-of-fact glance up and down the dock, made a few reasonably unflattering remarks about the place, and let it go at that, silently resolving to start inland as quickly as possible.

The other man at the table, when he was not talking, kept whistling aimless little tunes under his breath. He was a few years younger, of sturdier build, and astonishingly handsome, as the girl often told him, in his late Paramount way. Usually there was very little expression of any sort to be found on his smooth face, but the features were formed in such a manner that in repose they suggested a general bland contentment.

They stared out into the street's dusty afternoon glare.

'The war has certainly left its mark here.' Small, with blonde hair and an olive complexion, she was saved from prettiness by the intensity of her gaze. Once one had seen her eyes, the rest of the face grew vague, and when one tried to recall her image afterwards, only the piercing, questioning violence of the wide eyes remained.

'Well, naturally. There were troops passing through for a year or more.'

'It seems as though there might be some place in the world they could have left alone,' said the girl. This was to please her husband, because she regretted having felt annoyed with him about the maps a moment ago. Recognizing the gesture, but not understanding why she was making it, he paid no attention to it.

The other man laughed patronizingly, and he joined in.

'For your special benefit, I suppose?' said her husband.

'For us. You know you hate the whole thing as much as I do.'

'What whole thing?' he demanded defensively. 'If you mean this colourless mesa here that calls itself a town, yes. But I'd still a damned sight rather be here than back in the United States.'

She hastened to agree. 'Oh, of course. But I didn't mean this place or any other particular place. I meant the whole horrible thing that happens after every war, everywhere.'

'Come, Kit,' said the other man. 'You don't remember any other war.'

She paid him no attention. 'The people of each country get more like the people of every other country. They have no character, no beauty, no ideals, no culture – nothing, nothing.'

Her husband reached over and patted her hand. 'You're right. You're right,' he said smiling. 'Everything's getting grey, and it'll be greyer. But some places'll withstand the malady longer than you think. You'll see, in the Sahara here . . .'

Across the street a radio was sending forth the hysterical screams of a coloratura soprano. Kit shivered. 'Let's hurry up and get there,' she said. 'Maybe we could escape that.'

They listened fascinated as the aria, drawing to a close, made the orthodox preparations for the inevitable high final note.

Presently Kit said, 'Now that that's over, I've got to have another bottle of Oulmès.'

'My God, more of that gas? You'll take off.'

'I know, Tunner,' she said, 'but I can't get my mind off water. It doesn't matter what I look at, it makes me thirsty. For once I feel as if I could get on the wagon and stay there. I can't drink in the heat.'

'Another Pernod?' said Tunner to Port.

Kit frowned. 'If it were real Pernod –'

'It's not bad,' said Tunner, as the waiter set a bottle of mineral water on the table.

'*Ce n'est pas du vrai Pernod?*'

'*Si, si, c'est du Pernod,*' said the waiter.

'Let's have another set-up,' Port said. He stared at his glass dully. No one spoke as the waiter moved away. The soprano began another aria.

'She's off!' cried Tunner. The din of a tramcar and its bell passing across the terrace outside drowned the music for a moment. Beneath the awning they had a glimpse of the open vehicle in the sunshine as it rocked past. It was crowded with people in tattered clothes.

Port said, 'I had a strange dream yesterday. I've been trying to remember it, and just this minute I did.'

'No!' cried Kit with force. 'Dreams are so dull! Please!'

'You don't want to hear it!' he laughed. 'But I'm going to tell it to you anyway.' This last was said with a certain ferocity which on the surface appeared feigned, but as Kit looked at him she felt that on the contrary he actually was dissimulating the violence he felt. She did not say the withering things that were on the tip of her tongue.

'I'll be quick about it,' he smiled. 'I know you're doing me a favour by listening, but I can't remember it just thinking about it. It was daytime and I was on a train that kept putting on speed. I thought to myself: We're going to plough into a big bed with the sheets all in mountains.'

Tunner said archly, 'Consult Madame La Hiff's *Gypsy Dream Dictionary.*'

'Shut up. And I was thinking that if I wanted to, I could live over again – start at the beginning and come right on up to the present, having exactly the same life, down to the smallest detail.'

Kit closed her eyes unhappily.

'What's the matter?' he demanded.

'I think it's extremely thoughtless and egotistical of you to insist this way when you know how boring it is for us.'

'But I'm enjoying it so much.' He beamed. 'And I'll bet Tunner wants to hear it, anyway. Don't you?'

Tunner smiled. 'Dreams are my cup of tea. I know my La Hiff by heart.'

Kit opened one eye and looked at him. The drinks arrived. 'So I said to myself, "No! No!" I couldn't face the idea of all those God-awful fears and pains again, *in detail.* And then for no reason I looked out the window at the trees and heard myself say, "Yes!" Because I knew I'd be willing to go through the whole thing again just to smell the spring the way it used to smell when I was a kid. But then I realized it was too late, because while I'd been thinking "No!" I'd reached up and snapped off my incisors as if they'd been made of plaster. The train had stopped and I held my teeth in my hand, and I started to sob. You know those terrible dream sobs that shake you like an earthquake?'

Clumsily Kit rose from the table and walked to a door marked *Dames.* She was crying.

'Let her go,' said Port to Tunner, whose face showed concern. 'She's worn out. The heat gets her down.'

3

HE sat up in bed reading, wearing only a pair of shorts. The door between their two rooms was open, and so were the windows. Over the town and harbour a lighthouse played its beam in a wide, slow circle, and above the desultory traffic an insistent electric bell shrilled without respite.

'Is that the movie next door?' called Kit.

'Must be,' he said absently, still reading.

'I wonder what they're showing.'

'What?' He laid down his book. 'Don't tell me you're interested in going!'

'No.' She sounded doubtful. 'I just wondered.'

'I'll tell you what it is. It's a film in Arabic called *Fiancée for Rent*. That's what it says under the title.'

'It's unbelievable.'

'I know.'

She wandered into the room, thoughtfully smoking a cigarette, and walked about in a circle for a minute or so. He looked up.

'What is it?' he asked.

'Nothing.' She paused. 'I'm just a little upset. I don't think you should have told that dream in front of Tunner.'

He did not dare say, 'Is that why you cried?' But he said, 'In *front* of him! I told it *to* him, as much as to you. What's a dream? Good God, don't take everything so seriously! And why shouldn't he hear it? What's wrong with Tunner? We've known him for five years.'

'He's such a gossip. You know that. I don't trust him. He always makes a good story.'

'But who's he going to gossip with here?' said Port, exasperated.

Kit in turn was annoyed.

'Oh, not here!' she snapped. 'You seem to forget we'll be back in New York some day.'

'I know, I know. It's hard to believe, but I suppose we will. All right. What's so awful if he remembers every detail and tells it to everybody we know?'

'It's such a humiliating dream. Can't you see?'

'Oh, crap!'

There was a silence.

'Humiliating to whom? You or me?'

She did not answer. He pursued, 'What do you mean, you don't trust Tunner? In what way?'

'Oh, I trust him, I suppose. But I've never felt completely at ease with him. I've never felt he was a close friend.'

'That's nice, now that we're here with him!'

'Oh, it's all right. I like him very much. Don't misunderstand.'

'But you must mean something.'

'Of course I mean something. But it's not important.'

She went back into her own room. He remained a moment, looking at the ceiling, a puzzled expression on his face.

He started to read again, and stopped.

'Sure you don't want to see *Fiancée for Rent*?'

'I certainly don't.'

He closed his book. 'I think I'll take a walk for about a half an hour.'

He rose, put on a sports shirt and a pair of seersucker trousers, and combed his hair. In her room, she was sitting by the open window, filing her nails. He bent over her and kissed the nape of her neck, where the silky blonde hair climbed upward in wavy furrows.

'That's wonderful stuff you have on. Did you get it here?' He sniffed noisily, with appreciation. Then his voice changed when he said, 'But what did you mean about Tunner?'

'Oh, Port! For God's sake, stop *talking* about it!'

'All right, baby,' he said submissively, kissing her shoulder. And with an inflection of mock innocence, 'Can't I even *think* about it?'

She said nothing until he got to the door. Then she raised her head, and there was pique in her voice, 'After all, it's much more your business than it is mine.'

'See you soon,' he said.

4

He walked through the streets, unthinkingly seeking the darker ones, glad to be alone and to feel the night air against his face. The streets were crowded. People pushed against him as they passed, stared from doorways and windows, made comments openly to each other about him – whether with sympathy or not he was unable to tell from their faces – and they sometimes ceased to walk merely in order to watch him.

How friendly are they? Their faces are masks. They all look a thousand years old. What little energy they have is only the blind, mass desire to live, since no one of them eats enough to give him his own personal force. But what do they think of me? Probably nothing. Would one of them help me if I were to have an accident? Or would I lie here in the street until the police found me? What motive could any one of them *have* for helping me? They have no religion left. Are they Moslems or Christians? They don't know. They know money, and when they get it all they want is to eat. But what's wrong with that? Why do I feel this way about them? Guilt at being well fed and healthy among them? But suffering is equally divided among all men; each has the same amount to undergo . . . Emotionally he felt that this last idea was untrue, but at the moment it was a necessary belief: it is not always easy to support the stares of hungry people. Thinking that way he could walk on through the streets. It was as if either he or the people did not exist. Both suppositions were possible. The Spanish maid at the hotel had said to him that noon, '*La vida es pena.*' 'Of course,' he had replied, feeling false even as he spoke, asking himself if any American can truthfully accept a definition of life which makes it synonymous with suffering. But at the moment he had approved her sentiment because she was old, withered, so clearly of the people. For years it had been one of his superstitions that reality and true perception were to be found in the conversation of the labouring classes. Even though now he saw clearly that their formulas of thought and speech are as strict and as patterned, and thus as far removed from any profound expression of truth as those of any other class, often he found himself still in the act of waiting, with the unreasoning belief that gems of wisdom might yet issue from their mouths. As he walked along, his nervousness was made manifest to him by the sudden consciousness that he was repeatedly tracing rapid figure-eights with his right index finger. He sighed and made himself stop doing it.

His spirits rose a bit as he came out on to a square that was relatively brightly lighted. The cafés on all four sides of the little plaza had put tables and chairs not only across the sidewalks, but in the street as well, so that it would have been impossible for a vehicle to pass through without upsetting them. In the centre of the square was a tiny park adorned by four plane trees that had been trimmed to look like open parasols. Underneath the trees there were at least a dozen dogs of various sizes, milling about in a close huddle, and all barking frantically. He made his way slowly across the square, trying to avoid the dogs. As he moved along cautiously under the trees he became aware that at each step he was crushing something beneath his feet. The ground was covered with large insects; their hard shells broke with little explosions that were quite audible to him even amidst the noise the dogs were making. He was aware that ordinarily he would have experienced a thrill of disgust on contact with such a phenomenon, but unreasonably tonight he felt instead a childish triumph. I'm in a bad way and so what? The few scattered people sitting at the tables were for the most part silent, but when they spoke, he heard all three of the town's tongues: Arabic, Spanish and French.

Slowly the street began to descend; this surprised him because he imagined that the entire town was built on the slope facing the harbour, and he had consciously chosen to walk inland rather than toward the waterfront. The odours in the air grew ever stronger. They were varied, but they all represented filth of one sort or another. This proximity with, as it were, a forbidden element served to elate him. He abandoned himself to the perverse pleasure he found in continuing mechanically to put one foot in front of the other, even though he was quite clearly aware of his fatigue. Suddenly I'll find myself turning around and going back, he thought. But not until then, because he would not make the decision to do it. The impulse to retrace his steps delayed itself from moment to moment. Finally he ceased being surprised: a faint vision began to haunt his mind. It was Kit, seated by the open window, filing her nails and looking out over the town. And as he found his fancy returning more often, as the minutes went by, to that scene, unconsciously he felt himself the protagonist, Kit the spectator. The validity of his existence at that moment was predicated on the assumption that she had not moved, but was still sitting there. It was as if she could still see him from the window, tiny and far away as he was, walking rhythmically uphill and down, through light and shadow; it was as if only she knew when he would turn around and walk the other way.

The streetlights were very far apart now, and the streets had left off being paved. Still there were children in the gutters, playing with the garbage and screeching. A small stone suddenly hit him in the back. He wheeled about, but it was too dark to see where it had come from. A few seconds later another stone, coming from in front of him, landed against his knee. In the dim light, he saw a group of small children scattering before him. More stones came from the other direction, this time without hitting him. When he got beyond, to a point where there was a light, he stopped and tried to watch the two groups in battle, but they all ran off into the dark, and so he started up again, his gait as mechanical and rhythmical as before. A wind that was dry and warm, coming up the street out of the blackness before him, met him head on. He sniffed at the fragments of mystery in it, and again he felt an unaccustomed exaltation.

Even though the street became constantly less urban, it seemed reluctant to give up; huts continued to line it on both sides. Beyond a certain point there were no more lights, and the dwellings themselves lay in darkness. The wind, straight from the south, blew across the barren mountains that were invisible ahead of him, over the vast flat *sebkha* to the edges of the town, raising curtains of dust that climbed to the crest of the hill and lost themselves in the air above the harbour. He stood still. The last possible suburb had been strung on the street's thread. Beyond the final hut the garbage and rubble floor of the road sloped abruptly downward in three directions. In the dimness below were shallow, crooked, canyon-like formations. Port raised his eyes to the sky: the powdery course of the Milky Way was like a giant rift across the heavens that let the faint white light through. In the distance he heard a motor cycle. When its sound was finally gone, there was nothing to hear but an occasional cockcrow, like the highest part of a repeated melody whose other notes were inaudible.

He started down the bank to the right, sliding among the fish skeletons and dust. Once below, he felt out a rock that seemed clean and sat down on it. The stench was overpowering. He lit a match, saw the ground thick with chicken feathers and decayed melon rinds. As he rose to his feet he heard steps above him at the end of the street. A figure stood at the top of the embankment. It did not speak, yet Port was certain that it had seen him, had followed him, and knew he was sitting down there. It lit a cigarette, and for a moment he saw an Arab wearing a *chechia* on his head. The match, thrown into the air, made a fading parabola, the face disappeared, and only the red point of the cigarette remained. The cock crowed several times. Finally the man cried out.

'*Qu'est-ce ti cherches là?*'

Here's where the trouble begins, thought Port. He did not move.

The Arab waited a bit. He walked to the very edge of the slope. A dislodged tin can rolled noisily down toward the rock where Port sat.

'*Hé! M'sieu! Qu'est-ce ti vo?*'

He decided to answer. His French was good.

'Who? Me? Nothing.'

The Arab bounded down the bank and stood in front of him. With the characteristic impatient, almost indignant gestures he pursued his inquisition. What are you doing here all alone? Where do you come from? What do you want here? Are you looking for something? To which Port answered wearily: Nothing. That way. Nothing. No.

For a moment the Arab was silent, trying to decide what direction to give the dialogue. He drew violently on his cigarette several times until it glowed very bright, then he flicked it away and exhaled the smoke.

'Do you want to take a walk?' he said.

'What? A walk? Where?'

'Out there.' His arm waved toward the mountains.

'What's out there?'

'Nothing.'

There was another silence between them.

'I'll pay you a drink,' said the Arab. And immediately on that, 'What's your name?'

'Jean,' said Port.

The Arab repeated the name twice, as if considering its merits. 'Me,' tapping his chest, 'Smaïl. So, do we go and drink?'

'No.'

'Why not?'

'I don't feel like it.'

'You don't feel like it. What do you feel like doing?'

'Nothing.'

All at once the conversation began again from the beginning. Only the now truly outraged inflection of the Arab's voice marked any difference: '*Qu'est-ce ti fi là? Qu'est-ce ti cherches?*' Port rose and started to climb up the slope, but it was difficult going. He kept sliding back down. At once the Arab was beside him, tugging at his arm. 'Where are you going, Jean?' Without answering Port made a great effort and gained the top. '*Au revoir,*' he called, walking quickly up the middle of the street. He heard a desperate scrambling behind him; a moment later the man was at his side.

'You didn't wait for me,' he said in an aggrieved tone.

'No. I said goodbye.'

'I'll go with you.'

Port did not answer. They walked a good distance in silence. When they came to the first streetlight, the Arab reached into his pocket and pulled out a worn wallet. Port glanced at it and continued to walk.

'Look!' cried the Arab, waving it in his face. Port did not look.

'What is it?' he said flatly.

'I was in the Fifth Battalion of Sharpshooters. Look at the paper! Look! You'll see!'

Port walked faster. Soon there began to be people in the street. No one stared at them. One would have said that the presence of the Arab beside him made him invisible. But now he was no longer sure of the way. It would never do to let this be seen. He continued to walk straight ahead as if there were no doubt in his mind. 'Over the crest of the hill and down,' he said to himself, 'and I can't miss it.'

Everything looked unfamiliar: the houses, the streets, the cafés, even the formation of the town with regard to the hill. Instead of finding a summit from which to begin the downward walk, he discovered that here the streets all led perceptibly upward, no matter which way he turned; to descend he would have had to go back. The Arab walked solemnly along with him, now beside him, now slipping behind when there was not enough room to walk two abreast. He no longer made attempts at conversation; Port noticed with relish that he was a little out of breath.

I can keep this up all night if I have to, he thought, but how the hell will I get to the hotel?

All at once they were in a street which was no more than a passageway. Above their heads the opposite walls jutted out to within a few inches of each other. For an instant Port hesitated: this was not the kind of street he wanted to walk in, and besides, it so obviously did not lead to the hotel. In that short moment the Arab took charge. He said, 'You don't know this street? It's called Rue de la Mer Rouge. You know it? Come on. There are *cafés arabes* up this way. Just a little way. Come on.'

Port considered. He wanted at all costs to keep up the pretence of being familiar with the town.

'*Je ne sais pas si je veux y aller ce soir,*' he reflected, aloud.

The Arab began to pull Port's sleeve in his excitement. '*Si, si!*' he cried. '*Viens!* I'll pay you a drink.'

'I don't drink. It's very late.'

Two cats nearby screamed at each other. The Arab made a hissing noise and stamped his feet; they ran off in opposite directions.

'We'll have tea, then,' he pursued.

Port sighed. '*Bien,*' he said.

The café had a complicated entrance. They went through a low arched door, down a dim hall into a small garden. The air reeked of lilies, and it was also tinged with the sour smell of drains. In the dark they crossed the garden and climbed a long flight of stone steps. The staccato sound of a hand drum came from above, tapping indolent patterns above a sea of voices.

'Do we sit outside or in?' the Arab asked.

'Outside,' said Port. He sniffed the invigorating smell of hashish smoke, and unconsciously smoothed his hair as they arrived at the top of the stairs. The Arab noticed even that small gesture. 'No ladies here, you know.'

'Oh, I know.'

Through a doorway he caught a glimpse of the long succession of tiny, brightly lit rooms, and the men seated everywhere on the red matting that covered the floors. They all wore either white turbans or red *chechias* on their heads, a detail which lent the scene such a strong aspect of homogeneity that Port exclaimed, 'Ah!' as they passed by the door. When they were on the terrace in the starlight, with an oud being plucked idly in the dark nearby, he said to his companion, 'But I didn't know there was anything like this left in this city.' The Arab did not understand. 'Like this?' he echoed. 'How?'

'With nothing but Arabs. Like the inside there. I thought all the cafés were like the ones in the street, all mixed up: Jews, French, Spanish, Arabs together. I thought the war had changed everything.'

The Arab laughed. 'The war was bad. A lot of people died. There was nothing to eat. That's all. How would that change the cafés? Oh no, my friend. It's the same as always.' A moment later he said, 'So you haven't been here since the war! But you were here before the war?'

'Yes,' said Port. This was true; he had once spent an afternoon in the town when his boat had made a brief call there.

The tea arrived; they chatted and drank it. Slowly the image of Kit sitting in the window began to take shape again in Port's mind. At first, when he became conscious of it, he felt a pang of guilt. Then his fantasy took a hand, and he saw her face, tight-lipped with fury as she undressed and flung her flimsy pieces of clothing across the furniture. By now she had surely given up waiting and gone to bed. He shrugged his shoulders and grew pensive, rinsing what was left of his tea around and around in the bottom of the glass, and following with his eyes the circular motion he was making.

'You're sad,' said Smaïl.

'No, no.' He looked up and smiled wistfully, then resumed watching the glass.

'You live only a short time. *Il faut rigoler.*'

Port was impatient; he was not in the mood for café philosophizing.

'Yes, I know,' he said shortly, and he sighed. Smaïl pinched his arm. His eyes were shining.

'When we leave here, I'll take you to see a friend of mine.'

'I don't want to meet him,' said Port, adding, 'Thank you anyway.'

'Ah, you're really sad,' laughed Smaïl. 'It's a girl. Beautiful as the moon.'

Port's heart missed a beat. 'A girl,' he repeated automatically, without taking his eyes from the glass. He was perturbed to witness his own interior excitement. He looked at Smaïl.

'A girl?' he said. 'You mean a whore.'

Smaïl was mildly indignant. 'A whore? Ah, my friend, you don't know me. I wouldn't introduce you to that. *C'est de la saloperie, ça!* This is a friend of mine, very elegant, very nice. When you meet her, you'll see.'

The musician stopped playing the oud. Inside the café they were calling out numbers for the lotto game: '*Ouahad aou tletine! Arbaine!*'

Port said, 'How old is she?'

Smaïl hesitated. 'About sixteen. Sixteen or seventeen.'

'Or twenty or twenty-five,' suggested Port, with a leer.

Again Smaïl was indignant. 'What do you mean, twenty-five? I tell you she's sixteen or seventeen. You don't believe me? Listen. You meet her. If you don't like her, you just pay for the tea and we'll go out again. Is that all right?'

'And if I do like her?'

'Well, you'll do whatever you want.'

'But I'll pay her?'

'But of course you'll pay her.'

Port laughed. 'And you say she's not a whore.'

Smaïl leaned over the table towards him and said with a great show of patience, 'Listen, Jean. She's a dancer. She only arrived from her bled in the desert a few weeks ago. How can she be a whore if she's not registered and doesn't live in the quartier? Eh? Tell me! You pay her because you take up her time. She dances in the quartier, but she has no room, no bed there. She's not a whore. So now, shall we go?'

Port thought a long time, looked up at the sky, down into the garden, and all around the terrace before answering, 'Yes. Let's go. Now.'

Let It Come Down

This extract is the opening chapter of the novel Let It Come Down *(1952). Nelson Dyar, a man without aims or values, comes to North Africa to seek a sense of purpose, having given up his job as a bank clerk in New York. Drawn into the whirl of the Tangier expatriate community, Dyar finds himself swept along on a current of financial and sexual intrigue.*

A smuggling operation offers a chance of escape. Dyar flees to a lonely hut in the mountains of Spanish Morocco, where, his paranoia fuelled by drugs and isolation, he commits an act of horrifying violence.

It was night by the time the little ferry drew up alongside the dock. As Dyar went down the gangplank a sudden gust of wind threw warm raindrops in his face. The other passengers were few and poorly dressed; they carried their things in cheap cardboard valises and paper bags. He watched them standing resignedly in front of the customs house waiting for the door to be opened. A half-dozen disreputable Arabs had already caught sight of him from the other side of the fence and were shouting at him. 'Hotel Metropole, mister!' 'Hey, Johnny, come on!' 'You want hotel?' 'Grand Hotel, hey!' It was as if he had held up his American passport for them to see. He paid no attention. The rain came down in earnest for a minute or so. By the time the official had opened the door he was uncomfortably wet.

The room inside was lighted by three oil lamps placed along the counter, one to an inspector. They saved Dyar until last, and all three of them went through his effects very carefully, without a gleam of friendliness or humour. When he had repacked his grips so they would close they marked them with lavender chalk and reluctantly let him pass. He had to wait in line at the window over which was printed *Policia.* While he was standing there a tall man in a visored cap caught his attention, calling 'Taxi!' The man was decently dressed, and so he signalled yes with his head. Straightway the man in the cap was embroiled in a struggle with the others as he stepped to take the luggage. Dyar was the only prey that evening. He turned his head away disgustedly as the shouting figures followed the taxi-driver out the door. He felt a little sick, anyway.

And in the taxi, as the rain pelted the windshield and the squeaking wipers rubbed painfully back and forth on the glass, he went on feeling sick. He was really here now; there was no turning back. Of course there never had been any question of turning back. When he had written he would take the job and had bought his passage from New York, he had known his decision was irrevocable. A man does not change his mind about such things when he has less than five hundred dollars left. But now that he was here, straining to see the darkness beyond the wet panes, he felt for the first time the despair and loneliness he thought he had left behind. He lit a cigarette and passed the pack to the driver.

He decided to let the driver determine for him where he would stay. The man was an Arab and understood very little English, but he did know the words cheap and clean. They passed from the breakwater on to the mainland, stopped at a gate where two police inspectors stuck their heads in through the front windows, and then they drove slowly for a while along a street where there were a few dim lights. When they arrived at the hotel the driver did not offer to help him with his luggage, nor was there any porter in sight. Dyar looked again at the entrance: the façade was that of a large modern hotel, but within the main door he saw a single candle burning.

He got down and began pulling out his bags. Then he glanced questioningly at the driver who was watching him empty the cab of the valises; the man was impatient to be off.

When he had set all his belongings on the sidewalk and paid the driver, he pushed the hotel door open and saw a young man with smooth black hair and a dapper moustache sitting at the small reception desk. The candle provided the only light. He asked if this were the Hotel de la Playa, and he did not know whether he was glad or sorry to hear that it was. Getting his bags into the lobby by himself took a little while. Then, led by a small boy who carried a candle, he climbed the stairs to his room: the elevator was not working because there was no power.

They climbed three flights. The hotel was like an enormous concrete resonating chamber; the sound of each footstep, magnified, echoed in all directions. The building had the kind of intense and pure shabbiness attained only by cheap new constructions. Great cracks had already appeared in the walls, bits of the decorative plaster mouldings around the doorways had been chipped off, and here and there a floor tile was missing.

When they reached the room the boy went in first and touched a match to a new candle that had been stuck in the top of an empty Cointreau bottle. The shadows shot up along the walls. Dyar sniffed the close air with displeasure. The odour in the room suggested a mixture of wet plaster and unwashed feet.

'Phew! It stinks in here,' he said. He looked suspiciously at the bed, turned the stained blue spread back to see the sheets.

Opposite the door there was one large window which the boy hastened to fling open. A blast of wind rushed in out of the darkness. There was the faint sound of surf. The boy said something in Spanish, and Dyar supposed he was telling him it was a good room because it gave on the beach. He did not much care which way the room faced: he had not come here on a vacation. What he wanted at the moment was a bath. The boy shut the window and hurried downstairs to get the luggage. In one corner, separated from the rest of the room by a grimy partition, was a shower with grey concrete walls and floor. He tried the tap marked *caliente* and was surprised to find the water fairly hot.

When the boy had brought the valises, piled them in the wrong places, received his tip, had difficulty in closing the door, and finally gone away leaving it ajar, Dyar moved from the window where he had been standing fingering the curtains, looking out into the blackness. He slammed the door shut, heard the key fall tinkling to the floor in the corridor. Then he threw himself on the bed and lay awhile staring at the ceiling. He must call Wilcox immediately, let him know he had arrived. He turned his head and tried to see if there was a telephone on the low night table by the bed, but the table lay in the shadow of the bed's footboard, and it was too dark there to tell.

This was the danger point, he felt. At this moment it was almost as though he did not exist. He had renounced all security in favour of what everyone had assured him, and what he himself suspected, was a wild-goose chase. The old thing was gone beyond recall, the new thing had not yet begun. To make it begin he had only to telephone Wilcox, yet he lay still. His friends had told him he was crazy, his family had remonstrated with him both indignantly and sadly, but for some reason about which he himself knew very little, he had shut his ears to them all. 'I'm fed up!' he would cry, a little hysterically. 'I've stood at that damned window in the bank for ten years now. Before the war, during the war, and after the war. I can't take it any longer, that's all!' And when the suggestion was made that a visit to a doctor might be indicated, he laughed scornfully, replied, 'There's nothing wrong with me that a change won't cure. Nobody's meant to be confined in a cage like that year after year. I'm just fed up, that's all.' 'Fine, fine,' said his father. 'Only what do you think you can do about it?' He had no answer to that. During the Depression, when he was twenty, he had been delighted to get a job in the Transit Department at the bank. All his friends had considered him extremely fortunate; it was only his father's friendship with one of the vice-presidents which had made it possible for him to be taken on at such a time. Just before the war he had been made a teller. In those days when change was in the air nothing seemed permanent, and although Dyar knew he had a heart murmur, he vaguely imagined that in one way or another it would be got around so that he would be given some useful wartime work. Anything would be a change and therefore welcome. But he had been flatly rejected; he had gone on standing in his cage. Then he had fallen prey to a demoralizing sensation of motionlessness. His own life was a dead weight, so heavy that he would never be able to move it from where it lay. He had grown accustomed to the feeling of intense hopelessness and depression which had settled upon him, all the while resenting it bitterly. It was not in his nature to be morose, and his family noticed it. 'Just do things as they come along,' his father would say. 'Take it easy. You'll find there'll be plenty to fill each day. Where does it get you to worry about the future? Let it take care of itself.' Continuing, he would issue the familiar warning about heart trouble. Dyar would smile wryly. He was quite willing to let each day take care of itself – the future was furthest from his thoughts. The present stood in its way; it was the minutes that were inimical. Each empty, overwhelming minute as it arrived pushed him a little further back from life. 'You don't get out enough,' his father objected. 'Give yourself a chance. Why, when I was your age I couldn't wait for the day to be finished so I could get out on the tennis court, or down to the old river fishing, or home to press my pants for a dance. You're unhealthy. Oh, I don't mean physically. That little heart business is nothing. If you live the way you should it ought never to give you any trouble. I mean your attitude. That's unhealthy. I think the whole generation's unhealthy. It's either one thing or the other. Overdrinking and passing out on the sidewalk, or else mooning around about life not being worth living. What the hell's the matter with all of you?' Dyar would smile and say times had changed. Times always change, his father would retort, but not human nature.

Dyar was not a reader; he did not even enjoy the movies. Entertainment somehow made the stationariness of existence more acute, not only when the amusement was over, but even during the course of it. After the war he made a certain effort to reconcile himself to his life. Occasionally he would go out with two or three of his friends, each one taking a girl. They would have cocktails at the apartment of one of the girls, go on to a Broadway movie, and eat afterward at some Chinese place in the neighbourhood where there was dancing. Then there was the long process of taking the girls home one by one, after which they usually went into a bar and drank fairly heavily. Sometimes, not very often, they would pick up something cheap in the bar or in the street, take her to Bill Healy's room, and lay her in turn. It was an accepted pattern; there seemed to be no other to suggest in its place. Dyar kept thinking: Any life would be better than this, but he could find no different possibility to consider. 'Once you accept the fact that life isn't *fun,* you'll be much happier,' his mother said to him. Although he lived with his parents, he never discussed with them the way he felt; it was they who, sensing his unhappiness, came to him and, in vaguely reproachful tones, tried to help him. He was polite with them but inwardly contemptuous. It was so clear that they could never understand the emptiness he felt, nor realize the degree to which he felt it. It was a progressive paralysis, it gained on him constantly, and it carried with it the fear that when it arrived at a certain point something terrible would happen.

He could hear the distant sound of waves breaking on the beach outside: a dull roll, a long silence, another roll. Someone came into the room over his, slammed the door, and began to move about busily from one side of the room to the other. It sounded like a woman, but a heavy one. The water was turned on and the wash-basin in his room bubbled as if in sympathy. He lit a cigarette, from time to time flicking the ashes on to the floor beside the bed. After a few minutes the woman – he was sure it was a woman – went out of the door, slammed it, and he heard her walk down the hall into another room and close that door. A toilet flushed. Then the footsteps returned to the room above.

I must call Wilcox, he thought. But he finished his cigarette slowly, making it last. He wondered why he felt so lazy about making the call. He had taken the great step, and he believed he had done right. All the way across on the ship to Gibraltar, he had told himself that it was the healthy thing to have done, that when he arrived he would be like another person, full of life, delivered from the sense of despair that had weighed on him for so long. And now he realized that he felt exactly the same. He tried to imagine how he would feel if, for instance, he had his whole life before him to spend as he pleased, without the necessity to earn his living. In that case he would not have to telephone Wilcox, would not be compelled to exchange one cage for another. Having made the first break, he would then make the second, and be completely free. He raised his head and looked slowly around the dim room. The rain was spattering the window. Soon he would have to go out.

There was no restaurant in the hotel, and it was surely a long way to town. He felt the top of the night table; there was no telephone. Then he got up, took the candle, and made a search of the room. He stepped out into the corridor, picked his key off the floor, locked his door and went downstairs thinking: I'd have him on the wire by now if there'd only been a phone by the bed.

The man was not at the desk. 'I've got to make a call,' he said to the boy who stood beside a potted palm smirking. 'It's very important. Telephone! Telephone!' he shouted, gesturing, as the other made no sign of understanding. The boy went to the desk, brought an old-fashioned telephone out from behind and set it on top. Dyar took the letter out of his pocket to look for the number of Wilcox's hotel. The boy tried to take the letter, but he copied the number on the back of the envelope and gave it to him. A fat man wearing a black raincoat came in and asked for his key. Then he stood glancing over a newspaper that lay spread out on the desk. As the boy made the call Dyar thought: If he's gone out to dinner I'll have to go through this all over again. The boy said something into the mouthpiece and handed Dyar the receiver.

'Hello?'

'Hotel Atlantide.'

'Mr Wilcox, please.' He pronounced the name very carefully. There was a silence. Oh, God! he thought, annoyed with himself that he should care one way or the other whether Wilcox was in. There was a click.

'Yes?'

It was Wilcox. For a second he did not know what to say. 'Hello?' he said.

'Hello. Yes?'

'Jack?'

'Yes. Who's this?'

'This is Nelson. Nelson Dyar.'

'Dyar! Well, for God's sake! So you got here after all. Where are you? Come on over. You know how to get here? Better take a cab. You'll get lost. Where are you staying?'

Dyar told him.

'Jesus! That –' Dyar had the impression he had been about to say: that dump. But he said, 'That's practically over the border. Well, come on up as soon as you can get here. You take soda or water?'

Dyar laughed. He had not known he would be so pleased to hear Wilcox's voice. 'Soda,' he said.

'Wait a second. Listen. I've got an idea. I'll call you back in five minutes. Don't go out. Wait for my call. Just stay put. I just want to call somebody for a second. It's great to have you here. Call you right back. OK?'

'Right.'

He hung up and went to stand at the window. The rain that was beating against the glass had leaked through and was running down the wall. Someone had put a rag along the floor to absorb it, but now the cloth floated in a shallow pool. Two or three hundred feet up the road from the hotel there was a streetlight. Beneath it in the wind the glistening spears of a palm branch charged back and forth. He began to pace from one end of the little foyer to the other; the boy, standing by the desk with his hands behind him, watched him intently. He was a little annoyed at Wilcox for making him wait. Of course he thought he had been phoning from his room. He wondered if Wilcox were making good money with his travel agency. In his letters he had said he was, but Dyar remembered a good deal of bluff in his character. His enthusiasm need have meant nothing more than that he needed an assistant and preferred it to be someone he knew (the wages were low enough, and Dyar had paid his own passage from New York), or that he was pleased with a chance to show his importance and magnanimity; it would appeal to Wilcox to be able to make what he considered a generous gesture. Dyar thought it was more likely to be the latter case. Their friendship never had been an intimate one. Even though they had known each other since boyhood, since Wilcox's father had been the Dyars' family doctor, each had never shown more than a polite interest in the other's life. There was little in common between them – not even age, really, since Wilcox was nearly ten years older than he. During the war Wilcox had been sent to Algiers, and afterward it never had occurred to Dyar to wonder what had become of him. One day his father had come home saying, 'Seems Jack Wilcox has stayed on over in North Africa. Gone into business for himself and seems to be making a go of it.' Dyar had asked what kind of business it was, and had been only vaguely interested to hear that it was a tourist bureau.

He had been walking down Fifth Avenue one brilliant autumn twilight and had stopped in front of a large travel agency. The wind that moved down from Central Park had the crispness of an October evening, carrying with it the promise of winter, the season that paralyses; to Dyar it gave a foretaste of increased unhappiness. In one side of the window was a large model ship, black and white, with shiny brass accessories. The other side represented a tropical beach in miniature, with a sea of turquoise gelatine and tiny palm trees bending up out of a beach of real sand. BOOK NOW FOR WINTER CRUISES, said the sign. The thought occurred to him that it would be a torturing business to work in such a place, to plan itineraries, make hotel reservations and book passages for all the places one would never see. He wondered how many of the men who stood inside there consulting their folders, schedules, lists and maps felt as trapped as he would have felt in their place; it would be even worse than the bank. Then he thought of

Wilcox. At that moment he began to walk again, very fast. When he got home he wrote the letter and took it out to post immediately. It was a crazy idea. Nothing could come of it, except perhaps that Wilcox would think him a goddam fool, a prospect which did not alarm him.

The reply had given him the shock of his life. Wilcox had spoken of coincidence. 'There must be something in telepathy,' he had written. Only then did Dyar mention the plan to his family, and the reproaches had begun.

Moving regretfully away from the desk, the fat man walked back to the stairway. The telephone rang. The boy started for it, but Dyar got there ahead of him. The boy glared at him angrily. It was Wilcox, who said he would be at the Hotel de la Playa in twenty minutes. 'I want you to meet a friend of mine,' he said. 'The Marquesa de Valverde. She's great. She wants you to come to dinner too.' And as Dyar protested, he interrupted. 'We're not dressing. God, no! None of that here. I'll pick you up.'

'But, Jack, listen –'

'So long.'

Dyar went up to his room, nettled at not having been given the opportunity of deciding to accept or refuse the invitation. He asked himself if it would raise him in Wilcox's estimation if he showed independence and begged off. But obviously he had no intention of doing such a thing, since when he got to his room he tore off his clothes, took a quick shower, whistling all the while, opened his bags, shaved as well as he could by the light of the lone candle, and put on his best suit. When he had finished he blew out the candle and hurried downstairs to wait at the front entrance.

The Spider's House

This is the prologue of The Spider's House *(1955), the longest of Bowles's novels, which is set in 1954. Four foreigners are the only guests remaining at a hotel in the Medina at Fez, one of the world's great medieval cities, and it seems to them an enchanted labyrinth. But it is also the headquarters of the Moroccan nationalists at a time when the struggle for independence from France is reaching crisis point.*

It was just about midnight when Stenham left Si Jaffar's door. 'I don't need anyone to come with me,' he had said, smiling falsely to belie the sound of his voice, for he was afraid he had seemed annoyed or been abrupt, and Si Jaffar, after all, was only exercising his rights as a host in sending this person along with him.

'Really, I don't need anybody.' For he wanted to go back alone, even with all the lights in the city off. The evening had been endless, and he felt like running the risk of taking the wrong turnings and getting temporarily lost; if he were accompanied, the long walk would be almost like a continuation of sitting in Si Jaffar's salon.

But in any case, it was too late now. All the male members of the household had come to the door, even stood out in the wet alley, insisting that the man go with him. Their adieux were always lengthy and elaborate, as if he were leaving for the other side of the world rather than the opposite end of the Medina, and he consciously liked that, because it was a part of what he thought life in a medieval city should be like. However, it was unprecedented for them to force upon him the presence of a protector, and he felt there was no justification for it.

The man strode ahead of him in the darkness. Where'd they get him from? he thought, seeing again the tall bearded Berber in tattered mountain garb as he had looked when he had first caught sight of him in the dim light of Si Jaffar's patio. Then he recalled the fluttering and whispering that had gone on at one end of the room about an hour and a half earlier. Whenever these family discussions arose in Stenham's presence, Si Jaffar made a great effort to divert his attention from them by embarking on a story. The story usually began promisingly enough, Si Jaffar smiling, beaming through his two pairs of spectacles, but with his attention clearly fixed on the sound of voices in the corner. Slowly, as the whispered conversation over there subsided, his words would come more haltingly, and his eyes would dart from side to side as his smile became paralysed and meaningless. The tale would never be completed. Suddenly, 'Ahah!' he would cry triumphantly, apropos of nothing at all. Then he would clap his hands for snuff, or orange-flower water, or chips of sandalwood to throw on to the brazier, look still more pleased, and perhaps whack Stenham's knee playfully. A similar comedy had been played this evening about half past ten. As he thought it over now, Stenham decided that the occasion for it had been the family's sudden decision to provide him with someone to accompany him back to the hotel. Now he remembered that after the discussion Abdeltif, the eldest son, had disappeared for at least half an hour; that must have been when the guide had been fetched.

The man had been crouching in the dark patio entrance just inside the door when they had gone out. It was embarrassing, because he knew Si Jaffar was not a well-to-do man, and while a little service like this was not abnormally expensive, still, it had to be paid for; Si Jaffar had made that clear. 'Don't give this man anything,' he had said in French. 'I have already seen to that.'

'But I don't need him,' Stenham had protested. 'I know the way. Think of all the times I've gone back alone.' Si Jaffar's four sons, his cousin and his son-in-law had all murmured, 'No, no, no,' together, and the old man had patted his arm affectionately. 'It's better,' he said, with one of his curiously formal little bows. There was no use in objecting. The man would stay with him until he had delivered him over to the watchman at the hotel, and then he would disappear into the night, go back to whatever dark corner he had come from, and Stenham would not see him again.

The streets were completely without passers-by. It would have been quite possible to go most of the way along somewhat more frequented thoroughfares, he reflected, but obviously his companion preferred the empty ones. He took out his little dynamo flashlight and began to squeeze it, turning the dim ray downward to the ground at the man's feet. The insect-like whirring it made caused him to turn around, a look of surprise on his face.

'Light,' said Stenham.

The man grunted. 'Too much noise,' he objected.

He smiled and let the light die down. How these people love games, he thought. This one's playing cops and robbers now; they're always either stalking or being stalked. 'The Oriental passion for complications, the involved line, Arabesques,' Moss had assured him, but he was not sure it was that. It could just as easily be a deep sense of guilt. He had suggested this, but Moss had scoffed.

The muddy streets led down, down. There was not a foot of level ground. He had to move forward stiff-ankled, with the weight all on the balls of his feet. The city was asleep. There was profound silence, broken only by the scuffing sound he made as he walked. The man, barefooted, advanced noiselessly. From time to time, when the way led not through inner passages but into the open, a solitary drop of rain fell heavily out of the sky, as if a great invisible piece of wet cloth were hanging only a few feet above the earth. Everything was invisible, the mud of the street, the walls, the sky. Stenham squeezed the flashlight suddenly, and had a rapidly fading view of the man moving ahead of him in his brown djellaba, and of his giant shadow thrown against the beams that formed the ceiling of the street. The man grunted again in protest.

Stenham smiled: unaccountable behaviour on the part of Moslems amused him, and he always forgave it, because, as he said, no non-Moslem knows enough about the Moslem mind to dare find fault with it. 'They're far, far away from us,' he would say. 'We haven't an inkling of the things that motivate them.' There was a certain amount of hypocrisy in this attitude of his; the truth was that he hoped principally to convince *others* of the existence of this almost unbridgeable gulf. The mere fact that he could then even begin to hint at the beliefs and purposes that lay on the far side made him feel more sure in his own attempts at analysing them and gave him a small sense of superiority to which he felt he was entitled, in return for having withstood the rigours of Morocco for so many years. This pretending to know something that others could not know, it was a little indulgence he allowed himself, a bonus for seniority. Secretly he was convinced that the Moroccans were much like any other people, that the differences were largely those of ritual and gesture, that even the fine curtain of magic through which they observed life was not a complex thing, and did not give their perceptions any profundity. It delighted him that this anonymous, barefoot Berber should want to guide him through the darkest, least frequented tunnels of the city; the reason for the man's desire for secrecy did not matter. These were a feline, nocturnal people. It was no accident that Fez was a city without dogs. I wonder if Moss has noticed that, he thought.

Now and then he had the distinct impression that they were traversing a street or an open space that he knew perfectly well, but if that were so, the angle at which they had met it was unexpected, so that the familiar walls (if indeed they *were* familiar walls) were dwarfed or distorted in the one swiftly fading beam of light that he played on them. He began to suspect that the power plant had suffered a major collapse: the electricity was almost certainly still cut off, because it would be practically impossible to go so far without coming upon at least one streetlight. However, he was used to moving around the city in the darkness. He knew a good many ways across it in each direction, and he could have found his way blindfolded along several of these routes. Indeed, wandering through the Medina at night was very much like being blindfolded; one let one's ears and nose do most of the work. He knew just how each section of a familiar way sounded when he walked it alone at night. There were two things to listen for: his feet and the sound of the water behind the walls. The footsteps had an infinite variety of sound, depending on the hardness of the earth, the width of the passageway, the height and configuration of the walls. On the Lemtiyine walk there was one place between the tannery and a small mosque where the echo was astounding: taut, metallic reverberations that shuddered between the walls like musical pistol shots. There were places where his footfalls were almost silent, places where the sound was strong, single and compact, died straightway, or where, as he advanced along the deserted galleries, each succeeding step produced a sound of an imperceptibly higher pitch, so that his passage was like a finely graded ascending scale, until all at once a jutting wall or a sudden tunnel dispersed the pattern and began another section in the long nocturne which in turn would slowly disclose its own design. And the water was the same, following its countless courses behind the partitions of earth and stone. Seldom visible but nearly always present, it rushed beneath the sloping alleyways, here gurgled, here merely dripped, here beyond the wall of a garden splashed or dribbled in the form of a fountain, here fell with a high hollow noise into an invisible cistern, here all at once was unabashedly a branch of the river roaring over the rocks (so that sometimes the cold vapour rising was carried over the wall by the wind and wet his face), here by the bakery had been dammed and was almost still, a place where the rats swam.

The two simultaneous sound-tracks of footsteps and water he had experienced so often that it seemed to him he must know each portion by heart. But now it was all different, and he realized that what he knew was only one line, one certain sequence whose parts became unrecognizable once they were presented out of their accustomed context. He knew, for instance, that in order to be as near the main branch of the river as they were now, at some point they had had to cross the street leading from the Karouine Mosque to the Zaouia of Si Ahmed Tidjani, but it was impossible for him to know when that had been; he had recognized nothing.

Suddenly he realized where they were: in a narrow street that ran the length of a slight eminence above the river, just below the mass of walls that formed the Fondouk el Yihoudi. It was far out of their way, not on any conceivable route between Si Jaffar's house and the hotel. 'Why have we come out here?' he asked with indignation. The man was unnecessarily abrupt in his reply, Stenham thought. 'Walk and be quiet.'

But they always are, he reminded himself; he would never be able to take for granted their curious mixture of elaborate circumspection and brutal bluntness, and he almost laughed aloud at the memory of how the ridiculous words had sounded five seconds ago: *Rhir zid o skout*. And in another few minutes they had circumnavigated the Fondouk el Yihoudi and were going through a wet garden under banana trees; the heavy tattered leaves showered cold drops as they brushed against them. 'Si Jaffar has outdone himself this time.' He decided to telephone him tomorrow and make a good story of it. *Zid o skout*. It would be a hilarious slogan over the tea glasses for the next fortnight, one in which the whole family could share.

It was a freakish summer night; a chill almost like that of early spring paralysed the air. A vast thick cloud had rolled down across the Djebel Zalagh and formed a ceiling low over the city, enclosing it in one great room whose motionless air smelled only of raw, wet earth. As they went silently back into the streets higher up the hill, an owl screamed once from somewhere above their heads.

When they had arrived at the hotel's outer gate, Stenham pushed the button that rang a bell down in the interior of the hotel in some little room near the office where the watchman stayed. For a moment he thought: It won't ring; the power's off tonight. But then he remembered that the hotel had its own electric system. It was usually a good five minutes before the light came on in the courtyard, and then another two or three before the watchman got to the gate. Tonight the light came on immediately. Stenham stepped close to the high doors and peered through the crack between them. The watchman was at the far end of the courtyard talking to someone. '*Ah, oui,*' he heard him say. A European in the court at this hour, he thought with some curiosity, trying to see more. The watchman was approaching. Like a guilty child, Stenham stepped quickly back and put his hands in his pockets, looking nonchalantly toward the side wall. Then he realized that his guide had disappeared. There was no sound of retreating footsteps; he was merely gone. The heavy bolt of the gate was drawn back and the watchman stood there in his khaki duster and white turban, the customary anxious expression on his face.

'*Bon soir, M'sio Stonamm,*' he said. Sometimes he spoke in Arabic, sometimes in French; it was impossible to know which he would choose for a given occasion. Stenham greeted him, looking across the courtyard to see who was there with him. He saw no one. The same two cars stood there: the hotel's station wagon and an old Citroën that belonged to the manager, but which he never used. 'You came quickly tonight,' he said.

'*Oui, M'sio Stonamm.*'

'You were outside, near the gate, perhaps?'

The watchman hesitated. '*Non, m'sio.*'

He abandoned it rather than become exasperated with the man, which he knew he would do if he went on. A lie is not a lie; it is only a formula, a substitute, a long way around, a polite manner of saying: None of your business.

He had his key in his pocket, and so he went directly up the back way to his room, a little ashamed of himself for having started to pry. But when he stood in his room in the tower, looking out over the invisible city spread below, he found that he could justify his inquisitiveness. It was not merely the watchman's patent lie which had prodded him; much more than that was the fact of its having come directly on the heels of the Berber's strange behaviour: the unnecessary detour, the gruff injunctions to silence, the inexplicable disappearance before he had had a chance to hand him the thirty francs he had ready to give him. Not only that, he decided, going further back to Si Jaffar. The whole family had so solemnly insisted that he be accompanied on his way home to the hotel. That too seemed to be a part of the conspiracy. 'They're all crazy tonight,' he told himself with satisfaction. He refused to tie all these things together by attributing them to the tension that was in the city. Ever since that day a year ago when the French, more irresponsible than usual, had deposed the Sultan, the tension had been there, and he had known it was there. But it was a political thing, and politics exist only on paper; certainly the politics of 1954 had no true connection with the mysterious medieval city he knew and loved. It would have been too simple to make a logical relationship between what his brain knew and what his eyes saw; he found it more fun to play this little game with himself.

Each night when Stenham had locked his door, the watchman climbed up the steep stairs into the tower of the *ancien palais* and snapped off the lights in the corridors, one by one. When he had gone back down, and the final sounds of his passage had died away, there was only the profound silence of the night, disturbed, if a wind blew, by the rustle of the poplars in the garden. Tonight, when the slow footsteps approached up the staircase, instead of the familiar click of the switch on the wall outside the door, there was a slight hesitation, and then a soft knock. Stenham had taken off his tie, but he was still fully dressed. Frowning, he opened the door. The watchman smiled apologetically at him – certainly not out of compunction for the lie in the courtyard, he commented, seeing that wistful, vanquished face. In the five seasons he had spent here at the hotel Stenham had never seen this man wear another expression. If the world went on he would grow old and die, night watchman at the Mérinides Palace, no other possibility having suggested itself to him. This time he spoke in Arabic. '*Smatsi.* M'sio Moss has sent me. He wants to know if you'll go to see him.'

'Now?' said Stenham incredulously.

'Now. Yes.' He laughed deprecatingly, with infinite gentleness, as if he meant to imply that his understanding of the world was vast indeed.

Stenham's first thought was: I can't let Moss start this sort of thing. Temporizing, he said aloud, 'Where is he?'

'In his room. Number Fourteen.'

'I know the number,' he said. 'Are you going to his room again, to take him my message?'

'Yes. Do I tell him you'll come?'

Stenham sighed. 'For a minute. Yes.' This would be disregarded, of course; the man would simply tell Moss that Monsieur Stonamm was coming, and disappear. Now he bowed, said, '*Ouakha*', and shut the door.

He stood before the mirror of the armoire, putting his necktie back on. It was the first time Moss had ever sent him a message at night, and he was curious to know what had made the Englishman decide to vary his code of strict discretion. He looked at his watch: it was twenty minutes past one. Moss would begin with florid apologies for having disturbed his work, whether he believed he had caused such an interruption or not, for Stenham encouraged his acquaintances to hold the impression that he worked evenings as well as mornings. It assured him more privacy, and besides, occasionally, if the weather were bad, he went to bed early and did manage to add an extra page to the novel that was still far from completed. Rain and wind outside the window in the darkness provided the incentive necessary to offset fatigue. Tonight, in any case, he would not have worked: it was far too late. Day in Fez began long before dawn, and it made him profoundly uneasy to think that he might not be asleep before the early call to prayer set off the great sound of cockcrow that spread slowly over the city and never abated until it was broad daylight. If he were still awake once the muezzins began their chant, there was no hope of further sleep. At this time of year they started about half past three.

He looked at the typed pages lying on the table, placed a fat porcelain ashtray on top of them, and turned to go out. Then he thought better of it, and put the entire manuscript in the drawer. He went to the door, cast a brief longing glance back at his bed, stepped out and locked the door behind him. The key had a heavy nickel tag attached to it; it felt like ice in his pocket. And there was a strong, chill draught coming up the tower's narrow stairwell. He went down as quietly as he could (not that there was anyone to disturb), felt his way through the dim lobby, and walked on to the terrace. The light from the reception hall streamed out across the wet mosaic floor. No isolated raindrops fell from the sky now; instead, a faint breeze moved in the air. In the lower garden it was very dark; a thin wrought-iron grill beside the Sultana's pool guided him to the patio where on sunny days he and Moss sometimes ate their lunch. The lanterns outside the great door of Number Fourteen had not been turned on, but slivers of light came through from the room between the closed blinds. As he knocked, a startled animal, a rat or a ferret perhaps, bolted, scurried through the plants and dead leaves behind him. The man who opened the door, standing stiffly aside to let him pass, was not someone he had ever seen before.

Moss stood in the centre of the room, directly under the big chandelier, nervously smoothing his moustache, an expression of consternation in his eyes. The only feeling of which Stenham could be conscious at the moment was a devout wish that he had not knocked on the door, that he could still be standing outside in the dark where he had been five seconds ago. He disregarded the man who stood beside him. 'Good evening,' he called to Moss, his intonation carrying a hint of casual heartiness. But Moss remained taut.

'Will you please come in, John?' he said dryly. 'I must talk to you.'

Up Above the World

The following extract, Chapter 30, comes from the end of this novel. Up Above the World *(1966) is an extraordinary book, which leads the reader into a strange world of imagination and high emotion. An elderly American couple are on holiday in Latin America. There they meet Grove, a young man of striking good looks and charm, and his seventeen-year-old girlfriend. The encounter opens the door to a nightmare as Grove leads his victims on a terrifying journey through hallucination to death.*

LATER, when it was daylight and the old American and his wife had left, and the servants were clattering in the kitchen, he went in again and finished his work. Driving back to the bungalow he felt a glow of pleasure as he recalled the speed and precision with which he had accomplished this last part of the venture. Grove was waiting for him outside the bungalow, sitting on a palm stump. They drove inland through the green world of a banana plantation to the top of a hill behind the town, where they stopped and watched until the fire was brought under control. The plaza was black with people. Then they cut through the jungle along a narrow back trail and came out on to the coast-capital highway.

It was all done, and done in the only way possible, as Thorny saw it, yet Grove was not content; he was fretting about the American girl. Over and over he said he would never be sure what she had seen. She had gone on her way quietly, yes, but how could he know she hadn't happened on to the truth (it must have been fairly evident, if for any reason she had really looked), and rather than see herself getting involved had merely shut the door and gone away, free to tell everything later?

'That's got to be changed,' Grove said with finality.

'It's a little late in the day to change anything,' Thorny told him, stung to realize that Grove did not consider his work a brilliant success.

Grove said nothing. As they rounded a curve, Thorny stole a glance at him, and decided that he had been shut out. Grove was going to do something crazy, and without taking him into his confidence.

Even so, he could scarcely believe Grove was serious when, two days later after getting him down to Los Hermanos, he expounded the outrageous new project to him.

'You *want* trouble, don't you?' he said slowly. 'Have you got to walk another tightrope now, when everything's all right?'

'The answer is yes,' Grove snapped. 'You'll be stuck here for a few days, that's all. They're coming down tonight.'

He did not ask Grove why the girl never appeared. Three mornings later, after they had managed to calm the old man somewhat, Grove remarked, 'It's a good thing she's responsive to treatment. If she were anything like him, Paloma'd never be able to manage her.'

Forbearing to criticize, since criticism was useless, Thorny merely said, 'The old guy's a handful.' He would not have thought Grove capable of such protracted nonsense. Instead of living a normal life, waiting quietly for word from London and Montreal, he was hysterically involved in a round-the-clock game with two American tourists: feeding them LSD, shooting them full of scopolamine and morphine, putting them under and bringing them out again, and providing special sound effects for each phase of the programme. (This preoccupation with the tape recorders struck him as the most infantile bit of all. The room at Los Hermanos had to be kept dark, and at times there was an endless whispering, scarcely loud enough to hear unless he remained in there purposely to listen; then the repeated phrases seemed to grow in volume and fill every corner.)

That period had been a strain; Thorny and Dirk worked in four-hour shifts. The schedule had to be observed with absolute precision. Each day Grove made three round trips up to the capital; on arriving back at Los Hermanos he was often short-tempered.

'Anyway,' Thorny said, the morning they drove to the station and he helped Grove carry the old man on to the train for San Felipe, 'whatever happens now, we've done everything we could.' He knew better than to say, I've done everything. But Grove turned on him with irritation.

'What is this always about things happening?' he demanded. 'Things don't happen. It depends on who comes along.'

'You're right,' he agreed, and he recalled the remark shortly afterward at the ranch. Grove had telephoned him the following day, saying he needed him; when he arrived he was waiting for him in the little library off his own bedroom. He got up and shut the door.

'You'll eat in here,' he told him. 'Your job is to tune in on all conversations, whatever room we're in, and tape everything. She's not being honest with me.'

'I thought you said she was responsive,' said Thorny, trying not to grin.

'That doesn't mean she's being honest now.'

Thorny listened before, during, and after mealtimes, and was impressed. There was no doubt that neither of them remembered anything at all about Puerto Farol; they were convinced that they had first met Grove down there at the dock.

'There's something she's holding back,' Grove complained, after he had studied the recordings.

'Get her mad if you can. Catch her off guard,' Thorny advised.

'She's going to give me trouble yet.'

With that in his mind, Grove could be counted on to react badly to the news about the bonfire; with misgivings Thorny went in to tell him. Earlier in the day Grove had handed him a pile of papers to burn, most of them typewritten notes of the sort he was always making. He would not have bothered to call it to Grove's attention had he not seen the girl wandering around out there in the garden, near the spot where he had burned them. When she had gone in, he left his hammock in the bamboo brake and walked over to check. One of the servants, before going off to the fiesta, must have spilled water on the fire, he decided, for the papers had not burned completely. He picked up those that remained and carried them into the kitchen, pinching off the charred edges on the way. At the sink he washed his hands, and while he dried them he glanced over the top fragment.

fer
as scaffolding f
(Note: for therap
rd day – tape of beach at La Lib
h 'Dawn will be breaking soon.'
nto RED notebook a

It went on in this way; there was not even another complete sentence – only bits of phrases and truncated words. However, there was nothing to do but take the stuff in and report what had happened.

'What?' Grove sprang up out of his chair, grabbed the papers.

Thorny was silent. He heard the steady spray of a sprinkler in the courtyard rattling as it hit the big banana leaves. After a lapse, Grove said, looking fixedly at him, 'This makes it bad.'

'For Christ's sake! She just walked past!'

Grove still glared at him. He raised his voice, 'Believe me when I say it's bad.'

'I believe you.' Thorny moved toward the door.

'Stay here,' said Grove sharply, beginning to walk around the centre of the room. Then for nearly ten minutes he talked without stopping. Finally he threw himself on to the divan and stretched out at full length. 'It's as though I'd known all along it was going to be this way. Unbelievable how things can dovetail.'

Thorny looked at the floor. 'It depends on who comes along. Isn't that what you said?'

Grove's glance was cold. 'I'm as much against it as you are. It's just where the whole thing is now. You can see that.'

'You know what you're doing.'

It was not much later when Thorny went out into the courtyard and saw the girl standing on the rocks down below; quickly Grove brought an immersion heater and made the doctor his tea.

A good while after dark, while Grove and the girl were in the kitchen, Thorny went down and got Pablo, who had stayed on at the generator. ('There's a señor who's sick, and I have to take him to San Felipe.') Together they carried the old man from the bed to the truck. Thorny got in and shut the door. Then he drove off alone in the dark, down the trail that ultimately led to Barrancas, until he got to the dangerous stretch edging the cliff. If there was even a mule coming along here, you had to stop the car. In the daytime, far below, you could see the round tops of the big trees down there. He had to do the rest alone, but, even so, it did not take more than two minutes. Then he went on down a mile or so until he came to a place where he could turn the car.

No one ever went down into that part of the country; it was empty land. Scrub mimosa and cactus at the foot of the cliff, and then terrible formless thickets of thorned bramble, like rolls of barbed wire. And still lower, the tufted forest of high green trees. And nothing lasted long down there, in any case, he thought, glancing out over the vast moonlit lands below: the buzzards, flopping and tugging, and the ants hurrying in endless lines, night and day.

'Why don't you go to bed?' Grove asked him when he got back.

'Yeah,' he said, and went down to see Pablo at the generator. Earlier they had made some *grifas* together. Now they sat smoking in the moonlight, listening to the radio. Before he relaxed completely, for he had no idea how long he might stay down there with Pablo, he made himself stand up and go over to the truck: he had left the keys in the ignition. He was almost down to the generator again when Pablo called out, and it was a shock to find the girl standing there; he had imagined she would be with Grove. The only thing possible was to go up to the house for a consultation.

Grove's face grew nasty when Thorny told him. 'Oh, she wants it to be at San Felipe, does she? OK, take her. It's perfect!' Then he explained, and told Thorny exactly what to do.

'You're out of your bloody mind!' said Thorny, in spite of himself.

Grove smiled broadly. 'I'll give you ten minutes' start.'

Bravado, thought Thorny, tramping back down to the generator. It was dangerous enough anyway, without the acrobatics. He stopped for a moment beside a high cactus and finished off a partly smoked *grifa* from his pocket.

He was very high driving up to San Felipe, and the girl had decided to be hostile. The confusion of the *alameda*, the fireworks and the yelling, made him even more nervous. When he had spotted Grove and knew Grove had seen him and the girl, he pushed into the crowd, looking straight ahead, and fought his way through to the open. Quickly he passed between the rows of silent seated Indians, and into the dark street where he had parked.

PART II

STORIES

Doña Faustina

This was written in 1949 and is taken from the collection Call at Corazón *(1988).*

1

No one could understand why Doña Faustina had bought the inn. It stood on one of the hairpin curves in the old highway leading up from the river valley to the town, but the route had been made useless by the building of the new paved road. Now it was impossible to reach the inn except by climbing up a stony path over the embankment and walking several hundred feet down the old road which, no longer kept in repair, already was being washed away by the rains and strangled by the shiny vegetation of that lowland region.

On Sundays the people used to walk out from the town, the women carrying parasols and the men guitars (for this was before the days of the radio, when almost everyone knew how to make a little music); they would get as far as the great bread-fruit tree and look up the road at the faded façade of the building, more than half hidden by young bamboo and banana plants, stare a few seconds, and turn around to go back. 'Why does she leave the sign up?' they would say. 'Does she think anyone would ever spend the night there now?' And they were quite right: no one went near the inn any more. Only the people of the town knew that it existed, and they had no need of it.

There remained the mystery of why she had bought it. As usual when there is something townspeople cannot understand, they invented a whole series of unpleasant explanations for Doña Faustina's behaviour. The earliest and most common one, which was that she had decided to transform the place into a house of ill-repute, soon fell to pieces, for there was absolutely nothing to substantiate such a theory. No one had been seen to go near the inn for weeks, except Doña Faustina's younger sister Carlota who arrived from Jalapa, and the old servants José and Elena, who went to market each morning and minded their business strictly enough to satisfy even the most vicious gossips. As for Carlota, she appeared occasionally at mass, dressed in black. It was said that she had taken their father's death very much to heart, and would probably not remove the mourning, ever.

The other suppositions evolved by the people of the town in their effort to bring light to the mystery proved as unlikely as the first. It was rumoured that Doña Faustina was giving asylum to Chato Morales, a bandit whom the police of the region had been trying for months to capture, but he was caught soon afterwards in a distant part of the province. Then it was said that the inn was a depository for a drug ring; this also proved to be false. The leaders of the ring, having been arrested, divulged their secrets, and the cache proved to be in a room above the Farmacia Ideal. There were darker hints to the effect that Carlota might be luring lone voyagers to the inn, where they met the fate that traditionally befalls such solitary visitors to lonely inns. But people did not take such suggestions seriously. The opinion grew that Doña Faustina had merely gone a little mad, and that her madness, having taken an anti-social turn, had induced her to retire to the outskirts of town where she could live without ever seeing anyone. To be sure, this theory was contested by certain younger members of the community who claimed that she was no more crazy than they, that on the contrary she was extremely crafty. They said that having a great deal of money she had bought the inn because of the ample lands which surrounded it, and that there in the privacy of the plant-smothered gardens and orchards she had devised all kinds of clever ways of hiding her riches. The older citizens of the town took no stock in this, however, since they clearly remembered both her husband and her father, neither of whom had evinced any unusual prowess in collecting money. And she had bought the inn for practically nothing. 'Where would she have got the pesos?' they said sceptically. 'Out of the trees, perhaps?'

2

ONCE when a child disappeared from the town (small children were often stolen in those days and taken off to distant places where they were made to work), the parents insisted that the police search the inn. Doña Faustina, who was a large women in the prime of life, met the little policeman at the door and refused to let him in. Indeed, she was so brusque with him and glared at him with such malignity that he felt obliged to go back to the *comisaría* and get reinforcements. When he and the three extra men returned to the inn, they made a complete but unrewarding search of the place, followed at every step by Doña Faustina, who did not cease to shower them with insults until they had left the premises. But they returned to town with a story. The rooms were a shambles, they said, the furniture was broken, there was rubbish and garbage everywhere in the corridors, the railing of the second-storey balcony had given way and been replaced by a single strand of barbed wire, and the place looked generally as though innumerable picnic parties had been held there over a period of years. This report helped to fortify people in their belief that Doña Faustina had more or less lost her mind, and for a time the town ceased thinking about her.

Some time afterwards it was noted that she and her sister had taken to making trips to neighbouring towns; they had been seen in such widely separated places as Tlacotalpam and Zempoala. But even these peregrinations failed to elicit true interest. Heads were shaken, sympathetically or otherwise, and it was remarked that Doña Faustina was growing less and less sane, but that was all.

When the mistresses of the house were absent they did not return for three or four days, and José and Elena remained alone to guard the property, not even venturing forth to the town for marketing until the two reappeared. On their return the sisters would take an old covered carriage that went each day to the station to await the train. They would pile their numerous bundles and baskets in and drive as far as the curve, where they would get down, the driver helping them up the embankment with their effects and then leaving them to get to the house in whatever way they could. Carlota would go and bring up José to help carry the things, but Doña Faustina always insisted on carrying the heaviest baskets herself. A few trips would be made back and forth through the undergrowth, and then the abandoned road would be quiet again until the old servants went to market the next morning.

In another fortnight or so they would set out once more, always to a new place; necessarily this led them further and further afield. Someone even claimed to have seen them once in Vera Cruz, although, given the number of false stories which were circulated about the two women, there was no particular reason to believe this.

Before the house had been made into an inn it had been a prosperous *finca,* with terraced lands planted with fruit trees, leading downward rather steeply for a mile or so to a high bluff above the river. For fifty years or more the land had been totally neglected, so that now it was hard to find the avocado and mango trees in the tangle of new, eager parasites which had sprung up on every side and often reached above even the tallest of the older trees. Lianas looped down from the branches, climbing plants stretched up to clutch at them, and a person could not stray more than fifty feet down one of the orchard paths from the house without coming face to face with an impenetrable curtain of leaves. And now no one really knew how far it was from the house to the river, because the borders of the property gave on even thicker jungle.

3

NOT even José would have known the tank existed, if he had not strayed a bit further down than usual one afternoon, to see if he could find some mameyes. In the deep silence of the undergrowth there, far beneath the regions where the sun could reach, he had heard a heavy splash not far distant, as though a boulder had been flung into deep water. He had listened intently, but there had been no other sound. The next afternoon during siesta time he went back to the same spot carrying a machete, and laboriously hacked his way through the stubborn vegetation. It was nearly twilight when he caught sight of the water ahead. Finally he stood near the edge of the tank. The stagnant water gave off a heavy odour, and insects hovered in swarms in the still air above it. And as he watched, it seemed to him that there was a faint movement down in the brown depths; for some reason the water was not completely motionless. For a while he stood there staring downward, lost in contemplation; then, as the light was fading, he turned and started back, resolving, without knowing why he did so, to say nothing about the tank to Elena when he returned to the house.

Several times in the course of the following months José

returned there, always with the hope of discovering what had made the splash. Even a man diving into the tank could scarcely have caused such a noise. There was a stone-paved ramp at the far end (the tank doubtless had been built to bathe cattle) and on two occasions he found the ramp partially wet, which merely added to his perplexity. The second time he noticed this, he began to cut his way through the vines along the edge, in order to examine the ramp closely. And halfway along he found the path. Someone had cleared a narrow but practicable passage to the tank from some point back near the house. Abandoning his project, he followed the path and came out in a corner of what had once been a rose garden, on a lower terrace between the door to the laundry and the ruined stables. As he stood blinking in the sunlight, Doña Faustina appeared coming down the short flight of steps outside the laundry door. By its handle she carried a basket with a newspaper tucked over the top. Automatically old José walked towards her to take the basket from her. Evidently she had not been expecting to see him, for when she looked up and realized he was near her, her face took on an extraordinary expression. But all she said was, 'What are you doing down here? Go to the kitchen.' Then she stepped to a stone bench under an arbour near her and sat down, putting the basket on the bench beside her.

As he went on up towards the house José thought he had never seen his *patrona* look quite so fierce. She was always severe, and often forbidding, but not to the point of being able to frighten him as she had today. It was as if a demon had peered out at him for a moment from beneath her heavy lids.

It must be true, he thought. Doña Faustina is going mad. What will become of Elena and me?

This time when he got to the kitchen he took Elena into a corner and whispered to her, telling her his fears, and of how strange the señora had looked in the garden. Elena crossed herself. 'Oh, God,' she murmured. But he did not mention the tank to her, either now or later. He did not even want to think about it, because he suspected that in some way it was connected with Doña Faustina's madness, and being the only one who knew about it gave him a certain feeling of security which he would have lost had he shared the knowledge with Elena.

4

ONE cold evening of *llovizna,* as the mealy fog slowly turned to water and drenched the countryside, there was a knock at the entrance door. Doña Faustina, who spent much of her time pottering about in the basement where the baths and laundry were, heard it from there, and straightway mounted the stairs, her face dark with fury. Carlota stood in the *comedor*, undecided as to whether she should answer. The knocking was repeated as Doña Faustina reached her.

'Again the police?' said Carlota a bit fearfully.

'*Ya veremos,*' muttered Doña Faustina. And she went out and stood behind the door, calling out in a loud voice, 'Who?'

There was no answer.

'Don't open it,' whispered Carlota, who stood behind her.

Doña Faustina made an impatient gesture to silence her sister. They waited several minutes, but the knock did not come again. There was only the irregular dripping of the water from the balcony above on to the ground.

'Stay here,' said Doña Faustina, and she went through the *comedor,* down the stairs and into the laundry again. Here she gathered up all the refuse that strewed the floor and the washtubs, and, packing it into two large baskets, continued out of the side door which gave on the grape arbour. From here, descending the steps slowly, she disappeared into the darkness of the rose garden.

Within a half-hour she was back in the entrance hall where Carlota still stood listening by the door.

'Nothing,' said Carlota in answer to Doña Faustina's questioning gesture. Doña Faustina beckoned to her. They went into the *comedor* and whispered together. One candle flame cowered behind a pitcher on the newspaper-covered sideboard.

'It's not the police,' said Doña Faustina. 'Your room has a key. Go immediately. Lock the door and go to bed.'

'But you . . . ?'

'I'm not afraid.'

Left alone in the *comedor*, Doña Faustina poured herself a glass of water and drank it. Then she took the candle and went up the long staircase to her room. She closed the door and set the candle down. By her sagging bed, around which Elena had draped the patched mosquito-net, stood a man. Swiftly he stepped over to her, and, putting one arm around her neck tightly, stuffed a crumpled cloth into her mouth. She swung her arms about wildly, and managed to hit him once in the face, but almost immediately he had tied her wrists together. There was no further struggle. He propelled her roughly to the bed, yanked aside the netting and pushed her down. She looked at him: he was a tall young man, a *mestizo* probably, and badly dressed. As he moved about the room looking into the crates and boxes that lay in wild disorder about the floor, he snorted with distaste. Finally he overturned a chair in anger and with a scornful gesture swept all the empty bottles and piles of newspapers off the bureau on to the floor. He approached the bed again and looked at Doña Faustina in the wavering light. Then, to her surprise (although it cannot be said to her annoyance), he lay down and had his way with her quietly, impersonally. A few minutes later he sat up and pulled the cloth out of her mouth. She lay perfectly still and looked up at him.

Finally she said, 'What do you want here? I have no money.'

'Who knows if you have or not?'

'I tell you there is none.'

'We'll see.'

He got up. Again he spent a quarter of an hour or so searching the room, scuffing piles of refuse under the tables, kicking the furniture over to examine the under part, emptying drawers of their dust and litter. He lit a small cigar and returned to the bed. His oblique eyes looked almost closed in the light of the candle.

'Where is it?' he said.

'There is none. But I have something more precious.'

'What?' He looked at her with scornful disbelief. What could be more precious than money?

'Untie my hands.'

He gave her the use of one hand, holding the other arm firmly while she fumbled in her clothing. In a moment she drew forth a small parcel done up in newspaper, and handed it to him. He placed it on the bed and bound her hands together. Then in a gingerly fashion he lifted the parcel and smelled it. It was soft, and slightly wet.

'What is it?'

'Open it, *hombre,* Eat it. You know what it is.'

Suspiciously he removed the outer layer of paper and held the contents close to the candle.

'What is this?' he cried.

'*Ya sabes, hombre,*' she said calmly. '*Cómelo.*'

'What is it?' he said again, trying to sound stern; but there was fear in his voice.

'Eat it, son. You don't have the chance every day.'

'Where did you get it?'

'Ah!' Doña Faustina looked mysterious and wise, and gave no further answer.

'What do I want of it?' said the young man presently, looking down at the little object in his hand.

'Eat it! Eat it and have the power of two,' she said cajolingly.

'*Brujerías!*' he exclaimed, still without putting the thing down.

A moment later he added, speaking slowly, 'I don't like witchcraft. I don't like it.'

'Bah!' Doña Faustina snorted. 'Don't be stupid, son. Don't ask questions. Eat it, and go on your way with the force of two. Who will ever know? Tell me that! Who?'

This argument appeared to weigh with the young man. Suddenly he lifted the thing to his mouth and bit into it as if it had been a plum. While he ate he looked once at Doña Faustina darkly. When he had finished, he walked around the room tentatively for a moment, his head slightly on one side. Doña Faustina watched him closely.

'How do you feel?' she inquired.

'*Bien,*' he said.

'Two,' she reminded him. 'Now you have the power of two.'

As if inspired by the fortifying suggestion, he walked to the bed, threw himself down on it and lay with her again briefly. This time she kissed his forehead. When it was over he rose, and without undoing the rope that bound her hands, without saying a word, he went out of the door and down the stairs. A minute or so later she heard the front door close. At the same time the candle, which had burned down to its base, began to flicker wildly, and soon the room was in darkness.

5

All night Doña Faustina lay perfectly still on her bed, sleeping now and then, and during the periods of wakefulness listening to the slow dripping of the mist outside her windows. In the morning Carlota, still fearful, opened her door a crack, and apparently finding everything in the corridors in a normal state went to Doña Faustina's room.

'*Ay, Dios!*' she cried when she saw Doña Faustina lying with her clothing partially ripped away and her hands lashed together. 'Oh God! Oh God!'

But Doña Faustina was calm. As Carlota undid the rope, she said, 'He did no harm. But I had to give him the heart.'

Carlota looked at her sister with horror.

'You're mad!' she cried. 'The police will be here any minute.'

'No, no,' Doña Faustina reassured her, and she was right: no police arrived to search the house again. Nothing happened. At the end of two weeks they made another trip, and a little while later still another. Two days after they had returned from this one, Doña Faustina called Carlota into her room and said to her, 'There will be a child.'

Carlota sat down slowly on the bed.

'How terrible!'

Doña Faustina smiled. 'No, no. It's perfect. Think. It will have the power of thirty-seven.'

But Carlota did not seem convinced. 'We don't know about those things,' she said. 'It may be a vengeance.'

'No, no, no,' said Doña Faustina, shaking her head. 'But now we must be more careful than ever.'

'No more trips?' said Carlota hopefully.

'I shall think about it.'

A few days later they were both in the rose garden sitting on a bench.

'I have thought,' said Doña Faustina. 'And there will be no more trips.'

'Good,' replied Carlota.

Towards the end of the year Doña Faustina was confined to bed, awaiting the birth of the child. She lay back comfortably in the crooked old bed, and had Elena come and sweep out the room for the first time in many months. Even when the floor was clean, the room still reeked of the garbage that had lain there for so long. Carlota had bought a tiny crib in the town; the purchase had reawakened interest in their activities on the part of the townspeople.

When the time arrived, Elena and Carlota were both in the room to assist at the birth. Doña Faustina did not scream once. The baby was washed and laid beside her in the bed.

'A boy,' said Elena, smiling down at her.

'Of course,' said Doña Faustina, beginning to nurse him.

Elena went down to the kitchen to tell José the good news. He shook his head gloomily.

'Something bad in all this,' he muttered.

'In all what?' said Elena sharply.

'Who is the father?' said José, looking up.

'That is Doña Faustina's secret,' Elena replied smugly, rather as if it had been her own.

'Yes. I think so too,' said José meaningfully. 'I think there is no father, if you want to know. I think she got the child from the Devil.'

Elena was scandalized. 'Shameless!' she cried. 'How can you say such a thing?'

'I have reasons,' said José darkly. And he would say no more.

Things went smoothly at the inn. Several months passed. The baby had been named Jesus Maria and was in perfect health – '*un torito,*' said Elena, 'a real little bull.'

'Of course,' Doña Faustina had replied on that occasion. 'He has the power of thirty-seven . . .' Exactly then Carlota had been taken with a violent fit of coughing which managed to cover the rest of the sentence. But Elena had noticed nothing.

The rainy season had finished again, and the bright days of sunlight and green leaves had come. José went in search of fruit once more, wandering down through the garden, crouching over most of the time to creep beneath the hanging walls of vines and tendrils. Again one day he cut his way to the tank, and stood on the edge of it looking towards the ramp. And this time he saw the monster just as it slid forward and disappeared beneath the surface of the water. His mouth dropped open. Only one word came out: '*Caimán!*'

He stood still for several minutes looking down at the dark water. Then he edged along the side of the tank to the place where the path had been the year before. It had completely disappeared. No one had been to the tank in many months; there was no indication that such a corridor had ever existed there in the mass of vegetation. He returned the way he had come.

It was a scandal, thought José, that such a beast should be living on Doña Faustina's property, and he determined to speak to her about it immediately. He found her in the kitchen talking with Elena. From his face she saw that something was wrong, and, fearful perhaps that he was going to say what he did say a moment later, she tried to get him out of the room.

'Come upstairs. I want you to do something for me,' she said, walking over to him and pulling him by the arm.

But José's excitement was too great. He did not even notice that she was touching him. 'Señora!' he cried. 'There is a crocodile in the garden!'

Doña Faustina looked at him with black hatred. 'What are you saying?' she said softly and with a certain concern in her voice, as if the old man needed to be treated with gentleness.

'An enormous *caimán!* I saw it!'

Elena looked at him apprehensively. 'He's ill,' she whispered to Doña Faustina.

José heard her. 'Ill!' he laughed scornfully. 'Come with me and wait a little. I'll show you who's ill! Just come!'

'You say in the garden?' repeated Doña Faustina incredulously. 'But where?'

'In the great tank, señora.'

'Tank? What tank?'

'The señora doesn't know about the tank? There's a tank down below in the orchard. *Sí, sí, sí,*' he insisted, seeing Elena's face. 'I've been there many times. It's not far. Come.'

Inasmuch as Elena seemed to be on the point of removing her apron and accepting his invitation, Doña Faustina changed her tactics. 'Stop this nonsense!' she shouted. 'If you're ill, José, go to bed. Or are you drunk?' She stepped close to him and sniffed suspiciously. 'No? *Bueno.* Elena, give him some hot coffee and let me know in an hour how he is.'

But in her room Doña Faustina began to worry.

6

THEY got out just in time. Carlota was not sure they ought to leave. 'Where shall we go?' she said plaintively.

'Don't think about that,' said Doña Faustina. 'Think about the police. We must go. I know. What good does it do me to have the power of thirty-seven if I pay no attention to what they tell me? They say we must leave. Today.'

As they sat in the train, ready to pull out of the station, surrounded by baskets, Doña Faustina held Jesus Maria up to the window and made his tiny arm wave goodbye to the town. 'The capital is a better place for him in any case,' she whispered.

They went to a small *fonda* in the capital, where the second day Doña Faustina conceived the idea of applying at the nearest *comisaría* for employment as police matron. Her physical build, plus the fact that, as she told the lieutenant, she was afraid of no human being, impressed those who interviewed her, and after various examinations, she was accepted into the force.

'You'll see,' she said to Carlota when she returned that evening in high spirits. 'From now on we have nothing to worry about. Nothing can harm us. We have new names. We are new people. Nothing matters but Jesus Maria.'

At that very moment the inn was swarming with police. The news of the *caimán,* which José in his obstinacy insisted was really there, first to Elena and then to others in the market, had reached them and awakened their curiosity once again. When it was found that there was not one but a pair of the beasts in the hidden tank, the police began to look more closely. No one really believed even now that it was Doña Faustina and her sister who were responsible for the disappearance of the dozens of infants who had vanished during the past two or three years, but it was felt that it would do no harm to investigate.

In a dark corner of the laundry, under one of the wash-tubs, they found a bundle of bloodstained rags which on closer inspection proved beyond a doubt to be the garments of an infant. Then they discovered other such rags stuffed in the windows to fill the spaces left by broken panes. 'They must be Jesus Maria's,' said the loyal Elena. 'The señora will be back in a day or so, and she will tell you.' The police leered.

The *jefe* came and looked around the laundry. 'She was not stupid,' he said admiringly. 'She did the work here, and *they*', he pointed out towards the orchard, 'took care of the rest.'

Little by little all the stories from round about concurred to make one unified mass of evidence; there was no longer much doubt as to Doña Faustina's guilt, but finding her was another matter. For a while the papers were full of the affair. Indignant articles were spread across the pages, and always there was the demand that the readers be on the look-out for the two monstrous women. But it turned out that no picture was available of either of them.

Doña Faustina saw the newspapers, read the articles, and shrugged her shoulders. 'All that happened long ago,' she said. 'It has no importance now. And even if it had, they could not catch me. I have too much power for them.' Soon the papers spoke of other things.

Fifteen years passed quietly. Jesus Maria, who was unusually bright and strong for his age, was offered a position as servant in the home of the Chief of Police. He had seen the boy about with his mother for several years, and liked him. This was a great triumph for Doña Faustina.

'I know you will be a great man,' she told Jesus Maria, 'and will never bring dishonour upon us.'

But eventually he did, and Doña Faustina was inconsolable.

After three years he grew bored with his menial work, and went into the army, carrying with him a recommendation from his employer to a close friend, a certain colonel who saw to it that Jesus Maria was pleasantly treated in the barracks. Everything went well for him; he was constantly promoted, so that by the time he was twenty-five he had become a colonel himself. It may be observed that to be a colonel in the Mexican army is not so great an attainment, nor is it necessarily a sign of exceptional merit. However, there is little doubt that Jesus Maria's military career would have continued its upward course had he not happened to be in Zacatecas at the time of the raids on the villages thereabout by Fermín Figueroa and his band. As one more privilege in the endless chain of favours granted him by his superiors he was put in charge of the punitive expedition that was sent out in pursuit of Figueroa. Jesus Maria could not have been completely without ability, none the less, since on the third day out he succeeded in taking the leader prisoner along with thirty-six of his men.

No one ever really knew what happened in the small mountain village where the capture took place, save that Figueroa and the bandits had all been tied up in a sheep corral, ready to be shot, and when a few hours later a corporal had arrived with six soldiers to carry out the execution the corral was empty. And it was even said, after Jesus Maria had been stripped of his rank, that a sheep-herder had seen him enter the corral in the bright afternoon sunlight when everyone else was asleep, loosen the ropes that bound Figueroa, and then hand him his knife, whereupon he turned his back and walked away. Few believed the sheep-herder's story: colonels do not do such things. Still, it was agreed that he had been inexcusably careless, and that it was entirely his fault that the thirty-seven bandits had escaped and thus lived to continue their depredations.

The evening Jesus Maria arrived back at his barracks in the capital, he stood alone in the latrine looking at himself in the fly-specked mirror. Slowly he began to smile, watching the movements of his facial muscles. 'No,' he said, and tried again. He opened his eyes wider and smiled with all his might. The man's face had looked something like that; he would never be able to get it exactly, but he would go on trying because it made him happy to recall that moment – the only time he had ever known how it feels to have power.

A Thousand Days for Mokhtar

This was written in 1948 and is taken from the collection of the same name (1989).

MOKHTAR lived in a room not far from his shop, overlooking the sea. There was a tiny window in the wall above his sleeping-mattress, through which, if he stood on tiptoe, he could see the waves pounding against the rocks of the breakwater far below. The sound came up, too, especially on nights when the Casbah was wrapped in rain and its narrow streets served only for the passage of unexpected gusts of wind. On these nights the sound of the waves was all around, even though he kept the window shut. Throughout the year there were many such nights, and it was precisely at such times that he did not feel like going home to be alone in his little room. He had been by himself ten years now, ever since his wife had died; his solitude never weighed on him when the weather was clear and the stars shone in the sky. But a rainy night put him in mind of the happy hours of his life, when in just such nocturnal wind and storm he and his great-eyed bride would pull the heavy blinds shut and live quietly in each other's company until dawn. These things he could not think about; he would go to the Café Ghazel and play dominoes hour after hour with anyone who came along, rather than return to his room.

Little by little the other men who sat regularly in the café had come to count on Mokhtar's appearance. 'It's beginning to rain: Si Mokhtar will be along soon. Save him the mat next to you.' And he never disappointed them. He was pleasant and quiet; the latter quality made him a welcome addition to a game, since the café's habitués considered each other far too talkative.

Sitting in the Café Ghazel tonight Mokhtar was unaccountably uneasy. He was disturbed by the bonelike sound of the dominoes as they were shuffled on the tables. The metallic scraping of the old phonograph in the inner room bothered him, and he looked up with an unreasoning annoyance at each new arrival who came in through the door, heralded by blasts of wet wind. Often he glanced out the window beside him at the vast blackness of the sea lying below at the foot of the city. On the other side of the glass, just at the edge of the cliff, a few tall stalks of bamboo caught the light from inside, stood out white against the blackness beyond, bending painfully before the gale.

'They'll break,' murmured Mokhtar.

'What?' said Mohammed Slaoui.

Mokhtar laughed, but said nothing. As the evening continued, his discomfort increased. In the inner room they had stopped the phonograph and were singing a strident song. Some of the men around him joined in the noise. He could no longer hear the wind. As that round of dominoes came to an end, he rose precipitately and said, 'Goodnight', not caring how strange his sudden departure might seem to the others.

Outside in the street it was scarcely raining at all, but the wind raged upward from the shore below, bringing with it the bloodlike smell of the sea; the crashing waves seemed very near, almost at his feet. He looked down as he walked along. At each mound of garbage there were cats; they ran across in front of him constantly from one pile to another. As Mokhtar reached his door and pulled out his key, he had the feeling that he was about to perform an irrevocable act, that stepping inside would be a gesture of finality.

What is happening? he asked himself. Am I going to die? He would not be afraid of that; still, he would like to know it a few moments in advance, if possible. He flexed his arms and legs before opening the door: there was no pain anywhere, everything appeared to be in good condition. It's my head, he decided. But his head felt clear, his thoughts moved forward in orderly fashion. Nevertheless, these discoveries did not reassure him; he knew something was wrong. He bolted the door behind him and began to mount the stairs in the dark. More clearly than anything else at the moment he sensed that this conviction of having entered into a new region of his life was only in the nature of a warning. 'Don't go on,' he was being told. Doing what? he asked himself as he undressed. He had no secrets, no involvements, no plans for the future, no responsibilities. He merely lived. He could not heed the warning because he could not understand it. And yet there was no doubt that it was there in his room, and it made itself most strongly felt when he lay down. The wind shook the blinds. The rain had begun to fall again; it showered violently on the panes of glass over the corridor, and rattled down the drainpipe from the roof. And the unappeased roaring of the waves went on, down at the base of the ramparts. He considered the sadness, the coldness of the damp blanket; he touched the straw-covered wall with his finger. In the black night he groaned, 'Al-lah!' and fell asleep.

But even in sleep he went on worrying; his dreams were a chaotic, relentless continuation of his waking state. The same accent of implicit warning was present in the sequences of streets and shops which unrolled before his eyes. He was at the entrance to the public market. A great many people were inside, where they had gone to get out of the rain. Although it was mid-morning, the day was so dark that all the stalls were blazing with electric lights. If only she could have seen this, he said to himself, thinking of how much pleasure it would have given his wife. Poor girl, in her day it was always dark here. And Mokhtar wondered if really he had the right to go on living and watching the world change, without her. Each month the world had changed a little more, had gone a little further away from what it had been when she had known it.

Also, since she is not here to eat it, what am I doing buying meat? He was standing before the stall of his friend Abdallah ben Bouchta, looking at the cuts that were displayed on the slab of white marble in front of him. And all at once he was embroiled in a quarrel with Bouchta. He felt himself seizing the old man by the throat; he felt his fingers pressing with increasing force: he was choking Bouchta and he was glad to be doing it. The violence of the act was a fulfilment and a relief. Bouchta's face grew black, he fell, and his glazed eyes stared like the eyes in a sheep's head served on a platter for the feast of Aïd el Kébir.

Mokhtar awoke, horrified. The wind was still blowing, carrying with it, above the town, wisps of the voice of the muezzin who at that moment was calling from the Jaamâa es Seghira. But the warnings had ceased, and this was comforting enough to make more sleep possible.

The morning was grey and cheerless. Mokhtar rose at the usual hour, made his daily visit to the great mosque for a few moments of prayer and a thorough wash, and proceeded through the rain to his shop. There were few people in the streets. The memory of his dream weighed upon him, saddening him even more than the prospect of a day of infrequent sales. As the morning progressed he thought often of his old friend; he was consumed with the desire to pass by the market, just to assure himself that Bouchta was there as always. There was no reason why he should not be, but once Mokhtar had seen him with his own eyes he would be content.

A little before noon he boarded up the front of his shop and set out for the market. When his eyes became accustomed to the dim inner light of the building, the first person he saw was

Bouchta standing behind the counter in his stall, chopping and slicing the meat the same as any other day. Feeling immensely relieved, Mokhtar wandered over to the counter and spoke to him. Perhaps the note of excessive cordiality in his voice surprised Bouchta, for he glanced up with a startled expression in his face, and seeing Mokhtar, said shortly, '*Sbalkheir.*' Then he resumed hacking at a piece of meat for a customer. His rather unfriendly look was lost on Mokhtar, who was so pleased to see him there that he was momentarily unable to perceive anything but that one fact. However, when Bouchta, on completing the sale, turned to him, and said abruptly, 'I'm busy this morning', Mokhtar stared at him, and again felt his fear stir within him.

'Yes, Sidi?' he said pleasantly.

Bouchta glared. 'Twenty-two douro would be a more welcome offering than your foolish smile,' he said.

Mokhtar looked confused. 'Twenty-two douro, Sidi?'

'Yes. The twenty-two douro you never paid me for the lamb's head at last Aïd el Kébir.'

Mokhtar felt the blood leap upward in him like a fire. 'I paid you for that the following month.'

'*Abaden!* Never!' cried Bouchta excitedly. 'I have eyes and a head too! I remember what happens! You can't take advantage of me the way you did of poor old Tahiri. I'm not that old yet!' And he began to call out unpleasant epithets, brandishing his cleaver.

People had stopped in their tracks and were following the conversation with interest. As Mokhtar's anger mounted, he suddenly heard, among the names that Bouchta was calling him, one which offended him more than the rest. He reached across the counter and seized Bouchta's djellaba in his two hands, pulling on the heavy woollen fabric until it seemed that it would surely be ripped off the old man's back.

'Let go of me!' shouted Bouchta. The people were crowding in to see whatever violence might result. 'Let go of me!' he kept screaming, his face growing steadily redder.

At this point the scene was so much like his dream that Mokhtar, even while he was enjoying his own anger and the sight of Bouchta as he became the victim of such a senseless rage, was suddenly very much frightened. He let go of the djellaba with one hand, and turning to the onlookers said loudly, 'Last night I dreamed that I came here and killed this man, who is my friend. I do not want to kill him. I am not going to kill him. Look carefully. I am not hurting him.'

Bouchta's fury was reaching grotesque proportions. With one hand he was trying to pry Mokhtar's fingers from his garment, and with the other, which held the cleaver, he was making crazy gyrations in the air. All the while he jumped quickly up and down, crying, 'Let go! Let go! *Khalli!*'

At any moment he is going to hit me with the cleaver, thought Mokhtar, and so he seized the wrist that held it, pulling Bouchta against the counter. For a moment they struggled and panted, while the slabs of meat slid about under their arms and fell heavily on to the wet floor. Bouchta was strong, but he was old. Suddenly he relaxed his grasp on the cleaver and Mokhtar felt his muscles cease to push. The crowd murmured. Mokhtar let go of both the wrist and the djellaba, and looked up. Bouchta's face was an impossible colour, like the sides of meat that hung behind him. His mouth opened and his head slowly tilted upward as if he were looking at the ceiling of the market. Then, as if someone had pushed him from behind, he fell forward on to the marble counter and lay still, his nose in a shallow puddle of pinkish water. Mokhtar knew he was dead, and he was a little triumphant as he shouted to everyone, 'I dreamed it! I dreamed it! I told you! Did I kill him? Did I touch him? You saw!' The crowd agreed, nodding.

'Get the police!' cried Mokhtar. 'I want everyone to be my witness.' A few people moved away quietly, not wishing to be involved. But most of them stayed, quite ready to give the authorities their version of the strange phenomenon.

In court the Qadi proved to be unsympathetic. Mokhtar was bewildered by his lack of friendliness. The witnesses had told the story exactly as it had happened; obviously they all were convinced of Mokhtar's innocence.

'I have heard from the witnesses what happened in the market,' said the Qadi impatiently, 'and from those same witnesses I know you are an evil man. It is impossible for the mind of an upright man to bring forth an evil dream. Bouchta died as a result of your dream.' And as Mokhtar attempted to interrupt, 'I know what you are going to say, but you are a fool, Mokhtar. You blame the wind, the night, your long solitude. Good. For a thousand days in our prison here you will not hear the wind, you will not know whether it is night or day, and you will never lack the companionship of your fellow prisoners.'

The Qadi's sentence shocked the inhabitants of the town, who found it of an unprecedented severity. But Mokhtar, once he had been locked up, was persuaded of its wisdom. For one thing, he was not unhappy to be in prison, where each night, when he had begun to dream that he was back in his lonely room, he could awaken to hear on all sides of him the comforting snores of the other prisoners. His mind no longer dwelled upon the earlier happy hours of his life, because the present hours were happy ones as well. And then, the very first day there, he had suddenly remembered with perfect clarity that, although he had intended to do so, he never had paid Bouchta the twenty-two douro for the lamb's head, after all.

The Wind at Beni Midar

First published in 1962, this was included in the collection Pages from Cold Point *(1968).*

At Beni Midar there is a barracks. It has many rows of small buildings, whitewashed, and everything is in the middle of big rocks, on the side of the mountain behind the town. A quiet place when the wind is not blowing. A few Spanish still live in the houses along the road. They run the shops. But now the people in the street are Moslems, mountain men with goats and sheep, or soldiers from the *cuartel* looking for wine. The Spanish sell wine to men they know. One Jew sells it to almost anybody. But there never is enough wine in the town for everybody who wants it. Beni Midar has only one street, that comes down out of the mountains, curves back and forth like a snake between the houses for a while, and goes on, back into the mountains. Sunday is a bad day, the one free time the soldiers have, when they can walk back and forth all day between the shops and houses. A few Spaniards in black clothes go into the church at the hour when the Rhmara ride their donkeys out of the souk. Later the Spaniards come out of the church and go home. Nothing else happens because all the shops are shut. There is nothing the soldiers can buy.

Driss had been stationed for eight months in Beni Midar. Because the *cabran* in charge of his unit had been a neighbour of his in Tetuan, he was not unhappy. The *cabran* had a friend with a motor cycle. Together they went each month to Tetuan. There the *cabran* always saw Driss's sister, who made a big bundle of food to send back to the barracks for him. She sent him chickens and cakes, cigarettes and figs, and always many hard-boiled eggs. He shared the eggs with two or three friends, and did not complain about being in Beni Midar.

Not even the brothels were open on Sunday. It was the day when everyone walked from one end of the town to the other, back and forth, many times. Sometimes Driss walked like this with his friends. Usually he took his gun and went down into the valley to hunt for hares. When he came back at twilight he stopped in a small café at the edge of the town and had a glass of tea and a few pipes of *kif*. If it had not been the only café he would never have gone into it. Shameful things happened there. Several times he had seen men from the mountains get up from the mat and do dances that left blood on the floor. These men were Djilala, and no one thought of stopping them, not even Driss. They did not dance because they wanted to dance, and it was this that made him angry and ashamed. It seemed to him that the world should be made in such a way that a man is free to dance or not as he feels. A Djilali can do only what the music tells him to do. When the musicians, who are Djilala too, play the music that has the power, his eyes shut and he falls on the floor. And until the man has shown the proof and tasted his own blood, the musicians do not begin the music that will bring him back to the world. They should do something about it, Driss said to the other soldiers who went with him to the café, and they agreed.

He had talked about it with his *cabran* in the public garden. The *cabran* said that when all the children in the land were going to school every day there would be no more djenoun. Women would no longer be able to put spells on their husbands. And the Djilala and the Hamatcha and all the others would stop cutting their legs and arms and chests. Driss thought about this for a long time. He was glad to hear that the government knew about these bad things. But if they know, he thought, why don't they do something now? The day they get every one of the children in school I'll be lying beside Sidi Ali el Mandri. He was thinking of the cemetery at Bab Sebta in Tetuan. When he saw the *cabran* again he said, 'If they can do something about it, they ought to do it now.' The *cabran* did not seem interested. 'Yes,' he said.

When Driss got his permission and went home he told his father what the *cabran* had said. 'You mean the government thinks it can kill all evil spirits?' his father cried.

'That's right. It can,' said Driss. 'It's going to.'

His father was old and had no confidence in the young men who now ran the government. 'It's impossible,' he said. 'They should let them alone. Leave them under their stones. Children have gone to school before, and how many were hurt by *djenoun*? But if the government begins to make trouble for them, you'll see what will happen. They'll go after the children first.'

Driss had expected his father to speak this way, but when he heard the words he was ashamed. He did not answer. Some of his friends were without respect for God. They ate during Ramadan and argued with their fathers. He was glad not to be like them. But he felt that his father was wrong.

One hot summer Sunday when the sky was very blue Driss lay in bed late. The men who slept in his room at the barracks had gone out. He listened to the radio. It would be good down in the valley on a day like this, he thought. He saw himself swimming in one of the big pools, and he thought of the hot sun on his back afterward. He got up and unlocked the cupboard to look at his gun. Even before he took it out he said, '*Yah latif!*' because he remembered that he had only one cartridge left, and it was Sunday. He slammed the cupboard door shut and got back into bed. The radio began to give the news. He sat up, spat as far out as he could from the bed, and turned it off. In the silence he heard many birds singing in the *safsaf* tree outside the window. He scratched his head. Then he got up and dressed. In the courtyard he saw Mehdi going toward the stairs. Mehdi was on his way to do sentry duty in the box outside the main gate.

'*Khaï!* Does four rials sound good to you?'

Mehdi looked at him. 'Is this number sixty, three, fifty-one?' This was the name of an Egyptian song that came over the radio nearly every day. The song ended with the word nothing. Nothing, nothing, sung over and over again.

'Why not?' As they walked along together, Driss moved closer, so that his thigh rubbed against Mehdi's.

'The price is ten, *khoya*.'

'With all its cartridges?'

'You want me to open it up and show you here?' Mehdi's voice was angry. The words came out of the side of his mouth.

Driss said nothing. They came to the top of the stairs. Mehdi was walking fast. 'You'll have to have it back here by seven,' he said. 'Do you want it?'

In his head Driss saw the long day in the empty town. 'Yes,' he said. 'Stay there.' He hurried back to the room, unlocked his cupboard, and took out his gun. From the shelf he pulled down his pipe, his *kif*, and a loaf of bread. He put his head outside the door. There was no one in the courtyard but Mehdi sitting on the wall at the other end. Then with the old gun in his hands he ran all the way to Mehdi. Mehdi took it and went down the stairs, leaving his own gun lying on the wall. Driss took up the gun, waited a moment, and followed him. When he went past the sentry box he heard Mehdi's voice say softly, 'I need the ten at seven, *khoya*.'

Driss grunted. He knew how dark it was in there. No officer ever stuck his head inside the door on Sundays. Ten rials, he thought, and he's running no risk. He looked around at the goats among the rocks. The sun was hot, but the air smelled sweet, and he was happy to be walking down the side of the mountain. He pulled the visor of his cap further down over his eyes and began to whistle. Soon he came out in front of the town, below it on the other side of the valley. He could see the people on the benches in the park at the top of the cliff, small but clear and black. They were Spaniards and they were waiting for the bell of their church to begin to ring.

He got to the highest pool about the time the sun was overhead. When he lay on the rocks afterward eating his bread, the sun burned him. No animals will move before three, he thought. He put his trousers on and crawled into the shade of the oleander bushes to sleep. When he awoke the air was cooler. He smoked all the *kif* he had, and went walking through the valley. Sometimes he sang. He found no hares, and so he put small stones on the tops of the rocks and fired at them. Then he climbed back up the other side of the valley and followed the highway into the town.

He came to the café and went in. The musicians were playing an *aaita* and singing. The tea drinkers clapped their hands with the music. A soldier cried, 'Driss! Sit down!' He sat with his friends and smoked some of their *kif*. Then he bought four rials' worth from the cutter who sat on the platform with the musicians, and went on smoking. 'Nothing was moving in the valley today,' he told them. 'It was dead down there.'

A man with a yellow turban on his head who sat nearby closed his eyes and fell against the man next to him. The others around him moved to a further part of the mat. The man toppled over and lay on the floor.

'Another one?' cried Driss. 'They should stay in Djebel Habib. I can't look at him.'

The man took a long time to get to his feet. His arms and legs had been captured by the drums, but his body was fighting, and he groaned. Driss tried to pay no attention to him. He smoked his pipe and looked at his friends, pretending that no Djilali was in front of him. When the man pulled out his knife he could not pretend any longer. He watched the blood running into the man's eyes. It made a blank red curtain over each hole. The man opened his eyes wider, as if he wanted to see through the blood. The drums were loud.

Driss got up and paid the *qahouaji* for his tea. He said goodbye to the others and went out. The sun would soon go below the top of the mountain. Its light made him want to shut his eyes, because he had a lot of *kif* in his head. He walked through the town to the higher end and turned into a lane that led up into another valley. In this place there was no one. Cacti grew high on each side of the lane, and the spiders had built a world of webs between their thorns. Because he walked fast, the *kif* began to boil in his head. Soon he was very hungry, but all the fruit had been picked from the cacti along the lane. He came to a small farmhouse with a thatched roof. Behind it on the empty mountainside there were more cacti still pink with hundreds of *hindiyats*. A dog in a shed beside the house began to bark. There was no sign of people. He stood still for a while and listened to the dog. Then he walked toward the cactus patch. He was sure no one was in the house. Many years ago his sister had shown him how to pick *hindiyats* without letting the needles get into the flesh of his hands. He laid his gun on the ground behind a low stone wall and began to gather the fruit. As he picked he saw in his head the two blind red holes of the Djilali's eyes, and under his breath he cursed all Djilala. When he had a great pile of fruit on the ground he sat down and began to eat, throwing the peels over his shoulder. As he ate he grew hungrier, and so he picked more. The picture he had in his head of the man's face shiny with blood slowly faded. He thought only of the *hindiyats* he was eating. It was almost dark there on the mountainside. He looked at his watch and jumped up, because he remembered that Mehdi had to have his gun at seven o'clock. In the dim light he could not see the gun anywhere. He searched behind the wall, where he thought he had laid it, but he saw only stones and bushes.

'It's gone, *Allah istir*,' he said. His heart pounded. He ran back to the lane and stood there a while. The dog barked without stopping.

It was dark before he reached the gate of the barracks. Another man was in the sentry box. The *cabran* was waiting for him in the room. The old gun Driss's father had given him lay on his bed.

'Do you know where Mehdi is?' the *cabran* asked him.

'No,' said Driss.

'He's in the dark house, the son of a whore. And do you know why?'

Driss sat down on the bed. The *cabran* is my friend, he was thinking. 'It's gone,' he said, and told him how he had laid the gun on the ground, and a dog had been barking, and no one had come by, and still it had disappeared. 'Maybe the dog was a *djinn*,' he said when he had finished. He did not really believe the dog had anything to do with it, but he could not think of anything else to say then.

The *cabran* looked at him a long time and said nothing. He shook his head. 'I thought you had some brains,' he said at last. Then his face grew very angry, and he pulled Driss out into the courtyard and told a soldier to lock him up.

At ten o'clock that night he went to see Driss. He found him smoking his *sebsi* in the dark. The cell was full of *kif* smoke. 'Garbage!' cried the *cabran*, and he took the pipe and the *kif* away from him. 'Tell the truth,' he said to Driss. 'You sold the gun, didn't you?'

'On my mother's head, it's just as I told you! There was only the dog.'

The *cabran* could not make him say anything different. He slammed the door and went to the café in the town to have a glass of tea. He sat listening to the music, and he began to smoke the *kif* he had taken from Driss. If Driss was telling the truth, then it was only the *kif* in Driss's head that had made him lose the gun, and in that case there was a chance that it could be found.

The *cabran* had not smoked in a long time. As the *kif* filled his head he began to be hungry, and he remembered the times when he had been a boy smoking *kif* with his friends. Always they had gone to look for *hindiyats* afterward, because they tasted better than anything else and cost nothing. They always knew where there were some growing. A *kouffa* full of good *hindiyats*, he thought. He shut his eyes and went on thinking.

The next morning early the *cabran* went out and stood on a high rock behind the barracks, looking carefully all around the valley and the bare mountainside. Not far away he saw a lane with cacti along it, and further up there was a whole forest of cactus. 'There,' he said to himself.

He walked among the rocks until he came to the lane, and he followed the lane to the farmhouse. The dog began to bark. A woman came to the doorway and looked at him. He paid no attention to her, but went straight to the high cacti on the hillside behind the house. There were many *hindiyats* still to be eaten, but the *cabran* did not eat any of them. He had no *kif* in his head and he was thinking only of the gun. Beside a stone wall there was a big pile of *hindiya* peelings. Someone had eaten a great many. Then he saw the sun shining on part of the gun's barrel under the peelings. 'Hah!' he shouted, and he seized the gun and wiped it all over with his handkerchief. On his way back to the barracks he felt so happy that he decided to play a joke on Driss.

He hid the gun under his bed. With a glass of tea and a

piece of bread in his hand he went to see Driss. He found him asleep on the floor in the dark.

'Daylight is here!' he shouted. He laughed and kicked Driss's foot to wake him up. Driss sat on the floor drinking the tea and the *cabran* stood in the doorway scratching his chin. He looked down at the floor, but not at Driss. After a time he said, 'Last night you told me a dog was barking?'

Driss was certain the *cabran* was going to make fun of him. He was sorry he had mentioned the dog. 'Yes,' he said, not sounding sure.

'If it was the dog,' the *cabran* went on, I know how to get it back. You have to help me.'

Driss looked up at him. He could not believe the *cabran* was being serious. Finally he said in a low voice, 'I was joking when I said that. I had *kif* in my head.'

The *cabran* was angry. 'You think it's a joke to lose a gun that belongs to the Sultan? You did sell it! You haven't got *kif* in your head now. Maybe you can tell the truth.'

He stepped toward Driss, and Driss thought he was going to hit him. He stood up quickly. 'I told you the truth,' he said. 'It was gone.'

The *cabran* rubbed his chin and looked down at the floor again for a minute. 'The next time a Djilali begins to dance in the café, we'll do it,' he told him. He shut the door and left Driss alone.

Two days later the *cabran* came again to the dark house. He had another soldier with him. 'Quick!' he told Driss. 'There's one dancing now.'

They went out into the courtyard and Driss blinked his eyes. 'Listen,' said the *cabran*. 'When the Djilali is drinking his own blood he has power. What you have to do is ask him to make the *djinn* bring me the gun. I'm going to sit in my room and burn *djaoui*. That may help.'

'I'll do it,' said Driss. 'But it won't do any good.'

The other soldier took Driss to the café. The Djilali was a tall man from the mountains. He had already taken out his knife, and he was waving it in the air. The soldier made Driss sit down near the musicians, and then he waited until the man began to lick the blood from his arms. Then, because he thought he might be sick if he watched any longer, Driss raised his right arm toward the Djilali and said in a low voice, 'In the name of Allah, *khoya*, make the *djinn* that stole Mehdi's gun take it now to Aziz the *cabran*.' The Djilali seemed to be staring at him, but Driss could not be sure whether he had heard his words or not.

The soldier took him back to the barracks. The *cabran* was sitting under a plum tree beside the kitchen door. He told the soldier to go away and jumped up. 'Come,' he said, and he led Driss to the room. The air was blue with the smoke of the *djaoui* he had been burning. He pointed to the middle of the floor. 'Look!' he cried. A gun was lying there. Driss ran and picked it up. After he had looked at it carefully, he said, 'It's the gun.' And his voice was full of fear. The *cabran* could see that Driss had not been sure the thing was possible, but that now he no longer had any doubt.

The *cabran* was happy to have fooled him so easily. He laughed. 'You see, it worked,' he said. 'It's lucky for you. Mehdi's going to be in the dark house for another week.'

Driss did not answer. He felt even worse than when he had been watching the Djilali slicing the flesh of his arms.

That night he lay in bed worrying. It was the first time he had had anything to do with a *djinn* or an *affrit*. Now he had entered into their world. It was a dangerous world and he did not trust the *cabran* any longer. What am I going to do? he thought. The men all around him were sleeping, but he could not close his eyes. Soon he got up and stepped outside. The leaves of the *safsaf* tree were hissing in the wind. On the other side of the courtyard there was light in one of the windows. Some of the officers were talking there. He walked slowly around the garden in the middle and looked up at the sky, thinking of how different his life was going to be now. As he came near the lighted window he heard a great burst of laughter. The *cabran* was telling a story. Driss stopped walking and listened.

'And he said to the Djilali, "Please, Sidi, would you ask the dog that stole my gun –"'

The men laughed again, and the sound covered the *cabran*'s voice.

He went quickly back and got into bed. If they knew he had heard the *cabran*'s story they would laugh even more. He lay in the bed thinking, and he felt poison come into his heart. It was the *cabran*'s fault that the *djinn* had been called, and now in front of his superior officers he was pretending that he had had nothing to do with it. Later the *cabran* came in and went to bed, and it was quiet in the courtyard, but Driss lay thinking for a long time before he went to sleep.

In the days that came after that, the *cabran* was friendly again, but Driss did not want to see him smile. He thought with hatred: In his head I'm afraid of him now because he knows how to call a *djinn*. He jokes with me now because he has power.

He could not laugh or be happy when the *cabran* was nearby. Each night he lay awake for a long time after the others had gone to sleep. He listened to the wind moving the hard leaves of the *safsaf* tree, and he thought only of how he could break the *cabran*'s power.

When Mehdi came out of the dark house he spoke against the *cabran*. Driss paid him his ten rials. 'A lot of money for ten days in the dark house,' Mehdi grumbled, and he looked at the bill in his hand. Driss pretended not to understand. 'He's a son of a whore,' he said.

Mehdi snorted. 'And you have the head of a needle,' he said. 'It all came from you. The wind blows the *kif* out your ears!'

'You think I wasn't in the dark house too?' cried Driss. But he could not tell Mehdi about the Djilali and the dog. 'He's a son of a whore,' he said again.

Mehdi's eyes grew narrow and stiff. 'I'll do his work for him. He'll think he's in the dark house himself when I finish.'

Mehdi went on his way. Driss stood watching him go.

The next Sunday Driss got up early and walked into Beni Midar. The souk was full of rows of mountain people in white clothes. He walked in among the donkeys and climbed the steps to the stalls. There he went to see an old man who sold incense and herbs. People called him El Fqih. He sat down in front of El Fqih and said, 'I want something for a son of a whore.'

El Fqih looked at him angrily. 'A sin!' He raised his forefinger and shook it back and forth. 'Sins are not my work.' Driss did not say anything. El Fqih spoke more quietly now. 'To balance that, it is said that each trouble in the world has its remedy. There are cheap remedies and remedies that cost a lot of money.' He stopped.

Driss waited. 'How much is this one?' he asked him. The old man was not pleased because he wanted to talk longer. But he said, 'I'll give you a name for five rials.' He looked sternly at Driss, leaned forward and whispered a name in his ear. 'In the alley behind the sawmill,' he said aloud. 'The blue tin shack with the canebrake in back of it.' Driss paid him and ran down the steps.

He found the house. The old woman stood in the doorway with a checked tablecloth over her head. Her eyes had turned white like milk. They looked to Driss like the eyes of an old dog. He said, 'You're Anisa?'

'Come into the house,' she told him. It was almost dark inside. He told her he wanted something to break the power of a son of a whore. 'Give me ten rials now,' she said. 'Come back at sunset with another ten. It will be ready.'

After the midday meal he went out into the courtyard. He met Mehdi and asked him to go with him to the café in Beni Midar. They walked through the town in the hot afternoon sun. It was still early when they got to the café, and there was plenty of space on the mats. They sat in a dark corner. Driss took out his *kif* and his *sebsi* and they smoked. When the musicians began to play, Mehdi said, 'The circus is back!' But Driss did not want to talk about the Djilala. He talked about the *cabran*. He gave the pipe many times to Mehdi, and he watched Mehdi growing more angry with the *cabran* as he smoked. He was not surprised when Mehdi cried, 'I'll finish it tonight!'

'No, *khoya*,' said Driss. 'You don't know. He's gone way up. He's a friend of all the officers now. They bring him bottles of wine.'

'He'll come down,' Mehdi said. 'Before dinner tonight. In the courtyard. You be there and watch it.'

Driss handed him the pipe and paid for the tea. He left Mehdi there and went into the street to walk up and down because he did not want to sit still any longer. When the sky was red behind the mountain he went to the alley by the sawmill. The old woman was in the doorway.

'Come in,' she said as before. When they were inside the room she handed him a paper packet. 'He has to take all of it,' she said. She took the money and pulled at his sleeve. 'I never saw you,' she said. 'Goodbye.'

Driss went to his room and listened to the radio. When dinner time came he stood inside the doorway looking out into the courtyard. In the shadows at the other end he thought he could see Mehdi, but he was not sure. There were many soldiers walking around in the courtyard, waiting for dinner. Soon there was shouting near the top of the steps. The soldiers began to run toward the other end of the courtyard. Driss looked from the doorway and saw only the running soldiers. He called to the men in the room. 'Something's happening!' They all ran out. Then with the paper of powder in his hand he went back into the room to the *cabran*'s bed and lifted up the bottle of wine one of the officers had given the *cabran* the day before. It was almost full. He pulled out the cork and let the powder slide into the bottle. He shook the bottle and put the cork back. There was still shouting in the courtyard. He ran out. When he got near the crowd, he saw Mehdi being dragged along the ground by three soldiers. He was kicking. The *cabran* sat on the wall with his head down, holding his arm. There was blood all over his face and shirt.

It was almost a half-hour before the *cabran* came to eat his dinner. His face was covered with bruises and his arm was bandaged and hung in a sling. Mehdi had cut it with his knife at the last minute when the soldiers had begun to pull them apart. The *cabran* did not speak much, and the men did not try to talk with him. He sat on his bed and ate. While he was eating he drank all the wine in the bottle.

That night the *cabran* moaned in his sleep. A dry wind blew between the mountains. It made a great noise in the *safsaf* tree outside the window. The air roared and the leaves rattled, but Driss still heard the *cabran*'s voice crying. In the morning the doctor came to look at him. The *cabran*'s eyes were open but he could not see. And his mouth was open but he could not speak. They carried him out of the room where the soldiers lived and put him somewhere else. Maybe the power is broken now, thought Driss.

A few days later a truck came to the barracks, and he saw two men carrying the *cabran* on a stretcher to the truck. Then he was sure that the *cabran*'s soul had been torn out of his body and that the power was truly broken. In his head he made a prayer of thanks to Allah. He stood with some other soldiers on a rock above the barracks watching the truck grow smaller as it moved down the mountain.

'It's bad for me,' he told a man who stood nearby. 'He always brought me food from home.' The soldier shook his head.

He of the Assembly

First published in 1960, this was included in the collection Pages from Cold Point *(1968).*

> He salutes all parts of the sky and the earth where it is bright. He thinks the colour of the amethysts of Aguelmous will be dark if it has rained in the valley of Zerekten. 'The eye wants to sleep,' he says, 'but the head is no mattress.' When it rained for three days and water covered the flat lands outside the ramparts, he slept by the bamboo fence at the Café of the Two Bridges.

It seems there was a man named Ben Tajah who went to Fez to visit his cousin. The day he came back he was walking in the Djemaa el Fna, and he saw a letter lying on the pavement. He picked it up and found that his name was written on the envelope. He went to the Café of the Two Bridges with the letter in his hand, sat down on a mat and opened the envelope. Inside was a paper which read: 'The sky trembles and the earth is afraid, and the two eyes are not brothers.' Ben Tajah did not understand, and he was very unhappy because his name was on the envelope. It made him think that Satan was nearby. He of the Assembly was sitting in the same part of the café. He was listening to the wind in the telephone wires. The sky was almost empty of daytime light. The eye wants to sleep, he thought, but the head is no mattress. I know what that is, but I have forgotten it. Three days is a long time for rain to keep falling on flat bare ground. If I got up and ran down the street, he thought, a policeman would follow me and call to me to stop. I would run faster, and he would run after me. When he shot at me I'd duck around the corners of houses. He felt the rough dried mud of the wall under his fingertips. And I'd be running through the streets looking for a place to hide, but no door would be open, until finally I came to one door that was open, and I'd go in through the rooms and courtyards until finally I came to the kitchen. The old woman would be there. He stopped and wondered for a moment why an old woman should be there alone in the kitchen at that hour. She was stirring a big kettle of soup on the stove. And I'd look for a place to hide there in the kitchen, and there'd be no place. And I'd be waiting to hear the policeman's footsteps, because he wouldn't miss the open door. And I'd look in the dark corner of the room where she kept the charcoal, but it wouldn't be dark enough. And the old woman would turn and look at me and say, 'If you're trying to get away, my boy, I can help you. Jump into the soup-kettle.' The wind sighed in the telephone wires. Men came into the Café of the Two Bridges with their garments flapping. Ben Tajah sat on his mat. He had put the letter away, but first he had stared at it a long time. He of the Assembly leaned back and looked at the sky. 'The old woman,' he said to himself. 'What is she trying to do? The soup is hot. It may be a trap. I may find there's no way out, once I get down there.' He wanted a pipe of *kif*, but he was afraid the policeman would run into the kitchen before he was able to smoke it. He said to the old woman, 'How can I get in? Tell me.' And it seemed to him that he heard footsteps in the street, or perhaps even in one of the rooms of the house. He leaned over the stove and looked down into the kettle. It was dark and very hot down in there. Steam was coming up in clouds, and there was a thick smell in the air that made it hard to breathe. 'Quick!' said the old woman, and she unrolled a rope ladder and hung it over the edge of the kettle. He began to climb down, and she leaned over and looked after him. 'Until the other world!' he shouted. And he climbed all the way down. There was a rowboat below. When he was in it he tugged on the ladder and the old woman began to pull it up. And at that instant the policeman ran in, and two more were with him, and the old woman had just the time to throw the ladder down into the soup. Now they are going to take her to the commissariat, he thought, and the poor woman only did me a favour. He rowed around in the dark for a few minutes, and it was very hot. Soon he took off his clothes. For a while he could see the round top of the kettle up above, like a porthole in the side of a ship, with the heads of the policemen looking down in, but then it grew smaller as he rowed, until it was only a light. Sometimes he could find it and sometimes he lost it, and finally it was gone. He was worried about the old woman, and he thought he must find a way to help her. No policeman can go into the Café of the Two Bridges because it belongs to the Sultan's sister. This is why there is so much *kif* smoke inside that a *berrada* can't fall over even if it is pushed, and why most customers like to sit outside, and even there keep one hand on their money. As long as the thieves stay inside and their friends bring them food and *kif*, they are all right. One day police headquarters will forget to send a man to watch the café, or one man will leave five minutes before the other gets there to take his place. Outside everyone smokes *kif* too, but only for an hour or two – not all day and night like the ones inside. He of the Assembly had forgotten to light his *sebsi.* He was in a café where no policeman could come, and he wanted to go away to a *kif* world where the police were chasing him. This is the way we are now, he thought. We work backwards. If we have something good, we look for something bad instead. He lighted the *sebsi* and smoked it. Then he blew the hard ash out of the *chqaf.* It landed in the brook beside the second bridge. The world is too good. We can only work forward if we make it bad again first. This made him sad, so he stopped thinking, and filled his *sebsi.* While he was smoking it, Ben Tajah looked in his direction, and although they were facing each other He of the Assembly did not notice Ben Tajah until he got up and paid for his tea. Then he looked at him because he took such a long time getting up off the floor. He saw his face and he thought: That man has no one in the world. The idea made him feel cold. He filled his *sebsi* again and lighted it. He saw the man as he was going to go out of the café and walk alone down the long road outside the ramparts. In a little while he himself would have to go out to the souks to try and borrow money for dinner. When he smoked a lot of *kif* he did not like his aunt to see him, and he did not want to see her. Soup and bread. No one can want more than that. Will thirty francs be enough the fourth time? The *qahouaji* wasn't satisfied last night. But he took it. And he went away and let me sleep. A Moslem, even in the city, can't refuse his brother shelter. He was not convinced, because he had been born in the mountains, and so he kept thinking back and forth in this way. He smoked many *chqofa,* and when he got up to go out into the street he found that the world had changed.

Ben Tajah was not a rich man. He lived alone in a room near Bab Doukkala, and he had a stall in the bazaars where he sold coathangers and chests. Often he did not open the shop because he was in bed with a liver attack. At such times he pounded on the floor from his bed, using a brass pestle, and the postman who lived downstairs brought him up some food. Sometimes he stayed in bed for a week at a time. Each morning and night the postman came in with a tray. The food was not very good because the postman's wife did not understand much about cooking. But he was glad to have it. Twice he had brought the postman a new chest to keep clothes and blankets in. One of the postman's wives a few years before had taken a chest with her when she had left him and gone back to her family in Kasba Tadla. Ben Tajah himself had tried having a wife for a while because he needed someone to get him regular meals and to wash his clothes, but the girl was from the mountains, and was wild. No matter how much he beat her she would not be tamed. Everything in the room got broken, and finally he had to put her out into the street. 'No more women will get into my house,' he told his friends in the bazaars, and they laughed. He took home many women, and one day he found that he had *en noua.* He knew that was a bad disease, because it stays in the blood and eats the nose from inside. 'A man loses his nose only long after he has already lost his head.' He asked a doctor for medicine. The doctor gave him a paper and told him to take it to the Pharmacie de l'Etoile. There he bought six vials of penicillin in a box. He took them home and tied each little bottle with a silk thread, stringing them so that they made a necklace. He wore this always around his neck, taking care that the glass vials touched his skin. He thought it likely that by now he was cured, but his cousin in Fez had just told him that he must go on wearing the medicine for another three months, or at least until the beginning of the moon of Chouwal. He had thought about this now and then on the way home, sitting in the bus for two days, and he had decided that his cousin was too cautious. He stood in the Djemaa el Fna a minute watching the trained monkeys, but the crowd pushed too much, so he walked on. When he got home he shut the door and put his hand in his pocket to pull out the envelope, because he wanted to look at it again inside his own room and be sure that the name written on it was beyond a doubt his. But the letter was gone. He remembered the jostling in the Djemaa el Fna. Someone had reached into his pocket and imagined his hand was feeling money, and taken it. Yet Ben Tajah did not truly believe this. He was convinced that he would have known such a theft was happening. There had been a letter in his pocket. He was not even sure of that. He sat down on the cushions. Two days in the bus, he thought. Probably I'm tired. I found no letter. He searched in his pocket again, and it seemed to him he could still remember how the fold of the envelope had felt. Why would it have my name on it? I never found any letter at all. Then he wondered if anyone had seen him in the café with the envelope in one hand and the sheet of paper in the other, looking at them both for such a long time. He stood up. He wanted to go back to the Café of the Two Bridges and ask the *qahouaji*, 'Did you see me an hour ago? Was I looking at a letter?' If the *qahouaji* said 'Yes,' then the letter was real. He repeated the words aloud: 'The sky trembles and the earth is afraid, and the two eyes are not brothers.' In the silence afterwards the memory of the sound of the words frightened him. If there was no letter, where are these words from? And he shivered because the answer to that was: 'From Satan.' He was about to open the door when a new fear stopped him. The *qahouaji* might say 'No', and this would be still worse, because it would mean that the words had been put directly into his head by Satan, that Satan had chosen him to reveal Himself to. In that case He might appear at any moment. '*Ach haddou laillaha ill'Allah* . . .' he prayed, holding his two forefingers up, one on each side of him. He sat down again and did not move. In the street the children were crying. He did not want to hear the *qahouaji* say, 'No. You had no letter.' If he knew that Satan was coming to tempt him, he would have that much less power to keep Him away with his prayers, because he would be more afraid.

He of the Assembly stood. Behind him was a wall. In his hand was the *sebsi*. Over his head was the sky, which he felt was about to burst into light. He was leaning back looking at it. It was dark on the earth, but there was still light up there behind the stars. Ahead of him was the *pissoir* of the Carpenters' Souk which the French had put there. People said only Jews used it. It was made of tin, and there was a puddle in front of it that reflected the sky and the top of the *pissoir.* It looked like a boat in the water. Or like a pier where boats land. Without moving from where he stood, He of the Assembly saw it approaching slowly. He was going toward it. And he remembered he was naked, and put his hand over his sex. In a minute the rowboat would be bumping against the pier. He steadied himself on his legs and waited. But at that moment a large cat ran out of the shadow of the wall and stopped in the middle of the street to turn and look at him with an evil face. He saw its two eyes and for a while could not take his own eyes away. Then the cat ran across the street and was gone. He was not sure what had happened, and he stood very still looking at the ground. He looked back at the *pissoir* reflected in the puddle and thought: It was a cat on the shore, nothing else. But the cat's eyes had frightened him. Instead of being like cats' eyes, they had looked like the eyes of a person who was interested in him. He made himself forget he had had this thought. He was still waiting for the rowboat to touch the landing pier, but nothing had happened. It was going to stay where it was, that near the shore but not near enough to touch. He stood still a long time, waiting for something to happen. Then he began to walk very fast down the street toward the bazaars. He had just remembered that the old woman was in the police station. He wanted to help her, but first he had to find out where they had taken her. I'll have to go to every police station in the Medina, he thought, and he was not hungry any more. It was one thing to promise himself he would help her when he was far from land, and another when he was a few doors from a commissariat. He walked by the entrance. Two policemen stood in the doorway. He kept walking. The street curved and he was alone. 'This night is going to be a jewel in my crown,' he said, and he turned quickly to the left and went along a dark passageway. At the end he saw flames, and he knew that Mustapha would be there tending the fire of the bakery. He crawled into the mud hut where the oven was. 'Ah, the jackal has come back from the forest!' said Mustapha. He of the Assembly shook his head. 'This is a bad world,' he told Mustapha. 'I've got no money,' Mustapha said. He of the Assembly did not understand. 'Everything goes backwards,' he said. 'It's bad now, and we have to make it still worse if we want to go forwards.' Mustapha saw that He of the Assembly was *mkiyif ma rassou* and was not interested in money. He looked at him in a more friendly way and said, 'Secrets are not between friends. Talk.' He of the Assembly told him that an old woman had done him a great favour, and because of that three policemen had arrested her and taken her to the police station. 'You must go for me to the commissariat and ask them if they have an old woman there.' He pulled out his *sebsi* and took a very long time filling it. When he finished it he smoked it himself and did not offer any to Mustapha, because Mustapha never offered him any of his. 'You see how full of *kif* my head is,' he said laughing. 'I can't go.' Mustapha laughed too and said it would not be a good idea, and that he would go for him.

'I was there, and I heard him going away for a long time, so long that he had to be gone, and yet he was still there, and his footsteps were still going away. He went away and there was nobody. There was the fire and I moved away from it. I wanted to hear a sound like a muezzin crying "*Allah akbar!*" or a French plane from the Pilot Base flying over the Medina, or news on the radio. It wasn't there. And when the wind came in the door it was made of dust high as a man. A night to be chased by dogs in the Mellah. I looked in the fire and I saw an eye in there, like the eye that's left when you burn *chibb* and you know there was a *djinn* in the house. I got up and stood. The fire was making a noise like a voice. I think it was talking. I went out and walked along the street. I walked a long time and I came to Bab el Khemiss. It was dark there and the wind was cold. I went to the wall where the camels were lying and stood there. Sometimes the men have fires and play songs on their *aouadas*. But they were asleep. All snoring. I walked again and went to the gate and looked out. The big trucks went by full of vegetables and I thought I would like to be on a truck and ride all night. Then in another city I would be a soldier and go to Algeria. Everything would be good if we had a war. I thought a long time. Then I was so cold I turned around and walked again. It was as cold as the belly of the oldest goat of Ijoukak. I thought I heard a muezzin and I stopped and listened. The only thing I heard was the water running in the *seguia* that carries the water out to the gardens. It was near the *mçid* of Moulay Boujemaa. I heard the water running by and I felt cold. Then I knew I was cold because I was afraid. In my head I was thinking: If something should happen that never happened before, what would I do? You want to laugh? Hashish in your heart and wind in your head. You think it's like your grandmother's prayer-mat. This is the truth. This isn't a dream brought back from another world past the customs like a teapot from Mecca. I heard the water and I was afraid. There were some trees by the path ahead of me. You know at night sometimes it's good to pull out the *sebsi* and smoke. I smoked and I started to walk. And then I heard something. Not a muezzin. Something that sounded like my name. But it came up from below, from the *seguia*, "*Allah istir!*" And I walked with my head down. I heard it again saying my name, a voice like water, like the wind moving the leaves in the trees, a woman. It was a woman calling me. The wind was in the trees and the water was running, but there was a woman too. You think it's *kif*. No, she was calling my name. Now and then, not very loud. When I was under the trees it was louder, and I heard that the voice was my mother's. I heard that the way I can hear you. Then I knew the cat was not a cat, and I knew that Aïcha Qandicha wanted me. I thought of other nights when perhaps she had been watching me from the eyes of a cat or a donkey. I knew she was not going to catch me. Nothing in the seven skies could make me turn around. But I was cold and afraid and when I licked my lips my tongue had no spit on it. I was under the *safsaf* trees and I thought: She's going to reach down and try to touch me. But she can't touch me from the front and I won't turn around, not even if I hear a pistol. I remembered how the policeman had fired at me and how I'd found only one door open. I began to yell, "You threw me the ladder and told me to climb down! You brought me here! The filthiest whore in the Mellah, with the pus coming out of her, is a thousand times cleaner than you, daughter of all the *padronas* and dogs in seven worlds." I got past the trees and I began to run. I called up to the sky so she could hear my voice behind: "I hope the police put a hose in your mouth and pump you full of salt water until you crack open!" I thought: Tomorrow I'm going to buy *fasoukh* and *tib* and *nidd* and *hasalouba* and *mska* and all the *bakhour* in the Djemaa, and put them in the *mijmah* and burn them, and walk back and forth over the *mijmah* ten times slowly, so the smoke can clean out all my clothes. Then I'll see if there's an eye in the ashes afterwards. If there is, I'll do it all over again right away. And every Thursday I'll buy the *bakhour* and every Friday I'll burn it. That will be strong enough to keep her away. If I could find a window and look through and see what they're doing to the old woman! If only they could kill her! I kept running. There were a few people in the streets. I didn't look to see where I was going, but I went to the street near Mustapha's oven where the commissariat was. I stopped running before I got to the door. The one standing there saw me before that. He stepped out and raised his arm. He said to me, "Come here."'

He of the Assembly ran. He felt as though he were on horseback. He did not feel his legs moving. He saw the road coming toward him and the doors going by. The policeman had not shot at him yet, but it was worse than the other time because he was very close behind and he was blowing his whistle. The policeman is old. At least thirty-five. I can run faster. But from any street others could come. It was dangerous and he did not want to think about danger. He of the Assembly let songs come into his head. When it rains in the valley of Zerekten the amethysts are darker in Aguelmous. The eye wants to sleep but the head is no mattress. It was a song. Ah, my brother, the ink on the paper is like smoke in the air. What words are there to tell how long a night can be? Drunk with love, I wander in the dark. He was running through the dye-souk, and he splashed into a puddle. The whistle blew again behind him, like a crazy bird screaming. The sound made him feel like laughing, but that did not mean he was not afraid. He thought: If I'm seventeen I can run faster. That has to be true. It was very dark ahead. He had to slow his running. There was no time for his eyes to get used to the dark. He nearly ran into the wall of the shop at the end of the street. He turned to the right and saw the narrow alley ahead of him. The police had tied the old woman naked to a table with her thin legs wide apart and were sliding electrodes up inside her. He ran ahead. He could see the course of the alley now even in the dark. Then he stopped dead, moved to the wall, and stood still. He heard the footsteps slowing down. He's going to turn to the left. And he whispered aloud, 'It ends that way.' The footsteps stopped and there was silence. The policeman was looking into the silence and listening into the dark to the left and to the right. He of the Assembly could not see him or hear him, but he knew that was what he was doing. He did not move. When it rains in the valley of Zerekten. A hand seized his shoulder. He opened his mouth and swiftly turned, but the man had moved and was pushing him from the side. He felt the wool of the man's djellaba against the back of his hand. He had gone through a door and the man had shut it without making any noise. Now they both stood still in the dark, listening to the policeman walking quickly by outside the door. Then the man struck a match. He was facing the other way, and there was a flight of stairs ahead. The man did not turn around, but he said, 'Come up,' and they both climbed the stairs. At the top the man took out a key and opened a door. He of the Assembly stood in the doorway while the man lit a candle. He liked the room because it had many mattresses and cushions and a white sheepskin under the tea-tray in the corner on the floor. The man turned around and said, 'Sit down.' His face looked serious and kind and unhappy. He of the Assembly had never seen it before, but he knew it was not the face of a policeman. He of the Assembly pulled out his *sebsi*.

Ben Tajah looked at the boy and asked him, 'What did you mean when you said down there, "It ends that way"? I heard you say it.' The boy was embarrassed. He smiled and looked at the floor. Ben Tajah felt happy to have him there. He had been standing outside the door downstairs in the dark for a long time, trying to make himself go to the Café of the Two Bridges and talk to the *qahouaji*. In his mind it was almost as though he already had been there and spoken with him. He had heard the *qahouaji* telling him that he had seen no letter, and he had felt his own dismay. He had not wanted to believe that, but he would be willing to say yes, I made a mistake and there was no letter, if only he could find out where the words had come from. For the words were certainly in his head: '. . . and the two eyes are not brothers.' That was like the footprint found in the garden the morning after a bad dream, the proof that there had been a reason for the dream, that something had been there after all. Ben Tajah had not been able to go or to stay. He had started and stopped so many times that now, although he did not know it, he was very tired. When a man is tired he mistakes the hopes of children for the knowledge of men. It seemed to him that He of the Assembly's words had a meaning all for him. Even though the boy might not know it, he could have been sent by Allah to help him at that minute. In a nearby street a police whistle blew. The boy looked at him. Ben Tajah did not care very much what the answer would be, but he said, 'Why are they looking for you?' The boy held out his lighted *sebsi* and his *mottoui* fat with *kif*. He did not want to talk because he was listening. Ben Tajah smoked *kif* only when a friend offered it to him, but he understood that the police had begun once more to try to enforce their law against *kif*. Each year they arrested people for a few weeks, and then stopped arresting them. He looked at the boy, and decided that probably he smoked too much. With the *sebsi* in his hand he was sitting very still listening to the voices of some passers-by in the street below. 'I know who he is,' one said. 'I've got his name from Mustapha.' 'The baker?' 'That's the one.' They walked on. The boy's expression was so intense that Ben Tajah said to him, 'It's nobody. Just people.' He was feeling happy because he was certain that Satan would not appear before him as long as the boy was with him. He said quietly, 'Still you haven't told me why you said: "It ends that way."' The boy filled his *sebsi* slowly and smoked all the *kif* in it. 'I meant,' he said, 'thanks to Allah. Praise the sky and the earth where it is bright. What else can you mean when something ends?' Ben Tajah nodded his head. Pious thoughts can be of as much use for keeping Satan at a distance as camphor or *bakhour* dropped on to hot coals. Each holy word is worth a high column of smoke, and the eyelids do not smart afterward. He has a good heart, thought Ben Tajah, even though he is probably a guide for the Nazarenes. And he asked himself why it would not be possible for the boy to have been sent to protect him from Satan. Probably not. But it could be. The boy offered him the *sebsi.* He took it and smoked it. After that Ben Tajah began to think that he would like to go to the Café of the Two Bridges and speak to the *qahouaji* about the letter. He felt that if the boy went with him the *qahouaji* might say there had been a letter, and that even if the man could not remember, he would not mind so much because he would be less afraid. He waited until he thought the boy was not nervous about going into the street, and then he said, 'Let's go out and get some tea.' 'Good,' said the boy. He was not afraid of the police if he was with Ben Tajah. They went through the empty streets, crossed the Djemaa el Fna and the garden beyond. When they were near the café, Ben Tajah said to the boy, 'Do you know the Café of the Two Bridges?' The boy said he always sat there, and Ben Tajah was not surprised. It seemed to him that perhaps he had even seen him there. He seized the boy's arm. 'Were you there today?' he asked him. The boy said 'Yes', and turned to look at him. He let go of the arm. 'Nothing,' he said. 'Did you ever see me there?' They came to the gate of the café and Ben Tajah stopped walking. 'No,' the boy said. They went across the first bridge and then the second bridge, and sat down in a corner. Not many people were left outside. Those inside were making a great noise. The *qahouaji* brought the tea and went away again. Ben Tajah did not say anything to him about the letter. He wanted to drink the tea quietly and leave trouble until later.

When the muezzin called from the minaret of the

Koutoubia, He of the Assembly thought of being in the Agdal. The great mountains were ahead of him and the olive trees stood in rows on each side of him. Then he heard the trickle of water and he remembered the *seguia* that is there in the Agdal, and he swiftly came back to the Café of the Two Bridges. Aïcha Qandicha can be only where there are trees by running water. 'She comes only for single men by trees and fresh moving water. Her arms are gold and she calls in the voice of the most cherished one.' Ben Tajah gave him the *sebsi.* He filled it and smoked it. 'When a man sees her face he will never see another woman's face. He will make love with her all the night, and every night, and in the sunlight by the walls, before the eyes of children. Soon he will be an empty pod and he will leave this world for his home in Jehennem.' The last carriage went by, taking the last tourists down the road beside the ramparts to their rooms in the Mamounia. He of the Assembly thought: The eye wants to sleep. But this man is alone in the world. He wants to talk all night. He wants to tell me about his wife and how he beat her and how she broke everything. Why do I want to know all those things? He is a good man but he has no head. Ben Tajah was sad. He said, 'What have I done? Why does Satan choose me?' Then at last he told the boy about the letter, about how he wondered if it had had his name on the envelope and how he was not even sure there had been a letter. When he finished he looked sadly at the boy. 'And you didn't see me.' He of the Assembly shut his eyes and kept them shut for a while. When he opened them again he said, 'Are you alone in the world?' Ben Tajah stared at him and did not speak. The boy laughed. 'I did see you,' he said, 'but you had no letter. I saw you when you were getting up and I thought you were old. Then I saw you were not old. That's all I saw.' 'No, it isn't,' Ben Tajah said. 'You saw I was alone.' He of the Assembly shrugged. 'Who knows?' He filled the *sebsi* and handed it to Ben Tajah. The *kif* was in Ben Tajah's head. His eyes were small. He of the Assembly listened to the wind in the telephone wires, took back the *sebsi* and filled it again. Then he said, 'You think Satan is coming to make trouble for you because you're alone in the world. I see that. Get a wife or somebody to be with you always, and you won't think about it any more. That's true. Because Satan doesn't come to men like you.' He of the Assembly did not believe this himself. He knew that Father Satan can come for anyone in the world, but he hoped to live with Ben Tajah, so he would not have to borrow money in the souks to buy food. Ben Tajah drank some tea. He did not want the boy to see that his face was happy. He felt that the boy was right, and that there never had been a letter. 'Two days on a bus is a long time. A man can get very tired,' he said. Then he called the *qahouaji* and told him to bring two more glasses of tea. He of the Assembly gave him the *sebsi*. He knew that Ben Tajah wanted to stay as long as possible in the Café of the Two Bridges. He put his finger into the *mottoui*. The *kif* was almost gone. 'We can talk,' he said. 'Not much *kif* is in the *mottoui*.' The *qahouaji* brought the tea. They talked for an hour or more. The *qahouaji* slept and snored. They talked about Satan and the bad thing it is to live alone, to wake up in the dark and know that there is no one else nearby. Many times He of the Assembly told Ben Tajah that he must not worry. The *kif* was all gone. He held his empty *mottoui* in his hand. He did not understand how he had got back to the town without climbing up out of the soup kettle. Once he said to Ben Tajah, 'I never climbed back up.' Ben Tajah looked at him and said he did not understand. He of the Assembly told him the story. Ben Tajah laughed. He said, 'You smoke too much *kif*, brother.' He of the Assembly put his *sebsi* into his pocket. 'And you don't smoke and you're afraid of Satan,' he told Ben Tajah. 'No!' Ben Tajah shouted. 'By Allah! No more! But one thing is in my head, and I can't put it out. The sky trembles and the earth is afraid, and the two eyes are not brothers. Did you ever hear those words? Where did they come from?' Ben Tajah looked hard at the boy. He of the Assembly understood that these had been the words on the paper, and he felt cold in the middle of his back because he had never heard them before and they sounded evil. He knew, too, that he must not let Ben Tajah know this. He began to laugh. Ben Tajah took hold of his knee and shook it. His face was troubled. 'Did you ever hear them?' He of the Assembly went on laughing. Ben Tajah shook his leg so hard that he stopped and said, 'Yes!' When Ben Tajah waited and he said nothing more, he saw the man's face growing angry, and so he said, 'Yes, I've heard them. But will you tell me what happened to me and how I got out of the soup-kettle if I tell you about those words?' Ben Tajah understood that the *kif* was going away from the boy's head. But he saw that it had not all gone, or he would not have been asking that question. And he said, 'Wait a while for the answer to that question.' He of the Assembly woke the *qahouaji* and Ben Tajah paid him, and they went out of the café. They did not talk while they walked. When they got to the Mouassine mosque, Ben Tajah held out his hand to say goodnight, but He of the Assembly said, 'I'm looking in my head for the place I heard your words. I'll walk to your door with you. Maybe I'll remember.' Ben Tajah said, 'May Allah help you find it.' And he took his arm and they walked to Ben Tajah's door while He of the Assembly said nothing. They stood outside the door in the dark. 'Have you found it?' said Ben Tajah. 'Almost,' said He of the Assembly. Ben Tajah thought that perhaps when the *kif* had gone out of the boy's head he might be able to tell him about the words. He wanted to know how the boy's head was, and so he said, 'Do you still want to know how you got out of the soup-kettle?' He of the Assembly laughed. 'You said you would tell me later,' he told Ben Tajah. 'I will,' said Ben Tajah. 'Come upstairs. Since we have to wait, we can sit down.' Ben Tajah opened the door and they went upstairs. This time He of the Assembly sat down on Ben Tajah's bed. He yawned and stretched. It was a good bed. He was glad it was not the mat by the bamboo fence at the Café of the Two Bridges. 'And so, tell me how I got out of the soup-kettle,' he said laughing. Ben Tajah said, 'You're still asking me that? Have you thought of the words?' 'I know the words,' the boy said. 'The sky trembles . . .' Ben Tajah did not want him to say them again. 'Where did you hear them? What are they? That's what I want to know.' The boy shook his head. Then he sat up very straight and looked beyond Ben Tajah, beyond the wall of the room, beyond the streets of the Medina, beyond the gardens, toward the mountains where the people speak Tachelhait. He remembered being a little boy. This night is a jewel in my crown, he thought. It went this way. And he began to sing, making up a melody for the words Ben Tajah had told him. When he had finished '. . . and the two eyes are not brothers,' he added a few more words of his own and stopped singing. 'That's all I remember of the song,' he said. Ben Tajah clapped his hands together hard. 'A song!' he cried. 'I must have heard it on the radio.' He of the Assembly shrugged. 'They play it sometimes,' he said. I've made him happy, he thought. But I won't ever tell him another lie. That's the only one. What I'm going to do now is not the same as lying. He got up off the bed and went to the window. The muezzins were calling the *fjer.* 'It's almost morning,' he said to Ben Tajah. 'I still have *kif* in my head.' 'Sit down,' said Ben Tajah. He was sure now there had been no letter. He of the Assembly took off his djellaba and got into bed. Ben Tajah looked at him in surprise. Then he undressed and got into bed beside him. He left the candle burning on the floor beside the bed. He meant to stay awake, but he went to sleep because he was not used to smoking *kif* and the *kif* was in his head. He of the Assembly did not believe he was asleep. He lay for a long time without moving. He listened to the voices of the muezzins, and he thought that the man beside him would speak or move. When he saw that Ben Tajah was surely asleep, he was angry. This is how he treats a friend who has made him happy. He forgets his trouble and his friend too. He thought about it more and he was angrier. The muezzins were still calling the *fjer.* Before they stop, or he will hear. Very slowly he got out of the bed. He put on his djellaba and opened the door. Then he went back and took all the money out of Ben Tajah's pockets. In with the banknotes was an envelope that was folded. It had Ben Tajah's name written across it. He pulled out the piece of paper inside and held it near the candle, and then he looked at it as he would have looked at a snake. The words were written there. Ben Tajah's face was turned toward the wall and he was snoring. He of the Assembly held the paper above the flame and burned it, and then he burned the envelope. He blew the black paper-ashes across the floor. Without making any noise he ran downstairs and let himself out into the street. He shut the door. The money was in his pocket and he walked fast to his aunt's house. His aunt awoke and was angry for a while. Finally he said, 'It was raining. How could I come home? Let me sleep.' He had a little *kif* hidden under his pillow. He smoked a pipe. Then he looked across his sleep to the morning and thought: A pipe of *kif* before breakfast gives a man the strength of a hundred camels in the courtyard.

The Garden

First published in 1964, this was included in the collection Pages from Cold Point *(1968).*

A man who lived in a distant town of the southern country was working in his garden. Because he was poor his land was at the edge of the oasis. All the afternoon he dug channels, and when the day was finished he went to the upper end of the garden and opened the gate that held back the water. And now the water ran in the channels to the beds of barley and the young pomegranate trees. The sky was red, and when the man saw the floor of his garden shining like jewels, he sat down on a stone to look at it. As he watched, it grew brighter, and he thought: There is no finer garden in the oasis.

A great happiness filled him, and he sat there a long time, and did not get home until very late. When he went into the house, his wife looked at him and saw the joy still in his eyes.

He has found a treasure, she thought; but she said nothing. When they sat face to face at the evening meal, the man was still remembering his garden, and it seemed to him that now that he had known this happiness, never again would he be without it. He was silent as he ate.

His wife too was silent. He is thinking of the treasure, she said to herself. And she was angry, believing that he did not want to share his secret with her. The next morning she went to the house of an old woman and bought many herbs and powders from her. She took them home and passed several days mixing and cooking them, until she had made the medicine she wanted. Then at each meal she began to put a little of the *tsoukel* into her husband's food.

It was not long before the man fell ill. For a time he went each day to his garden to work, but often when he got there he was so weak that he could merely sit leaning against a palm tree. He had a sharp sound in his ears, and he could not follow his thoughts as they came to him. In spite of this, each day when the sun went down and he saw his garden shining red in its light, he was happy. And when he got home at night his wife could see that there was joy in his eyes.

He has been counting the treasure, she thought, and she began to go secretly to the garden to watch him from behind the trees. When she saw that he merely sat looking at the ground, she went back to the old woman and told her about it.

'You must hurry and make him talk, before he forgets where he has hidden the treasure,' said the old woman.

That night the wife put a great amount of *tsoukel* into his food, and when they were drinking tea afterward she began to say many sweet words to him. The man only smiled. She tried for a long time to make him speak, but he merely shrugged his shoulders and made motions with his hands.

The next morning while he was still asleep, she went back to the old woman and told her that the man could no longer speak.

'You have given him too much,' the old woman said. 'He will never tell you his secret now. The only thing for you to do is go away quickly, before he dies.'

The woman ran home. Her husband lay on the mat with his mouth open. She packed her clothing and left the town that morning.

For three days the man lay in a deep sleep. The fourth day when he awoke, it was as if he had made a voyage to the other side of the world. He was very hungry, but all he could find in the house was a piece of dry bread. When he had eaten that, he walked to his garden at the edge of the oasis and picked many figs. Then he sat down and ate them. In his mind there was no thought of his wife, because he had forgotten her. When a neighbour came by and called to him, he answered politely, as if speaking to a stranger, and the neighbour went away perplexed.

Little by little the man grew healthy once more. He worked each day in the garden. When dusk came, after watching the sunset and the red water, he would go home and cook his dinner and sleep. He had no friends, because although men spoke to him, he did not know who they were, and he only smiled and nodded to them. Then the people in the town began to notice that he no longer went to the mosque to pray. They spoke about this among themselves, and one evening the imam went to the man's house to talk with him.

As they sat there, the imam listened for sounds of the man's wife in the house. Out of courtesy he could not mention her, but he was thinking about her and asking himself where she might be. He went away from the house full of doubts.

The man went on living his life. But the people of the town now talked of little else. They whispered that he had killed his wife, and many of them wanted to go together and search the house for her remains. The imam spoke against this idea, saying that he would go and talk again with the man. And this time he went all the way to the garden at the edge of the oasis, and found him there working happily with the plants and the trees. He watched him for a while, and then he walked closer and spoke a few words with him.

It was late in the afternoon. The sun was sinking in the west, and the water on the ground began to be red. Presently the man said to the imam, 'The garden is beautiful.'

'Beautiful or not beautiful,' said the imam, 'you should be giving thanks to Allah for allowing you to have it.'

'Allah?' said the man. 'Who is that? I never heard of him. I made this garden myself. I dug every channel and planted every tree, and no one helped me. I have no debts to anyone.'

The imam had turned pale. He flung out his arm and struck the man very hard in the face. Then he went quickly out of the garden.

The man stood with his hand to his cheek. He has gone mad, he thought, as the imam walked away.

That night the people spoke together in the mosque. They decided that the man could no longer live in their town. Early the next morning a great crowd of men, with the imam going at the head of it, went out into the oasis, on its way to the man's garden.

The small boys ran ahead of the men, and got there long before them. They hid in the bushes, and as the man worked they began to throw stones and shout insults at him. He paid no attention to them. Then a stone hit the back of his head. He jumped up quickly. As they ran away, one of them fell, and the man caught him. He tried to hold him still so he could ask him, 'Why were you throwing stones at me?' But the boy only screamed and struggled.

And the townspeople, who were on their way, heard the screaming, and they came running to the garden. They pulled the boy away from him and began to strike at the man with hoes and sickles. When they had destroyed him, they left him there with his head lying in one of the channels, and went back to the town, giving thanks to Allah that the boy was safe.

Little by little the sand covered everything. The trees died, and very soon the garden was gone. Only the desert was there.

Here to Learn

This was first published in the collection Midnight Mass *(1985).*

1

MALIKA needed no one to tell her she was pretty. From the beginning of her memory people had murmured about her beauty, for even when she was a baby girl the symmetry of her head, neck and shoulders was remarkable. Before she was old enough to go to the spring to fetch water she knew she had eyes like a gazelle and that her head was like a lily on its stalk. At least, these were the things older people said about her.

On a hill above the town stood a large building with palm-shaded walks leading up to it. This belonged to the Hermanas Adoratrices. Certain of these nuns, upon catching sight of Malika, had gone to her father, offering to take her in charge and teach her to speak Spanish and to embroider. Enthusiastically he had agreed. Allah has sent us here to learn, he would say. Malika's mother, who disapproved of her daughter's spending her time with Nazarenes, did her utmost to make him change his mind. Nevertheless Malika stayed with the sisters for five years, until her father died.

Malika's grandmother was fond of saying that when she had been Malika's age she had looked exactly like her, and that if it were possible for her to become a little girl again and stand beside Malika, no one would be able to tell them apart. At first Malika found this impossible to believe; she studied the old woman's ravaged face and straightway rejected the idea. After her grandmother had died, she began to understand what the old woman had meant when she said: Only Allah remains the same. One day she would no longer be pretty, but now she was. Thus, when she was able to go by herself to the spring and carry back two full pails of water, it meant nothing to her if the older boys and the young men called to her and tried to speak with her. They would do better, she thought, to say all those flattering things to girls who needed such reassurance.

A barracks full of soldiers stood just outside the town. The men were rough and brutal. When she caught sight of one of them, even in the distance, Malika would hide until he had disappeared. Fortunately the soldiers seldom strayed into the arroyo that lay between her house and the spring; they preferred to saunter in groups up and down the main road leading through the town.

There came a day when her mother insisted that she go to sell a hen at the market on the main highway. Her older sister always had done this, but she was at a neighbour's house helping prepare for a wedding. Malika begged her mother to lend her her *haïk* so she could cover her face.

Your sister's been a thousand times. She never wears a *haïk*.

Malika knew this was because no one paid any attention to her sister, but she could not say it to her mother. I'm afraid, she said, and burst into tears. Her mother had no patience with the silly behaviour of girls, and refused to let her take the *haïk*. As Malika ran out of the house, holding the hen by its legs, she snatched up a soiled bathtowel. As soon as she was out of sight, she wrapped it loosely around her head, so that when she got to the highway she could pull it down and cover at least a part of her face.

Several dozen women lined one side of the road, each sitting on the ground with her wares spread out around her. Malika went to the end of the row, which was opposite a small park where the soldiers sat on benches. People wandered past and picked up the hen to squeeze it and shake it, so that it constantly squawked and fluttered. She had pulled the towel down so far over her eyes that she could see only the earth at her feet.

After an hour or so had gone by, a woman came along who began to discuss the price of the hen with her. Eventually she bought it, and Malika, once she had tied the coins up in a piece of cloth, jumped to her feet. The towel slipped over her face and fell to the ground. She picked it up and started to hurry along the highway.

2

THE town was derelict; it smelled of the poverty in which its people were accustomed to live. Nor was there any indication that in some past era something more had existed. The wind from the sea raised the dust of the streets high into the air and showered it angrily over the countryside. Even the leaves of the fig trees were coated white. The hot sand flying stung the skin on the backs of her legs as she turned the corner of the side street that led to the lower end of the gully. She draped the towel over her head and held on to it with one hand. It had never occurred to her to hate the town, for she assumed that anywhere else would be more or less the same.

The street was scarcely more than an alley, with walls on either side. All at once she heard the sound of heavy boots pounding the earth behind her. She did not turn around. Then a hard hand seized her arm and pushed her roughly against the wall. It was a soldier, and he was smiling. He braced his arms against the wall on each side of her so she could not escape.

Malika said nothing. The man stood gazing at her. He was

breathing deeply, as though he had been running. Finally he said: How old are you?

She looked directly into his eyes. Fifteen.

He smelt of wine, tobacco and sweat.

Let me go, she said, and she tried desperately to duck under the barricade. The pain she felt as he twisted her arm made her open her eyes very wide, hut she did not cry out. Two men in djellabas were approaching from the direction of the gully, and she fixed her eyes on them. The soldier turned, saw them, and began to walk quickly back toward the highway.

When she got home, she tossed the bit of cloth with the money in it on to the *taifor*, and indignantly showed her mother the marks on her arm.

What's that?

A soldier grabbed me.

Her mother dealt her a stinging blow across the face. Malika had never seen her in such a rage.

You young bitch! she screamed. That's all you're good for!

Malika ran out of the house and down into the gully, where she sat on a rock in the shade, wondering if her mother might be going mad. The unexpectedness and injustice of the sudden blow had removed all thought of the soldier from her mind. She felt that she must find an explanation of her mother's behaviour; otherwise she would hate her.

That night at dinner things were not much better; her mother would not look at her, and directed all her remarks to her other daughter. This proved to be the pattern for the days that followed. It was as if she had decided that Malika no longer existed.

Good, thought Malika. If I'm not here, then she's not here. She's not my mother and I do hate her.

This silent war between them did not mean that Malika was exempt from having to continue to go to the market. Nearly every week she would be sent off to sell a hen or a basket of vegetables and eggs. She had no further trouble with the soldiers, perhaps because she now stopped on her way down the gully each time and smeared a little mud over her face. It was always dry by the time she reached the highway, and although the women there sometimes stared at her with surprise, the men paid her no attention. On her way home, going up the gully, she would wash her face.

There was always suspicion in her mother's glance now when she returned to the house. If you get into trouble, she said, I swear I'll kill you with my own hands. Malika sniffed and left the room. She knew what her mother meant, but it astonished her to see how little she knew about her own daughter.

3

ONE day as Malika sat in the front row of women and girls in the market on the highway, a long yellow car without a top drove up silently and stopped. There was only one man in it, and he was a Nazarene. The women began to murmur and cry out, for the man held a camera in his hands and was pointing it at them. A girl sitting next to Malika turned to her and said:

You speak Spanish. Tell him to go away.

Malika ran over to the car. The man lowered his camera and stared at her.

Señor, you mustn't take pictures here, she said, looking at him gravely. She pointed back at the row of indignant women.

The Nazarene was big, with light-coloured hair. He understood and smiled. *Muy bien, muy bien*, he said good-naturedly, still looking fixedly at her. She was suddenly conscious of the dirt on her face. Without thinking she rubbed her cheek with the back of her hand. The man's smile became broader.

Will you let me take your picture?

Malika's heart began to beat painfully. No! No! she cried, aghast. Then by way of explanation she added: I have to go and sell my eggs.

The Nazarene looked more pleased than ever. You have eggs for sale? Bring them over.

Malika went and fetched the little packet of eggs, tied in a cloth. A group of boys had caught sight of the dazzling yellow car, and now they surrounded it, demanding money. The Nazarene, trying to wave them away, opened the door for Malika and pointed to the empty seat. She laid the bundle on the leather cushion and bent to undo the knot, but the arms of the boys kept pushing in front of her and jostling her. The Nazarene shouted angrily at the urchins in a foreign language, but this deterred them only for an instant. Finally, in a rage, he said to Malika: Get in. She lifted the eggs and obeyed, seating herself with the bundle on her lap. The man reached in front of her and slammed the door shut. Then he raised the window. But two beggars now had joined the boys, and they were able to reach over the top of the window.

Without warning the Nazarene started up the motor with a great roar. The car shot forward. Startled, Malika turned to see some of the boys sprawling in the road. When she looked again, they were almost out of the town. The Nazarene still seemed to be very angry. She decided not to ask him how far he was going before he stopped and bought the eggs. Her emotions hovered between delight at being in the fine car and anxiety about walking back to the town.

The trees were going by very fast. It seemed to her that she had always known something strange like this would happen to her one day. It was a comforting thought, and it kept her from feeling actual fear.

4

SOON they turned on to a dirt road that burrowed deep into a eucalyptus grove. Here in the dubious shade the Nazarene shut off the motor and turned to Malika with a smile. He took the bundle of eggs from her lap and put it into the back of the car. From a basket behind her seat he brought out a bottle of mineral water and a napkin. He poured a little water on to the napkin and with one hand on her shoulder set to work wiping the streaks of mud from her cheeks. She let him rub, and she let him remove the towel wrapped around her head, so that her hair fell to her shoulders. Why shouldn't he see me? she thought. He's a good man. She had already noticed that he did not smell at all and his gentleness with her gave her a pleasant sensation.

Now shall I take your picture?

She nodded. There was no one to witness the shameful act. He made her sit lower in the seat, and held the camera above her. It clicked so many times, and he looked so peculiar with the big black apparatus in front of his face, that she began to laugh. She thought he might stop then, but he seemed even more pleased, and went on clicking the camera until it would click no more. Then he spread a blanket on the ground and set a basket of food in the centre of it. They sat with the basket between them and ate chicken, cheese and olives. Malika was hungry, and she thought this great fun.

When they had finished, he asked her if she wanted him to take her back to the market. It was as if darkness had fallen over the world. She thought of the women there, and of what they would say when they saw her. She shook her head vigorously. The present moment was real; she would not help it to end. No, not yet, she said lightly.

He looked at his watch. Shall we go to Tetuan?

Her eyes brightened. It was less than an hour's ride from her town, but she had only heard about it. The trees sped by again. Here a stiff breeze blew in from the Mediterranean, and Malika was chilly. The man took out a soft camel's-hair cape and put it around her shoulders.

Tetuan was very exciting with all its traffic. The guards in scarlet and white stood at attention in front of the Khalifa's palace. But she would not get out of the car and walk with him in the street. They were parked there in the Feddane, where the hot afternoon sun beat down on them. Finally the man shrugged and said: Well, if I'm going to get to Tangier tonight, I'd better take you back home.

Malika made a strange sound. She seemed to have become very small inside the cape.

What's the matter?

I can't!

The man stared at her. But you've got to go back home.

Malika began to wail. No, no! she cried. The man glanced nervously at the passers-by, and tried to comfort her with words. But a possibility had just revealed itself to her, and at that moment the idea was powerful enough to occupy her totally. Seeing her too immersed in inner turmoil even to hear him, he started the car and slowly made his way through the throng of people to the other side of the plaza. Then he drove along the principal street to the outskirts of the city, stopped the car by the side of the road, and lighted a cigarette.

He turned to her. One would almost have said that on the seat beside him there was nothing but the cape. He tugged at it, and heard a sob. Gently slipping his hand inside, he smoothed her hair for a moment. Finally she began to push herself upward into a sitting position, and her head appeared.

I'm going to take you with me to Tangier, he said. She made no reply to this, nor did she look at him.

They sped westward, the late afternoon sun in front of them. Malika was conscious of having made an irrevocable choice. The results, already determined by destiny, would be disclosed to her one by one, in the course of events. It was only slowly that she became aware of the landscape around her and of the summer air rushing past.

They came to a tiny café, alone on the mountainside, and stopped. Come in and we'll have some tea, he said. Malika shook her head, pulling the cape more tightly around her. The man went inside and ordered two glasses of tea. A quarter of an hour later a boy carried them to the car on a tray. The tea was very hot, and it took them a while to drink it. Even when the boy had come and taken away the tray, they went on sitting there. Eventually the man switched on the headlights, and they started down the mountainside.

5

MALIKA was frightened by the elevator, but she relaxed somewhat when the man had shown her into the apartment and shut the door behind them. There were thick rugs and soft couches piled with pillows, and lights that could be turned on and off by pushing a button. Most important of all, the Nazarene lived there by himself.

That night he showed her to a room, telling her it was to be hers. Before he said goodnight he took her head in his hands and kissed her on the forehead. When he had gone she wandered into the bathroom and amused herself for a long time turning the hot and cold taps on and off, to see if sooner or later one of them would make a mistake. Finally she undressed, put on the muslin gandoura the man had left for her, and got into the bed.

A pile of magazines lay on the table beside her, and she began to look at the pictures. There was one photograph which caught her attention and held it. The picture showed a luxurious room, with a beautiful woman lying back in a chaise longue. A wide collar of diamonds flashed from her neck, and in her hand she held a book. The book was open but she was not looking at it. Her head was raised, as though someone had just come into the room and found her reading. Malika studied the photograph, glanced at others, and returned to it. To her it illustrated the perfect pose to adopt when receiving guests, and she resolved to practise it by herself, so that when the time came she could put it to use. It would be a good idea to be able to read, too, she thought. One day she would ask the man to show her how.

They had breakfast on the terrace in the morning sun. The building overlooked a spacious Moslem cemetery. Beyond it was the water. Malika told him it was not good to live so near to a graveyard. Later, she looked over the railing, saw the elaborate domed mausoleum of Sidi Bou Araqia and nodded her head in approval. As they sat over their coffee, he answered more of her questions. His name was Tim, he was twenty-eight years old, but he had no wife and no children. He did not live in Tangier all the time. Sometimes he was in Cairo and sometimes in London. In each of these places he had a small flat, but he kept his car in Tangier because that was where he came when he was not working.

As they sat there Malika heard sounds inside the apartment. Presently a fat black woman in a yellow zigdoun came on to the terrace. *Bonjour*, she said, and she began to carry out the dishes. Each time she appeared Malika sat very straight, looking fixedly out across the water at the mountains in Spain.

Someone would be coming in a little while, Tim said, an

Italian woman who was going to take her measurements and make some clothes for her.

Malika frowned. What kind of clothes?

When he said: Whatever you want, she jumped up and went to her room, returning with a copy of *The New Yorker*, which she opened at a page showing a girl in a knit sports suit standing by a set of matched luggage. Like this one, she said. An hour or so later the Italian woman came in, very businesslike, tickled Malika with her tape measure for a while, and left, notebook in hand.

6

LATE that afternoon when the black woman had gone, Tim took Malika into her bedroom, pulled the curtains across the windows, and very gently gave her her first lesson in love. Malika did not really want this to happen then, but she had always known it would sooner or later. The slight pain was negligible, but the shame of being naked in front of the man was almost more than she could bear. It never had occurred to her that a body could be considered beautiful, and she did not believe him when he told her she was perfect in every part. She knew only that men used women in order to make children, and this preoccupied her, as she had no desire for a child. The man assured her that he was not hoping for children either, and that if she did as he told her there was no danger of having any. She accepted this as she accepted everything else he said. She was there in order to learn, and she intended to learn as much as possible.

When, during the next few weeks, she finally consented to go with him to the houses of his friends, he did not guess that she agreed to appear in public only because she had studied herself in the new clothes, and had found them sufficiently convincing to act as a disguise. The European garments made it possible for her to go into the streets with a Nazarene and not be reviled by other Moroccans.

After taking Malika to a photographer's studio and making several lengthy visits to the authorities, Tim returned triumphant one day, waving a passport at her. This is yours, he said. Don't lose it.

Nearly every day there were parties on the Mountain or picnics on the beach. Malika particularly loved the night picnics around a fire, with the sound of the waves breaking on the sand. Sometimes there were musicians, and everyone danced barefoot. One evening eight or ten of the guests jumped up and ran shouting toward the breakers to swim naked in the moonlight. Since the moon was very bright, and there were men and women together, Malika gasped and hid her face. Tim thought this amusing, but the incident caused her to question the fitness of the people in Tangier to be her models for the elegance she hoped to attain.

One morning Tim greeted her with a sad face. In a few days, he told her, he had to go to London. Seeing her expression of chagrin, he quickly added that in two weeks he would be back, and that she would go on living in the flat just as though he were there,

But how can I? she cried. You won't be here! I'll be all alone.

No, no. You'll have friends. You'll like them.

That evening he brought two young men to the apartment. They were handsome and well dressed, and very talkative. When Malika heard Tim address one of them as Bobby, she burst into laughter.

Only dogs are called Bobby, she explained. It's not a man's name.

She's priceless, said Bobby. A teenage Nefertiti.

Absolute heaven, agreed his friend Peter.

After they had gone, Tim explained that they were going to keep Malika company while he was in England. They would live in the apartment with her. On hearing this, she was silent for a moment.

I want to go with you, she said, as if anything else were inconceivable.

He shook his head. *Ni hablar.*

But I don't want love with them.

He kissed her. They don't make love with girls. 'That's why I asked them. They'll take good care of you.

Ah, she said, partially reassured, and at the same time thinking how clever Tim was to have been able to find two such presentable eunuchs with so little apparent effort.

As Tim had promised, Bobby and Peter kept her amused. Instead of taking her out to parties they invited their friends in to meet her. Soon she realized that there were a good many more eunuchs in Tangier than she had suspected. Since, according to Bobby and Peter, these tea-parties and cocktail hours were given expressly for Malika, she insisted on knowing exactly when the guests would be coming, so she could receive them in the correct position, lying back on the cushions of the divan with a book in her hand. When the new arrivals were shown in, she would raise her head slowly until its noble proportions were fully evident, fix her gaze on a point far behind anything in the room, and let the beginning of a smile tremble briefly on her lips before it vanished.

She could see that this impressed them. They told her they loved her. They played games and danced with each other and with her. They tickled her, nuzzled her, took her on their laps and fussed with her hair. She found them more fun to be with than Tim's friends, even though she was aware that the things they said had no meaning. To them everything was a game; there was nothing to learn from them.

7

TIM had been gone for more than a week when they first brought Tony to the flat. He was a tall, noisy Irishman for whom the others of the group seemed to have a certain respect. At first Malika assumed that this was because he was not a eunuch like them, but quickly she discovered that it was only because he had far more money to spend than they did. Tony's clothing always smelled delicious, and his car, a green Maserati, attracted even more attention than Tim's. One day he came by at noon, while Bobby and Peter were still at the market. The black woman had received orders from Bobby to let no one in under any circumstances, but Tony was an expert in getting around such things. Malika had been playing a record of Abdelwahab's; now she quickly silenced it and gave all her attention to Tony. In the course of their dialogue, he remarked casually that her clothes were pretty. Malika smoothed her skirt.

But I'd like to see you in some other clothes, he went on.

Where are they?

Not here. In Madrid.

They heard the door slam, and knew that Bobby and Peter had returned. The two had quarrelled and were communicating only in acid monosyllables. Malika saw that the game of dominoes they had promised to play with her when they got back would not take place. She sat and sulked for a while, turning the pages of one of Tim's financial magazines. Eunuchs were extremely childish, she reflected.

Bobby came into the room and stood at the other end,

arranging books on the bookshelves in silence. Soon the black woman appeared in the doorway and announced to him in French that Monsieur Tim had telephoned from London and would not be in Tangier until the eighteenth.

When Tony had translated the information into Spanish, Malika merely sat staring at him, an expression of despair on her face.

Bobby hurried out of the room. Ill at ease, Tony stood up and followed him. A moment later Bobby's sharp voice cried: No, she can't go out to eat with you. She can't go out at all, anywhere, unless we go along. One of Tim's rules. If you want to eat here, you can.

Very little was said at lunch. In the middle of the meal Peter flung down his napkin and left the room. Afterward the black woman served coffee on the terrace. Bobby and Peter were arguing further back in the flat, but their shrill voices were strangely audible.

For a while Malika sipped her coffee and said nothing. When she spoke to Tony, it was as if there had been no interruption to their earlier conversation. Can we go to Madrid? she said.

You'd like that? He grinned. But you see how they are. And he pointed behind him.

A mí me da igual cómo son. I only promised to stay with them for two weeks.

The next morning, while Bobby and Peter were at the market buying food, Tony and Malika put some valises into the Maserati and drove to the port to catch the ferry to Spain. Tony had left a short note for Bobby, saying that he had borrowed Malika for a few days, and would see to it that she telephoned.

8

THEY slept in Córdoba the first night. Before setting out for Madrid in the morning, Tony stopped at the cathedral to show it to her. When they walked up to the door, Malika hesitated. She peered inside and saw an endless corridor of arches extending into the gloom.

Go on in, said Tony.

She shook her head. You go. I'll wait here.

Driving out of the city, he scolded her a bit. You should look at things when you have the chance, he told her. That was a famous mosque.

I saw it, she said firmly.

The first day in Madrid they spent at Balenciaga's, morning and afternoon. You were right, Malika said to Tony when they were back in the hotel. The clothes here are much better.

They had to wait several days for the first items to be ready. The Prado was almost next door to the hotel, but Tony decided against making the attempt to entice Malika into it. He suggested a bullfight.

Only Moslems know how to kill animals, she declared.

They had been in Madrid for more than a week. One evening as they sat in the bar downstairs at the Ritz, Tony turned to her and said: Have you called Tangier? No, you haven't. Come.

Malika did not want to think of Tangier. Sighing, she rose and went with Tony up to his room, where he put in the call.

When finally he heard Bobby at the other end of the wire, he gestured and handed the telephone to Malika.

At the sound of her voice, Bobby immediately began to reproach her. She interrupted him to ask for Tim.

Tim can't get back to Tangier quite yet, he said, and the pitch of his voice rose as he added: But he wants *you* to come back right now!

Malika was silent.

Did you hear what I said? yelled Bobby. *Oíste?*

Yes, I heard. I'll let you know. She hung up quickly so as not to hear the sounds of outraged protest at the other end.

They went several more times to Balenciaga for fittings. Malika was impressed by Madrid, but she missed the comforting presence of Tim, particularly at night when she lay alone in her bed. While it was pleasant to be with Tony because he paid so much attention to her and constantly bought her gifts, she knew he did this only because he enjoyed dressing her the way he wanted her to look when they went out together, and not because he cared about her.

Although the deliveries continued to be made, and the gowns and ensembles were perfect, Malika's pleasure was somewhat lessened by her discovery that the only places where people really looked at what she was wearing were two restaurants and the bar downstairs. When she remarked about this to Tony, he laughed.

Ah! What you want is Paris, I can see that.

Malika brightened. Can we go there?

When the last garment had arrived, Tony and Malika ate a final dinner at Horcher, and started early the next morning for Paris. They spent the night in Biarritz, where the streets were rainswept and empty.

9

PARIS was far too big. She was frightened of it even before they arrived at the hotel, and she determined not to let Tony out of her sight unless she was safe in her room. At the Hôtel de la Trémoaille she watched him lying back on his bed, making one telephone call after the other while he joked, shouted, waved his legs, and screamed with laughter. When he was through telephoning he turned to her.

Tomorrow night I'm going to take you to a party, he said. And I know just what you'll wear. The oyster-coloured satin number.

Malika was excited by the sumptuous house and the guests in evening clothes. Here at last, she was certain, she had reached a place where the people were of the ultimate degree of refinement. When she found that they looked at her with approval, she was filled with a sense of triumph.

Soon Tony led her up to a tall, pretty girl with flashing black eyes. This is my sister Dinah, he announced. She speaks better Spanish than I do.

Indicating Malika, he added: And this is the new Antinea. He left the two together and disappeared into another room.

Dinah's manner with her made her feel that they had been friends for a long time. When they had chatted for a few minutes, she led her over to a group of South Americans. The women were covered with jewels and some of them carried the pelts of animals over their shoulders. Even the men wore huge diamonds on their fingers. Malika suspected that Tim would disapprove of these people, but then it occurred to her that perhaps he could not be relied upon as an arbiter of taste in a city like this.

Paris es muy grande, she said to a man who smiled at her invitingly. I never saw it until yesterday. I'm afraid to go out. Why did they make it so big?

The man, smiling more broadly, said he was at her service, and would be delighted to go with her wherever she wished, whenever it suited her.

Oh, she said, looking pensive. That would be nice.

Mañana?

Somehow Dinah had caught the end of their dialogue. Not tomorrow, I'm afraid, she said briskly, taking Malika's arm. As she led her away she whispered furiously: His wife was standing there watching you.

Malika stole a frightened glance over her shoulder. The man was still smiling after her.

During the next few days Dinah, who lived nearby in the Avenue Montaigne, came regularly to the hotel. She and Tony had long discussions while Malika listened to Radio Cairo. One afternoon when Tony had gone out and Malika was bored, she asked Dinah to put in a call to Bobby in Tangier. A half-hour later the telephone rang, and she heard Bobby's voice.

Hola, Bobby!

Malika! His voice was already shrill. You can't do this to me! Why are you in Paris? You've got to come back to Tangier.

Malika was silent.

We're waiting for you. What will Tim say if you're not here?

Tim! she said with scorn. Where is Tim?

He's coming back next week. I want to speak to Tony.

Tony's gone out.

Listen to me! Bobby shouted. What hotel are you in?

I don't know its name, she said. It's in Paris. It's a nice hotel. *Adiós*.

One morning not long afterward Tony announced abruptly that he was leaving for London in an hour. Dinah came in shortly before he set out. They seemed to be involved in a dispute, which ended only when he kissed each of them goodbye. After he had gone, Malika nodded her head sagely. London, she mused. He won't come back.

10

THE day after Malika moved into Dinah's flat the weather turned rainy and cold. Dinah often went out, leaving her alone with the housemaid and cook. She was just as glad to stay indoors where it was warm. Her wardrobe, impressive as it was, failed to include any kind of covering for cold weather. Dinah had told her that the cold was just beginning, and that it would not be warm again for many months. It seemed to Malika that somewhere in Paris there must be a *joteya*, where she could take two or three evening gowns and exchange them for a coat, but Dinah shook her head when she asked her about it.

The apartment was spacious, and there were plenty of magazines to study. Malika spent her time curled up on a divan, examining the details in the fashion photographs.

Tony called from London, postponing his return for a few days. When Dinah gave her the news, Malika smiled and said: *Claro*.

I'm having lunch today with a friend. She has mountains of clothes, said Dinah. I'll see if I can't get a coat for you.

What she brought back that afternoon was a mink coat badly in need of repairs. Malika gazed at the rips with visible distaste.

You haven't any idea of how lucky you are, Dinah told her. She shrugged.

When the garment had been fitted at the furrier's and the skins resewn, it looked completely new, as if it had just been made for Malika. She ran her fingers over its glistening surface and examined herself in the mirror, and quickly decided that it was a very fine coat after all.

Dinah's friend came to lunch. Her name was Daphne. She was not very pretty and she tried to speak Italian with Malika. During the course of the meal she invited them both to a house party at Cortina d'Ampezzo.

Dinah was enthusiastic. She brought out an album of photographs after Daphne had left, and spread it in Malika's lap. Malika saw that the ground was white and the people, whose clothing was not at all elegant, wore long boards on their feet. She was doubtful, but the strange white landscape and the groups of festive people intrigued her. It might be more interesting than Paris, which in the end had turned out to be rather dull.

They went to the office to book plane passage. Have you any money at all? Dinah asked her as they waited.

Malika was suddenly very much ashamed. Tony never gave me any.

It's all right, Dinah told her.

Before they left there was a lively argument between them as to whether Malika should take all her valises with her on the plane to Milano.

But you won't need all those clothes there, Dinah objected. And besides, it would cost so much.

I have to take everything, Malika said.

All of her belongings went with them on the plane. They had bad weather on the way to Milano, where Daphne's car met them. She was already in Cortina.

Malika had not enjoyed the plane ride. She did not understand why people with cars took planes. There was nothing to see but clouds, and the rocking of the plane made some of the passengers sick, so that by the end of the flight everyone seemed to be nervous and unhappy. For a while as they sped along the autostrada Malika thought she was back in Spain.

According to the driver, there were already so many friends staying at Daphne's chalet that no place was left for them. Daphne was putting them up in a hotel. Dinah received this news in silence; presumably she was displeased. Malika, when she understood the situation, secretly rejoiced. There would be many more people in the hotel than in the house.

11

It was cold in Cortina. At first Malika would not go out of the hotel. The air is like poison, she complained. Then she began to experiment a bit, finally discovering that it was an agreeable kind of cold.

She would sit with the others on the terrace of the hotel in the brilliant sunshine, wearing her warm coat, sipping hot chocolate while they had their cocktails. The red-cheeked jollity of the people around her was a new experience, and the snow never ceased to fascinate her. Each morning when Daphne and her guests came to fetch Dinah, Malika would watch the noisy group rush out toward the ski fields. Then she would wander through the public rooms. The employees were polite, and often smiled at her. There was a shop in the hotel that sold skis and the clothes that had to be worn when using them. The window displays were changed daily, so that Malika was often to be seen standing outside the door, inspecting the merchandise through the glass.

Twice a tall young man had sauntered up to the shop windows as she stood there, giving the impression that he was about to speak to her. Both times she had turned away and resumed her aimless meandering. Tony and Dinah had warned her repeatedly against entering into conversation with strangers, and she thought it better to observe the etiquette they considered so important. She had discovered that Otto the barman spoke Spanish, and in the morning when the bar was often empty she would go in and talk with him. One morning he asked her why she never went out to ski with her friends.

I can't, she said in a muffled voice.

At that moment, in the mirror behind the bar, she saw the tall young man come into the room and remain standing by the door, as if he were listening to their conversation. She hoped Otto would not continue it, but he did.

That's no reason, he said. Take lessons. There are plenty of good skiing professors in Cortina.

Malika shook her head slowly several times.

The young man stepped to the bar, saying, in Spanish: He's right, our friend Otto. That's what Cortina's for. Everybody skis here.

Now he leaned on the bar and faced Malika. I spend a lot of time south of the border myself, he said as though in confidence. I have a little hacienda down in Durango.

Malika stared at him. He was speaking in Spanish, but she had no idea of what he was talking about. He misunderstood her expression and frowned. What's the matter. Don't you like Durango?

She looked at Otto and back at the tall young man. Then she burst into laughter, and the sound filled the bar agreeably. The tall young man's face seemed to melt as he heard it.

She slid down from the barstool, smiled at him, and said: I don't understand. *Hasta luego*, Otto. While the young man was still making a visible effort to collect his thoughts, she turned and walked out of the bar.

This marked the beginning of a new friendship, one which grew to substantial proportions later that same day. At the end of the afternoon Malika and the young man, who said his name was Tex, went for a walk along the road outside the hotel, where the snow had been packed down. The peaks of the mountains around them were turning pink. She sniffed the air with enthusiasm.

I like it here, she said, as though the subject had been under discussion.

You'd like it more if you learned to ski, he told her.

No, no!

She hesitated, then went on quickly: I can't pay for lessons. I haven't any money. They don't give me any.

Who's they?

She walked on beside him without answering, and he took her arm. By the time they got back to the hotel she had agreed to let Tex pay for lessons, skis and clothes, on condition that the clothes be bought at a shop in the town and not at the hotel.

Once she had been fitted out, the lessons were begun, Tex being always present. Dinah did not like the idea at all. She said it was unheard of, and she asked Malika to point Tex out to her.

Malika, who had felt no resentment at being left each day to her own devices, could not understand Dinah's objections. She was delighted with her new friend, and arranged for Dinah to meet him in the bar, where she sat for a half-hour listening to them speak in English. Later that night Dinah told her Tex was uncivilized. Malika did not understand.

He's an idiot! Dinah cried.

Malika laughed, for she took this to mean that Dinah also liked him. He has a good heart, she replied calmly.

Yes, yes. You'll see that good heart soon enough, Dinah told her with a crooked smile.

Having observed that Tex's interest in her was due in part to the mystery with which she seemed to be surrounded, Malika offered him as little information about herself as possible. He was still under the impression that she was Mexican and a member of Dinah's family, and that for one reason or another Dinah was in charge of her. His misconception amused Malika and she did nothing to correct it. She knew Dinah and Daphne were persuaded that she and Tex were having an affair, and this pleased her, too, since it was not true.

Sometimes, in spite of Malika's efforts to restrain him, Tex drank too much whisky. This generally happened in the bar after dinner. At such moments his face often took on an expression that made her think of a fish dragged up on to the beach. His eyes bulging, his jaw slack, he would take one of her hands in both of his, and groan: Oh, Honey! To Malika this was an expression of momentary despair. She would sigh and shake her head, and try to comfort him by saying that he would feel better in a little while.

The lessons were going very well; Malika spent most of the daylight hours on the snow with Tex. She would have eaten at his table, too, if Dinah had not indignantly forbidden it.

One day at lunch Dinah lit a cigarette and said: You're going to have your last skiing lesson tomorrow. We're leaving for Paris on Thursday.

Malika saw that she was watching her closely to observe the effect of her announcement. She decided to look slightly crest-fallen, but not enough to give Dinah any satisfaction.

It's been a marvellous holiday, Dinah went on, and we've all had a fine time, but now it's over.

Así es la vida, murmured Malika with lowered head.

12

THAT afternoon when the lesson was over, Malika and Tex sat side by side in the snow, looking out across the valley in the fading light. All at once she found that she was sobbing. Tex stared at her in consternation, then drew her to him, trying to comfort her. Through her sobs, she repeated what Dinah had told her at lunch.

When she felt his arms around her, she knew that the only reason for her unhappiness was that she did not want to leave him. She leaned her head on his chest and sobbed: *Me quiero quedar contigo, Tex, contigo.*

These words transformed him. He began to glow. While he soothed her with gestures, he told her he would do anything in the world for her. If she wanted him to, he would take her away that very night. She stopped weeping and listened.

Before they rose from the snowbank, they had agreed upon the following morning for their departure, while Dinah would be out skiing. Tex was determined to have no further meeting with Dinah, but Malika made him leave a note behind for her, which she dictated.

> Dinah, I don't want to go to Paris now. Thank you and thank Daphne. I loved Cortina. Now I'm going to learn to ski. I'll be in Switzerland for a while. Good luck, Malika.

Tex had made arrangements to have a chauffeur-driven car large enough to hold Malika's many valises pick them up at the hotel at half past nine in the morning. Everything went off smoothly. Malika handed the note for Dinah to the receptionist. He did not mention the subject of her bill, which she had feared he might do, but merely nodded gravely.

As they left Cortina behind them, Malika said: Dinah's going to be very angry.

I'm thinking of that, said Tex. Will she make trouble?

She can't do anything. She never saw my passport. She doesn't even know my name.

Tex appeared to be stunned by this information, and began to put a whole series of questions to her, but she, being happy to see the beautiful white landscape outside, replied without answering them, seized his hand now and then to draw his attention to a detail in the landscape, and, by taking gentle command, succeeded in putting him off without his being aware of it.

They had lunch at a small restaurant in Mezzolombardo.

The waiter brought a bottle of wine and poured out two glasses. No, said Malika, pushing it away.

Your friend Dinah's not here now, Tex reminded her. You can do whatever you like.

Dinah! she scoffed. What's Dinah beside the words of God? He stared at her, mystified, without pursuing the matter further, and drank the bottle of wine by himself, so that he was in a happy and relaxed state when they got back into the car. As they rolled southward on the autostrada he devoted himself to crushing her hand in his, nuzzling her neck with his lips, and finally kissing her feverishly on the lips. Malika could not have hoped for more.

13

AT dinner that night in Milano she watched him drink two bottles of wine. Later in the bar he had several whiskies. At Cortina she would have begged him to stop, but this night she affected not to notice that he was resolutely sliding into a drunken state. Instead, she began to tell him a complicated story she had known since her childhood, about a female ghoul that lived in a cave and unearthed newly buried corpses to extract their livers. Seeing his expression of total bewilderment, she stopped halfway through the tale.

He shook his head. What an imagination! he said.

I want to learn how to speak English, Malika went on, leaving the ghoul behind. That's what I'm going to do in Switzerland.

Tex was drunk by the time they went upstairs. She regretted this, for she liked him much better when he was sober. But she suspected that he was going to want to sleep with her and she thought it wiser for their first time together that he be in a state of befuddlement. It was imperative that he believe himself to be the first to have had her.

In the morning when he awoke staring, trying to remember, she confided that it had not been as painful as she had expected. Tex was contrite; he nearly wept as he begged her forgiveness. She smiled and covered him with kisses.

Having won this much, she pressed on, not with any specific purpose in mind, but simply to gain a stronger foothold. While he was still in the slough of early-morning remorse, she made him promise to abjure whisky.

At the Grand Saint Bernard, as the police handed back their passports, Malika saw Tex stare at hers briefly with astonishment. When they were in the car, he asked to see the passport again. The Arabic characters seemed to cause him great excitement. He began to ask her questions about Morocco which she could not have answered even if she had been in the mood for such conversation. She assured him it was like any other country. Now I'm looking at Switzerland, she said.

They arrived in Lausanne at sunset and took rooms in a large hotel by the lake, at Ouchy. It was far grander than the hospice at Corona, and the people living there, not being dressed for skiing, seemed to Malika much more elegant.

I like it here, she said to Tex that night at dinner. How long can we stay?

The next morning, at Malika's insistence, they went together to the Berlitz School for intensive language courses: she in English and he in French. She saw that Tex imagined she would soon tire of the strict schedule, but she was determined not to leave Lausanne before she could converse in English. They spent each morning in their respective classes, had lunch together, and returned to the school at three for further tutoring.

Every Friday afternoon Tex would rent a car, and they would drive to Gstaad, stopping to have dinner on the way.

Saturdays and Sundays if no snow fell, they skied at Wasserngrat or Eggli. Sometimes he would insist on staying over until Monday, even though it meant missing their morning classes. Malika could see that if she had let him have his way he always would have done this, and very likely would have extended the weekends further and further. He approved of Malika's learning English, but he could not fathom her obsessive preoccupation with it. Nor, had he asked her, could she have explained it to him. She knew only that unless she kept on learning she was lost.

14

DURING the winter there in Lausanne they made no friends, being entirely satisfied with each other's company. One day as they were coming out of the Schweizerische Kreditanstalt, where Tex had opened an account for Malika, he turned to her and apropos of nothing asked her if she had ever thought of being married.

She looked at him wonderingly. I think of it all the time, she said. You know it makes me happy to be married to you.

He stared at her as if he had understood nothing she had said. After a moment he seized her arm and pulled her to him. It makes me happy, too, he told her. She could see, however, that something was on his mind. Later when they were alone, he said that of course it was true that they were married, but that what he had been speaking of was marriage with papers.

With papers or not with papers! It's the same thing, isn't it? If two people love each other, what have papers got to do with it?

It's the governments, he explained. They like married people to have papers.

Of course, she agreed. In Morocco, too. Many people are married with papers.

She was about to add that papers were important if you expected to produce children, but she checked herself in time, sensing that the observation bordered on dangerous ground. Already, from certain questions he had put to her, she suspected that he had begun to wonder if she were pregnant. His questions amused her, based as they were on the supposition that there had been no Tim before Tex, to show her how always to be safe.

One morning in early spring when she complained of feeling tired, he asked her outright.

You think Moroccan women don't know anything? she cried. If they want to make children they make them. If they don't, they don't make them.

He nodded dubiously. Those home remedies don't always work.

She saw that she was safe. He knew nothing about Morocco. Mine does, she said.

If she never mentioned America to him or asked about his family, it was because she could not envisage his life there with enough clarity to be curious about it. For his part, he spoke of America with increasing frequency. Never before had he stayed away for so long, he said. Malika interpreted these remarks as warnings that he had had enough of his present life and was contemplating a change. The thought struck terror to her heart, but she would not let him perceive this.

From time to time she would catch him in the act of staring at her, an expression of utter incomprehension on his face. By now, at Malika's insistence, they often spoke together in English. She thought it suited him much better than Spanish; he seemed to have an altogether different voice.

Would you like to be married? With papers, I mean.

Yes, if you want to.

And you? he insisted.

Of course I want to, if you want to.

They were married in the rectory office of a Protestant minister, who remarked in an aside to Tex that personally he was not in favour of marriage where the bride was as young as Malika. In my experience, he said, very few such unions prove to be permanent.

To Malika the episode was a bit of nonsense of the sort that Nazarenes appear so much to enjoy. Nevertheless she saw clearly that it was a matter of great importance to Tex. Indeed, his character seemed to have undergone a subtle metamorphosis since the ceremony, in that he was now more self-assertive. She liked him rather better this way, and concluded that secretly he was a very devout man. These papers were obviously a requirement of the Nazarene religion; now that he had them he felt more secure.

It was only a fortnight later that Tex, after drinking a little more wine than was his habit, announced to her that they were going home. Malika received the news with a sinking sensation. She could see that he was glad to be leaving the world of hotels and restaurants, and she suspected that life in a house would be very different and not nearly so much fun.

Once again she saw nothing from the plane, but this time the journey went on for such a long time that she grew worried. Tex was sleepy, nevertheless she disturbed him several times to ask: Where are we?

Twice he answered jovially: In the air. The next time he said: Somewhere over the ocean, I suppose. And he stole a glance at her.

We're not moving, she told him. We're standing still. The plane is stuck.

He only laughed, but in such a way that she realized she had made a mistake of some sort. I don't like this plane, she said.

Go to sleep, Tex advised her.

She shut her eyes and sat quietly, feeling that she had gone much too far away, so far that now she was nowhere. Outside the world, she whispered to herself in Arabic, and shivered.

15

BEING in Los Angeles persuaded Malika that she was right, that she had left behind everything that was comprehensible, and was now in a totally different place whose laws she could not know. They went from the airport to the top of the mountain, where a house was hidden in the woods. Tex had told her about it, but she had imagined something very different, like the Mountain in Tangier where the villas had big gardens around them. This house was buried among the trees; she could not see the rest of it even when they went up to the door.

In the middle of the forest, she said wonderingly.

An ugly little Filipino in a white jacket opened the door for them. He bowed low and made a short formal speech of welcome to Malika. She knew he was speaking English, but it was not the English she had been taught in Lausanne. At the end she thanked him gravely.

Later she asked Tex what the little man had been saying.

He was hoping you'd be happy here in your new house, that's all.

My house? But it's your house, not mine!

Of course it's yours! You're my wife, aren't you?

Malika nodded. She knew, no matter what anyone pretended, that when men grew tired of their wives they put them out, and took new ones. She loved Tex and trusted him, but she did not expect him to be different from other men. When the time came, she knew he would find a pretext to rid himself of her. The important point was to know how to fight off the fatal moment, to make it come as late as possible. She nodded again and said with a smile: I like this house, Tex.

The rooms had irregular shapes, with unexpected alcoves and niches where there were soft couches with piles of cushions. As she inspected the house she noted with satisfaction that the windows were barred with iron grille work. She had already seen the massive front door with its heavy bolts.

That night as they sat in front of the fireplace they heard the yapping of coyotes.

Jackals, murmured Malika, turning her head to listen. Very bad.

She found it incomprehensible that anyone should waste money building such a pretty house in a place so far from everything. Above all she could not understand why the trees had been left growing so close to the house. Silently, she determined never to go outside unless Tex accompanied her, and never under any circumstances to remain in the house without him.

The next morning, when Tex was about to drive down into the city, Malika began to run from room to room, crying: Wait! I'm going with you.

You'd be bored, he told her. I've got to go to a lawyer's office. You stay here with Salvador.

She could not let Tex know that she was afraid to stay in the house; it would be an unforgivable affront. No, no, no. I want to see the town, she said.

He kissed her and they set out for the city. It was a bigger car than the one he had rented at the airport the day before.

I always want to go with you no matter where you go, she confided, hoping that this declaration would aid in establishing a precedent.

During these weeks, when she watched the life in the streets, she could find no pattern to it. The people were always on their way somewhere else, and they were in a hurry. She knew better than to imagine that they were all alike; still, she had no way of knowing who was who. In Morocco, in Europe, there had been people who were busy doing things, and there had been others watching. Always, no matter where one was or what one was doing, there were watchers. She had the impression that in America everyone was going somewhere and no one sat watching. This disturbed her. She felt herself to be far, far away from everything she had ever known. The freeways inspired her with dread, for she could not rid herself of the idea that some unnameable catastrophe had occurred, and that the cars were full of refugees fleeing from the scene. She had ample opportunity to observe the miles of small houses set side by side, and compare these simple dwellings with the house on the mountain. As a result it occurred to her that perhaps she was fortunate to live where she did. One day as they drove into the city she turned to Tex and said: Do you have more money than these people?

What people?

She moved her hand. The ones who live in these houses.

I don't know about other people's money, he said. I know I never have enough of my own.

She looked out at the rows of frail wooden houses with their dusty shrubbery, and could not believe him. You *do* have more money, she declared. Why don't you want to say it?

This made him laugh. Whatever I have, I made myself. The day I was twenty-one my father handed me a cheque and said: Let's see what you can do with this. In three years I changed it into four and a half times as much. Is that what you meant, Dad? I asked him. That's what I meant, Son, he said.

Malika thought a moment, saying finally: And now when he needs money you give it to him.

Tex looked sideways at her and said gravely: Of course.

She wanted to ask him if he had no friends in Los Angeles. Since their arrival she had not met anyone, and she thought this strange. It could be a custom here for recently married couples to keep strictly to themselves during a specified period. Or perhaps Tex's friends here were all girls, which would automatically preclude her knowing them. When she asked him, he said he seldom came to Los Angeles. I'm generally with my family in Texas, he said, or down at the hacienda.

There was a studio upstairs with a wide sun-deck that was not hidden by trees in the middle of the day. Malika did not feel entirely at ease sitting out there, with nothing between her and the dark forest. She suspected that the trees harboured dangerous birds. Sometimes she and Tex sat up here between dips in the pool, which, being below inside the closed patio, she considered safe. Tex would observe her as she lay stretched on a mattress, and assure her she was more beautiful than ever. She had noticed this herself, but she was pleased to know that he too had seen it.

16

ONE day Tex told her that a man named F.T. was coming to dinner. F.T. was an old friend of his father's, who managed his financial affairs for him. Malika was interested to hear what such work entailed, so Tex made an effort to explain the mechanics of investment. She was quiet for a while. But then you can't make money unless you already have it, she said.

That's about it, Tex agreed.

F.T. was middle-aged and well dressed with a small grey

moustache. He was delighted with Malika, and called her Little Lady. This struck her as vaguely insulting, but since she could see that he was a pleasant and well-behaved man otherwise, she made no objections. Besides, Tex had told her: Remember. If you should ever need anything, anything at all, just call F.T.'s number. He's like my father.

During dinner she decided that she really liked F.T., even though he seemed not to take her very seriously. Afterward he and Tex talked together for a long time. The words went on for so long that Malika fell asleep on a divan and awoke only after F.T. had gone. She was apologetic for having been rude, but she blamed Tex for allowing it to happen.

He threw himself down beside her. F.T. thought you were great. He says you're beyond a doubt the most beautiful girl he's ever seen.

He's a nice man, she murmured.

Ever since her arrival in California, her life had seemed static. When she thought back about it, she decided that it had stopped moving when she had left the Berlitz School. Innocently she asked Tex if she might continue the lessons here. To her astonishment he ridiculed the suggestion, claiming that all she needed was practice in conversation. Because he was not in the habit of refusing her anything, she did not take him at his word, and continued to dwell on her desire for further instruction. All at once she saw that he was going to be firm; he seemed to consider her dissatisfaction a criticism of him. Finally she realized that he was angry.

You don't understand! she cried. I have to study English more before I can study anything else.

Study!

Of course, she said calmly. I'm always going to study. You think I want to stay like this?

I hope you do, Honey, for my sake. You're perfect.

He took hold of her, but she wriggled free.

That evening Tex said to her: I'm going to get an extra woman in the kitchen and let Salvador give you lessons in cooking. That's something you should learn, don't you think?

Malika was silent. Do you want me to learn? You know I want to make you happy.

She began to spend several hours each day in the kitchen with Salvador and Concha, a Mexican girl of whose work the little Filipino was scornful. It was a pleasant enough room, but the number of strange machines and little bells that kept sounding as Salvador rushed from one spot to another awed and confused her. She was even a bit afraid of Salvador, because his face never changed its fixed expression – that of a meaningless grin. It seemed to her that when he was annoyed the grin became even wider. She took care to pay strict attention to everything he told her. Soon he had her making simple dishes which they ate at lunch. If the recipe called for a béchamel or a chasseur, he made it himself and incorporated it, since the timing was more than Malika could manage. It gratified her to see that Tex thought her food good enough to be served at table. She continued to spend two hours in the kitchen each morning, and another hour or so before dinner in the evening. Sometimes she helped Salvador and Concha prepare a picnic hamper, and they went to the beach. She would have liked to tell Tex about the picnics on the beach at Tangier, but there was no way of doing that.

17

OCCASIONALLY, despite Malika's entreaties, Tex would take advantage of her morning session in the kitchen to drive the small car into the city on an errand. She would be uneasy until he returned, but he was always back in time for lunch, One morning he failed to appear at the usual hour. The telephone rang. Salvador wiped his hands and stepped into the butler's pantry to answer it, while Malika and Concha went on chatting together in Spanish. In a moment Salvador reappeared in the doorway, and with a radiant smile told Malika the police had called to say that Mister Tex had met with an accident and was in a hospital in Westwood.

Malika rushed at the little man and seized him by the shoulders. Telephone to F.T.!

She hopped up and down while he searched for the number and dialled it. As soon as she saw that he was speaking to F.T., she snatched the telephone from his hand.

F.T.! Come and get me! I want to see Tex.

She heard F.T.'s voice, calm and reassuring. Yes. Now you just wait quietly for me. I'll be there as soon as I can. Don't you worry. Let me speak to Salvador again.

She left Salvador talking into the telephone and rushed upstairs to the studio, where she began to walk back and forth. If Tex was in hospital, he probably would not be home to sleep that night, and she would not stay in the house without him. She went out on to the sun-deck and stared at the trees. Tex is dead, she thought.

It was mid-afternoon before F.T.'s car drew up at the door. He found her in the studio lying face down on a couch. When she heard his voice she sprang up, wide-eyed, and ran to him.

That night Malika slept at F.T.'s house. He had insisted upon taking her home with him and leaving her in the care of his wife. For it was true that Tex was dead; he had succumbed not long after reaching the hospital.

F.T. and his wife did not commiserate with Malika. Mrs F.T. said a show of sympathy could induce hysteria. Malika merely talked on and on, weeping intermittently. Sometimes she forgot that her listeners did not know Arabic or Spanish, until at their prompting she would go back into English. She had sworn to accompany Tex whenever he went out, and she had not done so, therefore he had been killed, he was the only being in the world she loved, and she was far from home, and what was going to become of her here alone?

That night as she lay in the dark listening to the occasional passing wail of a police siren, she was assailed afresh by the sensation she had felt on the plane, that of having gone too far for the possibility of return. Being with Tex had made it possible to accept the strangeness of the place; now she saw herself as someone shipwrecked on an unknown shore peopled by creatures whose intentions were unfathomable. And no one could come to rescue her, for no one knew she was there.

She slept at F.T.'s house for several nights. During the days she visited supermarkets and other points of interest with Mrs F.T. You've got to keep busy, her hostess told her. We can't have you brooding.

There was no way, however, of preventing Malika from worrying about what was to become of her, stranded in this unlikely land without a peseta to buy herself bread, and only the caprice of F.T. and his wife between her and starvation.

18

ONE morning F.T. himself drove Malika to his office. Out of respect for him she had dressed with great care in a severe grey silk suit front Balenciaga. Her entrance into the office with F.T. caused a stir of interest. When she sat facing him across his desk in a small inner room, he pulled a sheaf of papers from a drawer. As he leafed through them he began to talk.

Betty tells me you're worried about money.

Seeing Malika nod, he went on. I take it you haven't any at all. Is that right?

She felt in her handbag and pulled out a crumpled twenty-dollar bill that Tex had given her one day when they were shopping.

Only this, she said, showing him.

F.T. cleared his throat.

Well, I want you to stop worrying. As soon as we get everything cleared up you'll have a regular income. In the meantime I've opened a checking account for you at the bank downstairs in this building.

He saw anxiety flitting across her face, and added hastily: It's your money. You're his sole beneficiary. After taxes and all the rest, you'll still have a substantial capital. And if you're wise you'll leave it all just where it is, in certificates of deposit and treasury notes. So stop worrying.

Yes, she said, understanding nothing.

I never let Tex play with stocks, F.T. went on. He had no head for business.

She was shocked to hear F.T. denigrate poor Tex in this way, but she said: I see.

When we get everything straight and running smoothly, you ought to have around fifty thousand a month. Possibly a little more.

Malika stared at F.T. Is that enough? she asked cautiously.

He shot a quick glance at her over his spectacles. I think you'll find it's enough.

I hope so, she said with fervour. You see, I don't understand money. I never bought anything myself. How much does a thing cost? I don't know. Only in my own country.

Of course. F.T. pushed a cheque book along the top of the desk toward her. You understand, this is a temporary account for you to draw on now, until all the legal work is finished. I hope you won't overdraw. But I'm sure you won't.

He smiled encouragingly at her. Remember, he went on. There are only twenty-five thousand dollars there. So be a good girl and keep track of your cheques.

But I can't do what you tell me! she exclaimed. Please do it for me.

F.T. sighed. Can you write your name? he asked very quietly.

Tex showed me in Lausanne, but I've forgotten.

In spite of himself, F.T. raised his arms. But, my dear lady, how do you expect to live? You can't go on this way.

No, she said miserably.

F.T. pushed back his chair and stood up. Well, he said jovially, what you don't know you can always learn. Why don't you come up here every morning and study with Miss Galper? She's as smart as a whip. She'll teach you everything you need to know. That's my suggestion for you.

He was not prepared for her vehement response. She jumped up and hugged him. Oh, F.T.! That's what I want! That's what I want!

19

THE following day Malika moved her luggage into a hotel in Beverly Hills. Under F.T.'s advice she kept Salvador on, living in the house, but now functioning solely as chauffeur. Each morning he called at the hotel for her and drove her to F.T.'s office. She found this routine stimulating. Miss Galper, a pleasant young woman with glasses, would spend the forenoon working with her, after which they generally went to lunch together. There had not been much glamour in Miss Galper's life, and she was fascinated by Malika's accounts of Europe and Morocco. There remained a basic mystery in her story, nevertheless, since she never explained how she came to be living at Tim's flat in Tangier. In her version, she might have come into being during a picnic on the beach at Sidi Qacem.

When after two months F.T. saw that Malika was, if anything, even more serious and determined about pursuing her practical education, he suggested that the lessons continue at the hotel. Now it was Miss Galper whom Salvador drove to and from Beverly Hills. Occasionally they went shopping – small expeditions to Westwood that delighted Malika because for the first time she was aware of prices, and could gauge the buying power of her money. F.T. had told her that with what Tex had left for her she would be able to live better than most people. At the time she had supposed this was a part of his attempt to comfort her, but now that she understood the prices she realized that he had been stating a fact. She said nothing to Miss Galper of her surprise at finding the cost of goods so low. Instead, she overwhelmed her with a constant flow of small gifts.

You've got to stop this, Malika, Miss Galper told her.

The first month they had done nothing but arithmetic. After that there was the telling of time, the names of the days and the months. With some difficulty Miss Galper taught her to sign the two forms of her name: *Malika Hapgood* and *Mrs Charles G. Hapgood*. By the time the lessons were moved to the hotel, Malika had begun to practise writing out in words complicated sums given her in figures. They went back to dates, and she had to learn to write them correctly.

You can leave everything else to a secretary, Miss Galper told her. But you've got to take care of your money yourself.

To this end she gave Malika a course in reading bank statements, and another in spacing the purchase of securities to assure regular turnover.

As the months went by and Malika's insight into the functioning of the world around her grew, she began to understand the true extent of her ignorance, and she conceived a passionate desire to be able to read the texts of newspapers and magazines.

I'm not an English teacher, Miss Galper told her. F.T. doesn't pay me for that. We can get you a good professor whenever you want.

Malika, being persuaded that she could learn only from Miss Galper, consulted F.T. about it. After a certain amount of deliberation, he devised a plan which delighted Malika and pleased Miss Galper as well. He would give Miss Galper a year's holiday with salary if Malika wanted to take her on as a paid companion during that time. In this way, he implied to Malika, she would be able to get the reading lessons she wanted. He added that he did not think Miss Galper was the person to give them, but since Malika had her heart set on being taught by her, this seemed to him a viable strategy.

It was Miss Galper's idea to make a tour of Europe. F.T. suggested they buy a big car, put it on a freighter, and take Salvador along with them to pick it up over there and drive it. When Malika heard this, she asked why they could not all go on the ship with the car. It might be possible, F.T. told her.

Eventually F.T. had arranged to get Malika a new passport, had even helped Miss Galper and Salvador expedite theirs, and, accompanied by Mrs F.T., had bidden them a lengthy farewell at the dock in San Pedro. It was a comfortable Norwegian freighter bound for Panama and eventually for Europe.

The ship was already in tropical waters. Malika said she had imagined it could be this hot only in the Sahara, and certainly not on the sea. She had nothing to do all day. Salvador spent most of his time sleeping. Miss Galper sat in a deck chair reading. She had refused to give Malika any kind of lessons while they were on the ship. It would make me seasick, she assured her. But she noticed Malika's boredom, and talked with her for long periods of time.

20

MALIKA could not sit, as Miss Galper could, looking at the sea. The flat horizon on all sides gave her much the same sensation of unreality she had experienced on the plane with Tex. Panama came as a relief, making it clear that the ship had not been static during all those days, and that they had reached a very different part of the world.

It took all day to go through the canal. Malika stood on deck in the sun, waving back to the men working along the locks. But from Panama on, her restlessness increased daily. She was reduced to playing endless games of checkers with a yawning Salvador each afternoon in the narrow passengers' lounge. They never spoke during these sessions. From the beginning of the voyage the captain had urged Malika to visit the bridge. At some point Miss Galper had mentioned that he had the power to seize anyone on the ship and have him locked into a dark cell somewhere below. When Malika finally accepted his invitation she took Miss Galper along.

Standing at the prow, Malika stared ahead at the white buildings of Cádiz. As the ship moved into the port, the combination of the light in the air, the colour of the walls and the odours on the wind told her that she was back in her part of the world and close to home. For a long time she had refused to think about the little house above the gully. Now that it no longer frightened her, she was able to imagine it almost with affection.

It was her duty to go and visit her mother, however hostile a reception she might get from her. She would try to give her money, which she was certain she would refuse to take. But Malika was ready with a ruse. If her mother spurned the money, she would tell her she was leaving it next door with Mina Glagga. Once Malika was out of the way, her mother would lose no time in going to claim it.

Miss Galper had hoped to spend the night in Cádiz, but Malika insisted on driving straight to Algeciras. Now that she was so near home, she wanted to get there as soon as she could. I must see my mother, she said. I must see her first.

Of course, said Miss Galper. But you haven't seen her in two years or more and she isn't expecting you. One day sooner or later?

We can come back. Now I have to go and see my mother.

In Algeciras at the hotel that night they saw Salvador eating at the other end of the long dining room. He had changed from his uniform into a grey flannel suit. Malika observed him carefully, and said: He's drinking wine.

He'll be all right tomorrow, Miss Galper told her. They always drink, Filipinos.

He was at the door grinning when they came out of the hotel in the morning to be driven to the dock. Most of the passengers going to Tangier were Moroccans. Malika had forgotten the shameless intensity with which her countrymen stare at women. Now she was back among her own kind. The realization startled her; she felt both excitement and apprehension.

21

AFTER they had settled into their quarters at the hotel, Malika went down to the desk. She hoped to visit her mother in the evening, when she was sure to be in the house, and when there would be a valid excuse for not staying too long. She intended to reserve two rooms in Tetuan for the night, one for Salvador and one for herself, and return to Tangier in the morning. In the lobby they told her of a new hotel on the beach only a mile or so from her town. She asked them to telephone for reservations.

Miss Galper's room was down the corridor from hers. Malika knocked on her door and told her she would be leaving about five o'clock, in order to get to the hotel before dark.

Miss Galper looked at her searchingly. I'm glad you're doing it now and getting it over with, she said.

You can have a good time, Malika told her. There are bars where you can go.

No, thank you. The men here give me the creeps. They all try to talk to you.

Malika shrugged. What difference does it make? You can't understand what they're saying.

This was fortunate, she thought. The brutally obscene remarks made by the men to women passing in the street disgusted and infuriated her. Miss Galper was lucky not to know any Arabic.

She said a lame goodbye and hurried to her room. The prospect of seeing her mother had unsettled her. Mechanically she put a few articles of clothing into an overnight bag. On the way out she cashed some traveller's cheques at the office, and soon she and Salvador were on the road to Tetuan.

The mountains had scarves of white cloud trailing outward from their summits. Salvador criticized the narrow highway. Malika scarcely heard his complaints. Her heart was beating unusually fast. It was true that she was going back to help her mother; she was going because it was included in the pattern. Since the day she had run away, the vision of the triumphant return had been with her, when she would be the living proof that her mother had been mistaken, that she was not like the other girls of the town. Now that the moment was drawing near, she suspected that the visit was foredoomed to failure. Her mother would feel no pleasure at seeing her – only rancour and bitterness at the thought that she had been with Nazarenes.

Salvador said: In Pilipinas we got better roads than this one.

Don't go fast, she told him.

They skirted Tetuan and turned to the left along the road that led to her town. The sea wind rushed through the car. *Bismil'lah*, she murmured under her breath, for now she was entering the crucial part of the journey.

She did not even know they had reached the town until they were in the main street. It looked completely different. There were big new buildings and bright lights. The idea that the town might change during her absence had not occurred to her; she herself would change, but the town would remain an unmoving backdrop which would help her define and measure her transformation.

A moment later they had arrived at the new hotel, spread out along the beach in a glare of green floodlights.

22

MALIKA soon discovered that it was not a real hotel. There was no room service, and in the dining room they served only snack-bar food. Before eating, she changed into blue jeans, bought in Los Angeles at Miss Galper's suggestion. She wore a sweater and wrapped a silk kerchief tightly around her head. In this costume she felt wholly anonymous.

Salvador was already eating at the counter in the *comedor*. She sat on a stool near him and ordered pinchitos. Her stomach rebelled at the thought of eating, but she chewed and swallowed the meat because she had learned that to feel well she must eat regularly. Through the rasping of a transistor radio at the end of the counter she heard the dull, repeated sound of the waves breaking over the sand below. If her mother flew into a rage and began to beat her, she would go directly to Mina Glagga and give her the money, and that would finish it. She signed the chit and went into the wind to the car.

The town's new aspect confused her. They had moved the market; she could not see it anywhere, and she felt a wave of indignation at this betrayal. Salvador parked the car at the service station and they set out on foot up the narrow street that led to the house. There were streetlights only part of the way; beyond, it would have been dark had it not been for the moon. Salvador glanced ahead and said it would be better to turn around and come again in the morning.

You wait here, she said firmly. I'll come back as soon as I can. I know the way. And she quickly went on, before he could argue about it.

She made her way up along the empty moonlit street until she came to a small open square from which, in the daytime at least, her mother's house was visible ahead, at the edge of the barranca. Now, as she looked, the moon's light did not seem to strike at all; she could see no sign of it. She hurried on, already assailed by a nightmarish premonition, and then she stopped, her mouth open in disbelief. The house was not there. Even the land where it stood was gone. Mina Glagga's and all the houses bordering on the gully had disappeared. Bulldozers had made a new landscape of emptiness, a great embankment of earth, ashes and refuse that stretched downward to the bottom of the ravine. The little house with its garden had been just below where she now stood. She felt her throat tighten painfully as she told herself that it no longer existed.

Ceasing finally to stare at the meaningless terrain, she turned and went back to the square, where she knocked at the door of one of the houses. The woman who opened the door was a friend of her mother's whose name she had forgotten. She eyed Malika's blue jeans with distaste and did not ask her inside. They talked standing in the doorway. In an expressionless voice the woman told her that her mother had died more than a year earlier, during Ramadan. It was fortunate, she added, that she had not lived to see them destroy her house in order to build the new road. She thought Malika's sister had gone to Casablanca, but she was not certain.

By now the woman had pushed the door so that it was nearly shut. Malika thanked her and said goodnight.

She went over and stood at the landfill, staring down at the uniform surface of the hillside, unreal even in the careful light dropped over it by the moon. She had to force her eyes shut to clear them of the tears that kept forming, and she found it strange, for she had not felt tenderness for her mother. Then she saw more clearly. It was not for her mother that she felt like weeping; it was for herself. There was no longer any reason to do anything.

She let her gaze wander over the dim expanse toward the mountains beyond. It would be good to perish in the place where she had lived, to be buried along with the house under the hateful mass. She pounded the edge of it with her heel, lost her footing, and slid downward some distance through mounds of ashes and decayed food. In that instant she was certain it was happening, as a punishment for having wished to be dead a moment ago; her weight had started a landslide that would roll her to the bottom, leaving her under tons of refuse. Terrified, she lay still, listening. There were faint stirrings and clicks around her, but they quickly died away into silence. She scrambled up to the roadbed.

A cloud had begun to move across the moon. She hurried down the hill toward the streetlight where Salvador waited.

Points in Time

Points in Time *(1982) is a compendium of short pieces in which Bowles explores the folklore of Morocco and the essence of its people, encapsulating centuries of Moroccan history and tradition.*

A century and a half ago, in one of the twisting back streets of the Mellah in Fez, there lived a respectable couple, Haim and Simha Hachuel. There would be no record of them today had their daughter Sol not been favoured with exceptional beauty.

Since Jewish girls were free to walk in the streets unveiled, the beauty of Sol Hachuel soon became legendary throughout the city.

Moslem youths climbed up from the Medina to stroll through the Mellah in the hope of catching sight of Sol on her way to a fountain to fetch water.

Having seen her once, Mohammed Zrhouni came each day and waited until she appeared, merely to gaze upon her. Later he spoke with her, and still later suggested that they marry.

Sol's parents rejected the idea outright: it would entail her abandonment of Judaism.

The Zrhouni family likewise strongly disapproved: they did not want a Jewess in the house, and they believed, like most Moslems, that no Jew's conversion to Islam could be considered authentic.

Mohammed was not disposed in any case to take a Moslem bride, since that would involve accepting the word of his female relatives as to the girl's desirability; by the time he was finally able to see her face, he would already be married to her. Since the considerations of his family would necessarily be based on the bride-price, he strongly doubted that any girl chosen by them could equal the jewel he had discovered in the Mellah.

For her part, Sol was infatuated with her Moslem suitor. Her parents' furious tirades only increased the intensity of her obsession. Like Mohammed, she saw no reason to let herself be swayed by the opinions of her elders.

The inevitable occurred: she went out of the house one day and did not return. Mohammed covered her with a *haïk* and went with her down into the Medina and across the bridge to his parents' house in the Keddane.

Mohammed lived with his mother, aunts and sisters, his father having died the previous year. Out of deference to him the women of the household received his bride with correctness, if not enthusiasm, and the wedding, with its explicit conversion of the bride to Islam, was performed.

His mother remarked in an aside to Mohammed that at least the bride had cost nothing, and he understood that this was the principal reason for her grudging acceptance of Sol as her daughter-in-law.

Almost immediately Sol realized that she had made an error. Although she was conversant with Moslem customs, it had not occurred to her that she would be forbidden ever to go outside the Zrhouni house.

When she remonstrated with Mohammed, saying that she needed to go out for a walk in the fresh air, he answered that it was common knowledge that a woman goes out only three times during her life: once when she is born and leaves her mother's womb, once when she marries and leaves her father's house, and once when she dies and leaves this world. He advised her to walk on the roof like other women.

The aunts and sisters, instead of coming little by little to accept Sol as a member of the family, made her feel increasingly like an interloper. They whispered among themselves and grew silent when they saw her approaching.

The months went by. Sol pleaded to be allowed to visit her mother and father. They could not come to see her, since the house would be profaned by their presence.

It seemed unjust to Sol that women were not allowed to enter the mosque; if only it had been possible to go with Mohammed and pray, her life would have been easier to bear. She missed the regular visits to the synagogue where she sat upstairs with her mother and listened to her father as he chanted below with the other men.

The Zrhouni house had become a prison, and she resolved to escape from it. Accordingly, one day when she had managed to get hold of the key to the outer door, she wrapped herself in her *haïk* and quietly slipped out into the street. Not looking to right or to left, she hurried up the Talâa to the top, and then set out for the Mellah.

The happiness in the Hachuel home lasted one day. Enraged and humiliated by his wife's dereliction, Mohammed had gone directly to the *ulema* and told them the story. They listened, consulted together, and declared his wife to be guilty of apostasy from Islam.

On the following afternoon a squad of *mokhaznia* pounded on the door of the house in the Mellah, and amidst shrieks and lamentations, seized the girl. They pulled her out of the house and dragged her through the streets of Fez Djedid, with a great crowd following behind.

Outside Bab Segma the crowd spread out and formed a circle. Screaming and struggling against the ropes that bound her, Sol was forced to kneel in the dust.

A tall *mokhazni* unsheathed his sword, raised it high in the air, and beheaded her.

PART III

TRAVEL WRITING

Baptism of Solitude

'Baptism of Solitude' and the following piece, 'A Man Must Not Be Very Moslem', are taken from Bowles's travel book Their Heads Are Green. *First published in 1963, it ranges through Sri Lanka (then Ceylon), Turkey, Thailand and North Africa and, in the title piece, includes a description of his experiences with parrots of many countries.*

Immediately when you arrive in the Sahara, for the first or the tenth time, you notice the stillness. An incredible, absolute silence prevails outside the towns; and within, even in busy places like the markets, there is a hushed quality in the air, as if the quiet were a conscious force which, resenting the intrusion of sound, minimizes and disperses it straightway. Then there is the sky, compared to which all other skies seem faint-hearted efforts. Solid and luminous, it is always the focal point of the landscape. At sunset, the precise, curved shadow of the earth rises into it swiftly from the horizon, cutting it into light section and dark section. When all daylight is gone, and the space is thick with stars, it is still of an intense and burning blue, darkest directly overhead and paling toward the earth, so that the night never really grows dark.

You leave the gate of the fort or the town behind, pass the camels lying outside, go up into the dunes, or out on to the hard, stony plain and stand awhile, alone. Presently, you will either shiver and hurry back inside the walls, or you will go on standing there and let something very peculiar happen to you, something that everyone who lives there has undergone, and which the French call *le baptême de la solitude*. It is a unique sensation, and it has nothing to do with loneliness, for loneliness presupposes memory. Here, in this wholly mineral landscape lighted by stars like flares, even memory disappears; nothing is left but your own breathing and the sound of your heart beating. A strange, and by no means pleasant, process of reintegration begins inside you, and it remains to be seen whether you will fight against it, and insist on remaining the person you have always been, or whether you will let it take its course. For no one who has stayed in the Sahara for a while is quite the same as when he came.

Before the war for independence in Algeria, under the rule of the French military, there was a remarkable feeling of friendly sympathy among Europeans in the Sahara. It is unnecessary to stress the fact that the corollary of this pleasant state of affairs was the exercise of the strictest sort of colonial control over the Algerians themselves, a regime which amounted to a reign of terror. But from the European viewpoint the place was ideal. The whole vast region was like a small unspoiled rural community where everyone respected the rights of everyone else. Each time you lived there for a while, and left it, you were struck with the indifference and the impersonality of the world outside. If during your travels there, you forgot something, you could be sure of finding it later on your way back; the idea of appropriating it would not have occurred to anyone. You could wander where you liked, out in the wilderness or in the darkest alleys of the towns; no one would molest you.

At that time, no members of the indigent, wandering, unwanted proletariat from northern Algeria had come down here, because there was nothing to attract them. Almost everyone owned a parcel of land in an oasis and lived by working it. In the shade of the date palms, wheat, barley and corn were grown, and those plants provided the staple items of diet. There were usually two or three Arab or Negro shopkeepers who sold things like sugar, tea, candles, matches, carbide for lighting, and cheap European cotton goods. In the larger towns there was sometimes a shop kept by a European, but the merchandise was the same, because the customers were virtually all natives. Almost without exception, the only Europeans who lived in the Sahara were the military and the ecclesiastic.

As a rule, the military and their aides were friendly men, agreeable to be with, interested in showing visitors everything worth seeing in their districts. This was fortunate, as the traveller was often completely at their mercy. He might have to depend on them for his food and lodging, since in the smaller places there were no hotels. Generally he had to depend on them for contact with the outside world, because anything he wanted, like cigarettes or wine, had to be brought by truck from the military post, and his mail was sent in care of the post, too. Furthermore, the decision as to whether he was to have permission to move about freely in the region rested with the military. The power to grant those privileges was vested in, let us say, one lonely lieutenant who lived two hundred miles from his nearest countryman, ate badly (anathema to any Frenchman) and wished that neither camels, date palms, nor inquisitive foreigners had ever been created. Still, it was rare to find an indifferent or unhelpful commandant. He was likely to invite you for drinks and dinner, show you the curiosities he had collected during his years in the bled, ask you to accompany him on his tours of inspection, or even to spend a fortnight with him and his *peloton* of several dozen native *meharistes* when they went out into the desert to make topographical surveys. Then you would be given your own camel – not an ambling pack camel that had to be driven with a stick by someone walking beside it, but a swift, trained animal that obeyed the slightest tug of the reins.

More extraordinary were the Pères Blancs, intelligent and

well educated. There was no element of resignation in their eagerness to spend the remainder of their lives in distant outposts, dressed as Moslems, speaking Arabic, living in the rigorous, comfortless manner of the desert inhabitants. They made no converts, and expected to make none. 'We are here only to show the Moslem that the Christian can be worthy of respect,' they would explain. One used to hear the Moslems say that although the Christians might be masters of the earth, the Moslems were the masters of Heaven; for the military it was quite enough that the *indigène* recognize European supremacy here. Obviously the White Fathers could not be satisfied with that. They insisted upon proving to the inhabitants that the Nazarene was capable of leading as exemplary a life as the most ardent follower of Mohammed. It is true that the austerity of the Fathers' mode of life inspired many Moslems with respect for them, if not for the civilization they represented. And as a result of the years spent in the desert among the inhabitants, the Fathers acquired a certain healthy and unorthodox fatalism, an excellent adjunct to their spiritual equipment, and a highly necessary one in dealing with the men among whom they had chosen to live.

With an area considerably larger than that of the United States, the Sahara is a continent within a continent – a skeleton, if you like, but still a separate entity from the rest of Africa which surrounds it. It has its own mountain ranges, rivers, lakes and forests, but they are largely vestigial. The mountain ranges have been reduced to gigantic bouldery bumps that rise above the neighbouring countryside like the mountains on the moon. Some of the rivers appear as such for perhaps one day a year – others much less often. The lakes are of solid salt, and the forests have long since petrified. But the physical contours of the landscape vary as much as they do anywhere else. There are plains, hills, valleys, gorges, rolling lands, rocky peaks and volcanic craters, all without vegetation or even soil. Yet, probably the only parts that are monotonous to the eye are regions like the Tanezrouft, south of Reggan, a stretch of about five hundred miles of absolutely flat, gravel-strewn terrain, without the slightest sign of life, nor the smallest undulation in the land, to vary the implacable line of the horizon on all sides. After being here for a while, the sight of even a rock awakens an emotion in the traveller; he feels like crying, 'Land!'

There is no known historical period when the Sahara has not been inhabited by man. Most of the other larger forms of animal life, whose abode it formerly was, have become extinct. If we believe the evidence of cave drawings, we can be sure that the giraffe, the hippopotamus and the rhinoceros were once dwellers in the region. The lion has disappeared from North Africa in our own time, likewise the ostrich. Now and then a crocodile is still discovered in some distant, hidden oasis pool, but the occurrence is so rare that when it happens it is a great event. The camel, of course, is not a native of Africa at all, but an importation from Asia, having arrived approximately at the time of the end of the Roman Empire – about when the last elephants were killed off. Large numbers of the herds of wild elephants that roamed the northern reaches of the desert were captured and trained for use in the Carthaginian army, but it was the Romans who finally annihilated the species to supply ivory for the European market.

Fortunately for man, who seems to insist on continuing to live in surroundings which become increasingly inhospitable to him, gazelles are still plentiful, and there are, paradoxically enough, various kinds of edible fish in the water holes – often more than a hundred feet deep – throughout the Sahara. Certain species which abound in artesian wells are blind, having always lived deep in the subterranean lakes.

*

An often-repeated statement, no matter how incorrect, takes a long time to disappear from circulation. Thus, there is a popular misconception of the Sahara as a vast region of sand across which Arabs travel in orderly caravans from one white-domed city to another, and it still prevails. A generalization much nearer to the truth would be to say that it is an area of rugged mountains, bare valleys and flat, stony wasteland, sparsely dotted with Negro villages of mud. The sand in the Sahara, according to data supplied by the Geographical Service of the French Army, covers only about a tenth of its surface, and the Arabs, most of whom are nomads, form a small part of the population. The vast majority of the inhabitants are of Berber (native North African) and/or Negro (native West African) stock. But the Negroes of today are not those who originally peopled the desert. The latter never took kindly to the colonial designs of the Arabs and the Islamized Berbers who collaborated with them; over the centuries they beat a constant retreat toward the southeast until only a vestige of their society remains, in the region now known as the Tibesti. They were replaced by the more docile Sudanese, imported from the south as slaves to work the constantly expanding series of oases.

In the Sahara the oasis – which is to say, the forest of date palms – is primarily a man-made affair, and can continue its existence only if the work of irrigating its terrain is kept up unrelentingly. When the Arabs arrived in Africa twelve centuries ago, they began a project of land reclamation which, if the Europeans continue it with the aid of modern machinery, will transform much of the Sahara into a great, fertile garden. Wherever there was a sign of vegetation, the water was there not far below; it merely needed to be brought to the surface. The Arabs set to work digging wells, constructing reservoirs, building networks of canals along the surface of the ground and systems of subterranean water-galleries deep in the earth.

For all these important projects, the recently arrived colonizers needed great numbers of workers who could bear the climate and the malaria that is still endemic in the oases. Sudanese slaves seemed to be the ideal solution of the problem, and these came to constitute the larger part of the sedentary population of the desert. Each Arab tribe travelled about among the oases it controlled, collecting the produce. It was never the practice or the intention of the sons of Allah to live there. They have a saying which goes: 'No one lives in the Sahara if he is able to live anywhere else.' Slavery has, of course, been abolished officially by the French, but only recently, within our time. Probably the principal factor in the process by which Timbuctoo was reduced from its status of capital of the Sahara to its present abject condition was the closing of the slave market there. But the Sahara, which started out as a Negro country, is still a Negro country, and will undoubtedly remain so for a long time.

The oases, those magnificent palm groves, are the blood and bone of the desert; life in the Sahara would be unthinkable without them. Wherever human beings are found, an oasis is sure to be nearby. Sometimes the town is surrounded by the trees, but usually it is built just outside, so that none of the fertile ground will be wasted on mere living quarters. The size of an oasis is reckoned by the number of trees it contains, not by the number of square miles it covers, just as the taxes are based on the number of date-bearing trees, and not on the amount of land. The prosperity of a region is in direct proportion to the number and size of its oases. The one at Figuig, for instance, has more than two hundred thousand bearing palms, and the one at Timimoun is forty miles long, with irrigation systems that are of an astonishing complexity.

To stroll in a Saharan oasis is rather like taking a walk through a well-kept Eden. The alleys are clean, bordered on each side by hand-patted mud walls, not too high to prevent you from seeing the riot of verdure within. Under the high waving palms are the smaller trees – pomegranate, orange, fig, almond. Below these, in neat squares surrounded by narrow ditches of running water, are the vegetables and wheat. No matter how far from the town you stray, you have the same impression of order, cleanliness, and insistence on utilizing every square inch of ground. When you come to the edge of the oasis, you always find that it is in the process of being enlarged. Plots of young palms extend out into the glaring wasteland. Thus far they are useless, but in a few years they will begin to bear, and eventually this sun-blistered land will be a part of the green belt of gardens.

There are a good many birds living in the oases, but their songs and plumage are not appreciated by the inhabitants. The birds eat the young shoots and dig up the seeds as fast as they are planted, and practically every man and boy carries a sling-shot. A few years ago I travelled through the Sahara with a parrot; everywhere the poor bird was glowered at by the natives, and in Timimoun a delegation of three elderly men came to the hotel one afternoon and suggested that I stop leaving its cage in the window; otherwise there was no telling what its fate might be. 'Nobody likes birds here,' they said meaningfully.

It is the custom to build little summer-houses out in the oasis. There is often an element of play and fantasy in the architecture of these edifices which makes them captivating. They are small, toy palaces of mud. Here, men have tea with their families at the close of day, or spend the night when it is unusually hot in the town, or invite their friends for a game of *ronda* and a little music. If a man asks you to visit him in his summer-house, you find that the experience is invariably worth the long walk required to get there. You will have to drink at least the three traditional glasses of tea, and you may have to eat a good many almonds and smoke more *kif* than you really want, but it will be cool, there will be the gurgle of running water and the smell of mint in the air, and your host may bring out a flute. One winter I priced one of these houses that had particularly struck my fancy. With its garden and pool, the cost was the equivalent of twenty-five pounds. The catch was that the owner wanted to retain the right to work the land, because it was unthinkable to him that it should cease to be productive.

Even though people of dissimilar origins may behave alike in everyday life, the differences become apparent in festive observances. In the highly religious settlement of the M'Zab, it would be inconceivable for the women to take part in a celebration; they stay on the roofs where Moslem women belong. From here they scream exhortations to the men who are below in the street, undergoing the frenetic, self-immolating contortions of their dance. I once spent a night in Ghardaia watching a dozen men dance themselves into unconsciousness beside a bonfire of palm branches. Two burly guards were necessary to prevent them from throwing themselves into the flames. After each man had been heaved back from the fire several times, he finally ceased making his fantastic skyward leaps, staggered, and sank to the ground. He was immediately carried outside the circle and covered with blankets, his place being taken by a fresh adept. There was no music or singing, but there were eight drummers, each playing an instrument of a different size.

In other places, the dance is similar to the Berber *ahouache* of the Moroccan Atlas. The participants form a great circle holding hands, women alternating with men; their movements are measured, never frantic, and, although the trance is constantly suggested, it seems never to be arrived at collectively. In the performances I have seen, there has been a woman in the centre with her head and neck hidden by a cloth. She sings and dances, and the chorus around her responds antiphonally. It is all very sedate and low-pitched, but the irrational seems never very far away, perhaps because of the hypnotic effect produced by the slowly beaten, deep-toned drums.

The Touareg, in all probability an ancient offshoot of the Kabyle Berbers of Algeria, were unappreciative of the 'civilizing mission' of the Roman legions, and decided to put a thousand miles or more of desert between themselves and their would-be educators. They went straight south until they came to a land that seemed likely to provide them the privacy they desired, and they have remained throughout the centuries, their own masters almost until today. Through all the ages during which the Arabs dominated the surrounding regions, the Touareg retained their rule of the Hoggar, that immense plateau in the very centre of the Sahara. Their traditional hatred of the Arabs, however, does not appear to have been powerful enough to keep them from becoming partially Islamized, although they are by no means a completely Moslem people. Far from being a piece of property only somewhat more valuable than a sheep, the woman has an extremely important place in Targui society. The line of succession is purely maternal. Here, it is the men who must be veiled day and night. The veil is of fine black gauze, and is worn, so they explain, to protect the soul. But since soul and breath to them are identical, it is not difficult to find a physical reason, if one is desired. The excessive dryness of the atmosphere often causes disturbances in the nasal passages. The veil conserves the breath's moisture, is a sort of little air-conditioning plant, and this helps to keep out the evil spirits which otherwise would manifest their presence by making the nostrils bleed, a common occurrence in this part of the world.

It is scarcely fair to refer to these proud people as Touareg. The word is a term of opprobrium meaning 'lost souls', given them by their traditional enemies the Arabs, but one which, in the outside world, has stuck. They call themselves *imochagh,* the free ones. Among all the Berber-speaking peoples, they are the only ones to have devised a system of writing their language. No one knows how long their alphabet has been in use, but it is a true phonetical alphabet, quite as well planned and logical as the Roman one, with twenty-three simple and thirteen compound letters.

Unfortunately for them the Touareg have never been able to remain at peace among themselves; internecine warfare has gone on unceasingly among them for centuries. Until the French military put a stop to it, it had been a common practice for one tribe to set out on plundering expeditions against a neighbouring tribe. During these voyages, the wives of the absent men remained faithful to their husbands, the strict Targui moral code recommending death as a punishment for infidelity. However, a married woman whose husband was away was free to go at night to the graveyard dressed in her finest apparel, lie on the tombstone of one of her ancestors, and invoke a certain spirit called Idebni, who always appeared in the guise of one of the young men of the community. If she could win Idebni's favour, he gave her news of her husband; if not, he strangled her. The Touareg women, being very clever, always managed to bring back news of their husbands from the cemetery.

The first motor crossing of the Sahara was accomplished in 1923. At that time it was still a matter of months to get from, let us say, Touggourt to Zinder, or from the Tafilalet to Gao. In 1934, I was in Erfoud inquiring about caravans to Timbuctoo. Yes, they said, one was leaving in a few weeks; and it would take from sixteen to twenty weeks to make the voyage. How would I get back? The caravan would probably set out on its return trip at this time next year. They were surprised to see that this information lessened my interest. How could you expect to do it more quickly?

Of course, the proper way to travel in the Sahara is by camel, particularly if you are a good walker, since after about two hours of the camel's motion you are glad to get down and walk for four. Each succeeding day is likely to bring with it a greater percentage of time spent off the camel. Nowadays, if you like, you can leave Algiers in the morning by plane, and be fairly well into the desert by evening, but the traveller who gives in to this temptation, like the reader of a mystery story who skips through the book to arrive at the solution quickly, deprives himself of most of the pleasure of the journey. The practical means of locomotion here today for the person who wants to see something is the trans-Saharan truck, a compromise between camel and aeroplane.

There are only two trails across the desert at present (the Piste Impériale through Mauretania not being open to the public) and I should not recommend either to drivers of private automobiles. The trucks, however, are especially built for the region. If there is any sort of misadventure, the wait is not likely to be more than twenty-four hours, since the truck is always expected at the next town, and there is always an ample supply of water aboard. But the lone car that gets stuck in the Sahara is in trouble.

Usually, you can go to the fort of any town and telephone ahead to the next post, asking them to notify the hotelkeeper there of your intended arrival. Should the lines be down, a not unusual circumstance, there is no way of assuring yourself a room in advance, save by mail, which is extremely slow. Unless you travel with your own blankets this can be a serious drawback, arriving unannounced, for the hotels are small, often having only five or six rooms, and the winter nights are cold. The temperature goes to several degrees below freezing, reaching its lowest point just before dawn. The same courtyard that may show 125 when it is flooded with sun at two in the afternoon will register only 28 the following morning. So it is good to know you are going to have a room and a bed in your next stopping place. Not that there is heating of any sort in the establishments, but by keeping the window shut you can help the thick mud walls conserve some of the daytime heat. Even so, I have awakened to find a sheet of ice over the water in the glass beside my bed.

These violent extremes of temperatures are due, of course, to the dryness of the atmosphere, whose relative humidity is often less than five per cent. When you reflect that the soil attains a temperature of 175 degrees during the summer, you understand that the principal consideration in planning streets and houses should be that of keeping out as much light as possible. The streets are kept dark by building them underneath and inside the houses, and the houses have no windows in their massive walls. The French have introduced the window into much of their architecture, but their windows open on to wide, vaulted arcades, and thus, while they do give air, they let in little light. The result is that once you are out of the sun you live in a Stygian gloom.

Even in the Sahara there is no spot where rain has not been known to fall, and its arrival is an event that calls for celebration – drumming, dancing, firing of guns. The storms are violent and unpredictable. Considering their disastrous effects, one wonders that the people can welcome them with such unmixed emotions. Enormous walls of water rush down the dry river beds, pushing everything before them, isolating the towns. The roofs of the houses cave in, and often the walls themselves. A prolonged rain would destroy every town in the

Sahara, since the *tob,* of which everything is built, is softer than our adobe. And, in fact, it is not unusual to see a whole section of a village which has been forsaken by its occupants, who have rebuilt their houses nearby, leaving the walls and foundations of their former dwellings to dissolve and drop back into the earth of which they were made.

In 1932 I decided to spend the winter in the M'Zab of southern Algeria. The rattletrap bus started out from Laghouat at night in a heavy rain. Not far to the south, the trail crossed a flat stretch about a mile wide, slightly lower than the surrounding country. Even as we were in it, the water began to rise around us, and in a moment the motor died. The passengers jumped out and waded about in water that soon was up to their waists; in all directions there were dim white figures in burnouses moving slowly through the flood, like storks. They were looking for a shallow route back to dry land, but they did not find it. In the end they carried me, the only European in the party, all the way to Laghouat on their backs, leaving the bus and its luggage to drown out there in the rain. When I got to Ghardaia two days later, the rain (which was the first in seven years) had made a deep pond beside an embankment the French had built for the trail. Such an enormous quantity of water all in one place was a source of great excitement to the inhabitants. For days there was a constant procession of women coming to carry it away in jugs. The children tried to walk on its surface, and two small ones were drowned. Ten days later the water had almost disappeared. A thick, brilliant green froth covered what was left, but the women continued to come with their jugs, pushing aside the scum and taking what remained. For once, they were able to collect as much water as they could store in their houses. Ordinarily, it was an expensive commodity that they had to buy each morning from the town watersellers, who brought it in from the oasis.

Most of the towns are better supplied with water than Ghardaia was then. But the quality of the water varies greatly, and the traveller does well to look into the matter at each place before drinking it. It is better to know whether the minerals it contains are likely to cause death, illness, or merely acute alimentary disturbances. But it is not bad water so much as no water that one had to fear. It is impossible to have too much of it with you. People still die regularly of thirst in the Sahara, so one should take along, on every stage of the journey, more than one can imagine will be needed. Then, if strange explosions and groans are heard among the rocks, the traveller will be aware that it is only a result of the sudden shifts in temperature, and not the laughter of el Rhoul, the *djinn* who comes to watch the thirsty traveller in his death agonies.

There are probably few accessible places on the face of the globe where you can get less comfort for your money than the Sahara. In the past few years the prices in dollars or sterling have more than quintupled, and the accommodations are as miserable as ever. You can still get something flat to lie down on, stewed turnips and sand, noodles and jam, and a few tendons of something euphemistically called chicken to eat, and the stub of a candle to undress by at night, but you will pay heavily for these luxuries. Inasmuch as you must carry your own food and stove with you in any case, it sometimes seems scarcely worth while to bother with the 'meals' provided by the hotels. But if you depend entirely on your tinned goods, they give out too quickly. Everything disappears eventually anyway – your coffee, tea, sugar, cigarettes – and you settle down to a life devoid of these superfluities, using a pile of soiled clothing as a pillow for your head at night and your burnous for a blanket.

*

Perhaps the logical question to ask at this point is: Why go? The answer is that once you have been there and undergone the baptism of solitude you cannot help yourself. Once you have been under the spell of the vast, luminous, silent country, no other place is quite strong enough, no other surroundings can provide the supremely satisfying sensation of existing in the midst of something that is absolute. The traveller will return, whatever the cost in comfort and money, for the absolute has no price.

A Man Must Not Be Very Moslem

This piece was first published in 1963 in the collection Their Heads Are Green.

– *Aboard MS* Tarsus,
Turkish Maritime Lines

WHEN I announced my intention of bringing Abdeslam along to Istanbul, the general opinion of my friends was that there were a good many more intelligent things to do in the world than to carry a Moroccan Moslem along with one to Turkey. I don't know. He may end up as a dead weight, but my hope is that he will turn out instead to be a kind of pass-key to the place. He knows how to deal with Moslems, and he has the Moslem sense of seemliness and protocol. He has also an intuitive gift for the immediate understanding of a situation, and at the same time is completely lacking in reticence or inhibitions. He can lie so well that he convinces himself straightway, and he is a master at bargaining: it is a black day for him when he has to pay the asking price for anything. He never knows what is printed on a sign because he is totally illiterate; besides, even if he did know he would pay no attention, for he is wholly deficient in respect for law. If you mention that this or that thing is forbidden, he is contemptuous: 'Agh! A decree for the wind!' Obviously he is far better equipped than I to squeeze that last drop of adventure out of any occasion. I, unfortunately, *can* read signs, but can't lie or bargain effectively, and will forgo any joy rather than risk unpleasantness or reprimand from whatever quarter. At all events, the die is cast: Abdeslam is here on this ship.

My first intimation of Turkey came during tea this afternoon as the ship was leaving the Bay of Naples. The orchestra was playing a tango which finally established its identity, after several *reprises*, as the *Indian Love Call*, and the cliffs of Capri were getting in the way of the sunset. I glanced at a biscuit that I was about to put into my mouth, then stopped the operation to examine it more closely. It was an ordinary little arrowroot tea-biscuit, and on it were embossed the words HAYD PARK. Contemplating this edible titbit, I recalled what friends had told me of the amusing havoc that results when the Turks phoneticize words borrowed from other languages. These metamorphosed words have a way of looking like gibberish until you say them aloud, and then more likely than not they resolve themselves into perfectly comprehensible English or French, or even, occasionally, Arabic. SKOC TUID looks like nothing; suddenly it becomes Scotch Tweed. TUALET, TRENCKOT, OTOTEKNIK and SEKSOLOJI likewise reveal their messages as one stares at them. Synthetic orthography is a constantly visible reminder of Turkey's determination to be 'modern'. The country has turned its back on the East and on Eastern concepts, not with the simple yearning of other Islamic countries to be European or to acquire American techniques, but with a conscious will to transform itself from the core outward – even to destroy itself culturally, if need be.

– Tarabya, Bosphorus

THIS afternoon it was blustery and very cold. The water in the tiny Sea of Marmara was choppy and dark, laced with froth; the ship rolled more heavily than it had at any time during its three days out on the open Mediterranean. If the first sight of Istanbul was impressive, it was because the perfect hoop of a rainbow painted across the lead-coloured sky ahead kept one from looking at the depressing array of factory smokestacks along the western shore. After an hour's moving backward and forward in the harbour we were close enough to see the needles of the minarets (and how many of them!) in black against the final flare-up of the sunset. It was a poetic introduction, and, like the introductions to most books, it had very little to do with what followed. *Poetic* is not among the adjectives you would use to describe the disembarkation. The pier was festive; it looked like an elegant waterside restaurant or one of the larger Latin-American airports – brilliantly illumined, awnings flapping, its decks mobbed with screaming people.

The customs house was the epitome of confusion for a half-hour or so; when eventually an inspector was assigned us, we were fortunate enough to be let through without having to open anything. The taxis were parked in the dark on the far side of a vast puddle of water, for it had been raining. I had determined on a hotel in Istanbul proper, rather than one of those in Beyöglu, across the Golden Horn, but the taxi-driver and his front-seat companion were loath to take me there. 'All hotels in Beyöglu,' they insisted. I knew better, and did some insisting of my own. We shot into the stream of traffic, across the Galata Bridge, to the hotel of my choosing. Unhappily I had neglected, on the advice of various friends back in Italy, to reserve a room. There was none to be had. And so on, from hotel to hotel there in Istanbul, back across the bridge and up the hill to every establishment in Beyöglu. Nothing, nothing. There are three international conventions in progress here, and besides, it is vacation time in Turkey; everything is full. Even the MS *Tarsus,* from which we just emerged, as well as another ship in the harbour, has been called into service tonight to be used as a hotel. By half past ten I accepted the suggestion of being driven twenty-five kilometres up the

Bosphorus to this place, where they had assured me by telephone that they had space.

'Do you want a room with bath?' they asked. I said I did.

'We haven't any,' they told me.

'Then I want a room without bath.'

'We have one.' That was that.

Once we had left the city behind and were driving along the dark road, there was nothing for Abdeslam to do but catechize the two Turks in front. Obviously they did not impress him as being up-to-the-mark Moslems, and he started by testing their knowledge of the Koran. I thought they were replying fairly well, but he was contemptuous. 'They don't know anything,' he declared in Moghrebi. Going into English, he asked them, 'How many times one day you pray?'

They laughed.

'People can sleep in mosque?' he pursued. The driver was busy navigating the curves in the narrow road, but his companion, who spoke a special brand of English all his own, spoke for him. 'Not slep in mosque many people every got hoss,' he explained.

'You make sins?' continued Abdeslam, intent on unearthing the hidden flaws in the behaviour of these foreigners. 'Pork, wine?'

The other shrugged his shoulders. 'Moslem people every not eat pork not drink wine but maybe one hundred year ago like that. Now different.'

'*Never* different!' shouted Abdeslam sternly. 'You not good Moslems here. People not happy. You have bad government. Not like Egypt. Egypt have good government. Egypt one hundred per cent Moslem.'

The other was indignant. 'Everybody happy,' he protested. 'Happy with Egypt too for religion. But the Egypts sometimes fight with Egypts. Arab fight Arabs. Why? I no like Egypt. I in

Egypt. I ask my way. They put me say bakhshish. If you ask in Istanbul, you say go my way, he can bring you, but he no say give bakhshish. Before, few people up, plenty people down. Now, you make your business, I make my business. You take your money, I take my money. Before, *you* take *my* money. You rich with *my* money. Before, Turkey like Egypt with Farouk.' He stopped to let all this sink in, but Abdeslam was not interested. 'Egypt very good country,' he retorted, and there was no more conversation until we got here.

The driver's comrade was describing a fascinating new ideology known as democracy. From the beginning of the colloquy I had my notebook out, scribbling his words in the dark as he spoke them. They express the average uneducated Turk's reaction to the new concept. It was only in 1950 that the first completely democratic elections were held. (Have there been any since?) To Abdeslam, who is a traditionally minded Moslem, the very idea of democracy is meaningless. It is impossible to explain it to him: he will not listen. If an idea is not explicitly formulated in the Koran, it is wrong; it came either directly from Satan or via the Jews, and there is no need to discuss it further.

This hotel, built at the edge of the lapping Bosphorus, is like a huge wooden box. At the base of the balustrade of the grand staircase leading up from the lobby, one on each side, are two life-sized ladies made of lead and painted with white enamel in the hope of making them look like marble. The dining-room's decorations are of a more recent period – the early twenties. There are high murals that look as though the artist had made a study of Boutet de Monvel's fashion drawings of the era; long-necked, low-waisted females in cloches and thigh-length skirts, presumably picnicking on the shores of the Bosphorus.

At dinner we were the only people eating, since it was nearly midnight. Abdeslam took advantage of this excellent opportunity by delivering an impassioned harangue (partly in a mixture of Moghrebi and Standard Arabic and partly in English), with the result that by the end of the meal we had fourteen waiters and busboys crowded around the table listening. Then someone thought of fetching the chef. He arrived glistening with sweat and beaming; he had been brought because he spoke more Arabic than the others, which was still not very much. 'Old-fashioned Moslem,' explained the headwaiter. Abdeslam immediately put him through the *chehade*, and he came off with flying colours, reciting it word for word along with Abdeslam: '*Achhaddouanlaillahainallah* . . .' The faces of the younger men expressed unmistakable admiration, as well as pleasure at the approval of the esteemed foreigner, but none of them could perform the chef's feat. Presently the manager of the hotel came in, presumably to see what was going on in the dining-room at this late hour. Abdeslam asked for the bill, and objected when he saw that it was written with Roman characters. 'Arabic!' he demanded. 'You Moslem? Then bring bill in Arabic.' Apologetically the manager explained that writing in Arabic was 'dangerous', and had been known on occasion to put the man who did it into jail. To this he added, just to make things quite clear, that any man who veiled his wife also went to jail. 'A man must not be *very* Moslem,' he said. But Abdeslam had had enough. 'I *very very* Moslem,' he announced. We left the room.

The big beds stand high off the floor, and haven't enough covers on them. I have spread my topcoat over me: it is cold and I should like to leave the windows shut, but the mingled stenches coming from the combined shower-lavatory behind a low partition in the corner are so powerful that such a course is out of the question. The winds moving down from the Black Sea will blow over me all night. Sometime after we had gone to bed, following a long silence during which I thought he had fallen asleep, Abdeslam called over to me, 'That Mustapha Kemal was carrion! He ruined his country. The son of a dog!' Because I was writing, and also because I am not sure exactly where I stand in this philosophical dispute, I said, 'You're right. *Allah imsik bekhir.*'

– *Sirkeci*

WE are installed at Sirkeci on the Istanbul side, in the hotel I had first wanted. Outside the window is a taxi stand. From early morning onward there is the continuous racket of men's voices shouting and horns being blown in a struggle to keep recently arrived taxis from edging in ahead of those that have been waiting in line. The general prohibition of horn-blowing which is in effect everywhere in the city doesn't seem to apply here. The altercations are bitter, and everyone gets involved in them. Taxi-drivers in Istanbul are something of a race apart. They are the only social group who systematically try to take advantage of the foreign visitor. In the ships, restaurants, cafés, the prices asked of the newcomer are the same as those paid by the inhabitants. (In the bazaars buying is automatically a matter of wrangling; that is understood.) The cab-drivers, however, are more actively acquisitive. For form's sake, their vehicles are equipped with meters, but their method of using them is such that they might better do without them. You get into a cab whose meter registers seventeen liras thirty kurus, ask the man to turn it back to zero and start again; he laughs and does nothing. When you get out it registers eighteen liras eighty kurus. You give him the difference, or one lira and a half. Never! He may want two and a half or three and a half or a good deal more, but he will not settle for what seems equitable according to the meter. Since most tourists pay what they are asked and go on their way, he is not prepared for an argument, and he is likely to let his temper run away with him if you are recalcitrant. There is also the pre-arranged-price system of taking a cab. Here the driver goes as slowly and by as circuitous a route as possible, calling out the general neighbourhood of his destination for all the street to hear, so that he can pick up extra fares *en route*. He will, unless you assert yourself, allow several people to pile in on top of you until there is literally no room left for you to breathe.

The streets are narrow, crooked and often precipitous, traffic is very heavy, and there are many tramcars and buses. The result is that the taxis go like the wind whenever there is a space of a few yards ahead, rushing to the extreme left to get around obstacles before oncoming traffic reaches them. I am used to Paris and Mexico, both cities of evil repute where taxis are concerned, but I think Istanbul might possibly win first prize for thrill-giving.

One day when we had arranged the price beforehand and our driver, having picked up two extra men, had mercifully put them in front with him, he spied a girl standing on the kerb, and slowed down to take her in, too. A policeman saw his manoeuvre and did not approve: one girl with five men seemed too likely to cause a disturbance. He blew his whistle menacingly. The driver, rattled, swerved sharply to the left, to pretend he had never thought of such a thing as stopping to pick up a young lady. There was a crash and we were thrown off the seat. We got out; the last we saw of the driver, he was standing in the middle of the street by his battered car, screaming at the man whom he had hit, and holding up all traffic. Abdeslam took down his licence number, in the hope of persuading me to instigate a lawsuit.

Since the use of the horn is proscribed, taxi-drivers can

make their presence known only by reaching out the window and pounding violently on the outside of the door. The scraping of the tramcars and the din of the enormous horse-drawn carts thundering over the cobbled pavements make it difficult to judge just how much the horn interdiction reduces noise. The drivers also have a pretty custom of passing back a packet of cigarettes at the beginning of the journey; this is to soften up the victim for the subsequent kill. On occasion they sing for you. One morning I was entertained all the way from Süleymaniye to Taksim with 'Jezebel' and 'Come On-a My House'. In such cases the traffic warnings on the side of the car are done in strict rhythm.

Istanbul is a jolly place; it is hard to find any element of the sinister about it, notwithstanding all the spy novels for which it provides such a handsome setting. A few of the older buildings are of stone; but many more of them are built of wood which looks as though it had never been painted. The cupolas and minarets rise above the disorder of the city like huge grey fungi growing out of a vast pile of ashes. For disorder is the visual keynote of Istanbul. It is not slovenly – only untidy; not dirty – merely dingy and drab. And just as you cannot claim it to be a beautiful city, neither can you accuse it of being uninteresting. Its steep hills and harbour views remind you a little of San Francisco; its overcrowded streets recall Bombay; its transportation facilities evoke Venice, for you can go to so many places by boat, and the boats are continually making stops. (It costs threepence to get across to Usküdar in Asia.) Yet the streets in detail are strangely reminiscent of an America that has almost disappeared. Again and again I have been reminded of some New England mill town in the time of my childhood. Or a row of little houses will suggest a back street in Stapleton, on Staten Island. It is a city whose aesthetic is that of the unlikely and incongruous, a photographer's paradise.

There is no native quarter, or, if you like, it is all native quarter. Beyöglu, site of the so-called 'better' establishments, concerns itself as little with appearances as do the humbler regions on the other side of the bridges.

You wander down the hill toward Karaköy. Above the harbour with its thousands of caïques, rowboats, tugs, freighters, and ferries, lies a pall of smoke and haze through which you can see the vague outline of the domes and towers of Aya Sofia, Sultan Ahmet and Süleymaniye; but to the left and far above all that there is a pure region next to the sky where the mountains in Asia glisten with their snow. As you descend the alleys of steps that lead to the water's level, there are more and more people around you. In Karaköy itself just to make progress along the pavement requires the best part of your attention. You would think that all of the city's million and a quarter inhabitants were there, on their way to or from Galata Bridge. By Western European standards it is not a well-dressed crowd. The chaotic sartorial effect achieved by the populace in Istanbul is not necessarily due to poverty, but rather to a divergent conception of the uses to which European garments should be put. The mass is not an ethnically homogeneous one. Faces range in type from Levantine through Slavic to Mongoloid, the last belonging principally to the soldiers from eastern Anatolia. Apart from language there seems to be no one element which they all have in common, not even shabbiness, since there are usually, among the others, a few men and women who do understand how to wear their clothing.

Galata Bridge has two levels, the lower of which is a great dock whence the boats leave to go up the Golden Horn and the Bosphorus, across to the Asiatic suburbs, and down to the islands in the Sea of Marmara. The ferries are there, of all sizes and shapes, clinging to the edge like water-beetles to the side of a floating stick. When you get across to the other side of the bridge there are just as many people and just as much traffic, but the buildings are older and the streets narrower, and you begin to realize that you are, after all, in an oriental city. And if you expect to see anything more than the 'points of interest', you are going to have to wander for miles on foot. The character of Istanbul derives from a thousand disparate, non-evident details; only by observing the variations and repetitions of such details can you begin to get an idea of the patterns they form. Thus the importance of wandering. The dust is bad. After a few hours of it I usually have a sore throat. I try to get off the main arteries where the horses and drays clatter by, and stay in the alleyways which are too narrow for anything but foot traffic. These lanes occasionally open up into little squares with rugs hanging on the walls and chairs placed in the shade of the grapevines overhead. A few Turks will be sitting about drinking coffee; the narghiles bubble. Invariably, if I stop and gaze a moment, someone asks me to have some coffee, eat a few green walnuts, and share his pipe. An irrational disinclination to become involved keeps me from accepting, but today Abdeslam did accept, only to find to his chagrin that the narghile contained tobacco, and not *kif* or hashish as he had expected.

Cannabis sativa and its derivatives are strictly prohibited in Turkey, and the natural correlative of this proscription is that alcohol, far from being frowned upon as it is in other Moslem lands, is freely drunk; being a government monopoly it can be bought at any cigarette counter. This fact is no mere detail: it is of primary social importance, since the psychological effects of the two substances are diametrically opposed to each other. Alcohol blurs the personality by loosening inhibitions. The drinker feels, temporarily at least, a sense of participation. *Kif* abolishes no inhibitions; on the contrary it reinforces them, pushes the individual further back into the recesses of his own isolated personality, pledging him to contemplation and inaction. It is to be expected that there should be a close relationship between the culture of a given society and the means used by its members to achieve release and euphoria. For Judaism and Christianity the means has always been alcohol; for Islam it has been hashish. The first is dynamic in its effects, the other static. If a nation wishes, however mistakenly, to Westernize itself, first let it give up hashish. The rest will follow, more or less as a matter of course. Conversely, in a Western country, if a whole segment of the population desires, for reasons of protest (as has happened in the United States), to isolate itself in a radical fashion from the society around it, the quickest and surest way is for it to replace alcohol by cannabis.

– *Sirkeci*

TODAY in our wanderings we came upon the old fire tower at the top of the hill behind Süleymaniye, and since there was no sign at the door forbidding entry, we stepped in and began to climb the one hundred and eighty rickety wooden steps of the spiral staircase leading to the top. (Abdeslam counted them.) When we had got almost up, we heard strains of Indian music: a radio up there was tuned in to New Delhi. At the same moment a good deal of water came pouring down upon us through the cracks above. We decided to beat a retreat, but then the boy washing the stairs saw us and insisted that we continue to the top and sit awhile. The view up there was magnificent; there is no better place from which to see the city. A charcoal fire was burning in a brazier, and we had tea and listened to some Anatolian songs which presently came over the air. Outside the many windows the wind blew, and the city below, made quiet by distance, spread itself across the rolling landscape on every side, its roof tiles pink in the autumn sun.

Later we sought out Pandeli's, a restaurant I had heard about but not yet found. This time we managed to discover it, a delapidated little building squeezed in among harness-shops and wholesale fruit stores. We had *pirinc corba*, *beyendeli kebap*, *barbunya fasulya*, and other good things. In the middle of the meal, probably while chewing on the *taze makarna*, I bit my lip. My annoyance with the pain was not mitigated by hearing Abdeslam remark unsympathetically, 'If you'd keep your mouth open when you chew, like everybody else, you wouldn't have accidents like this.' Pandeli's is the only native restaurant I have seen which doesn't sport a huge refrigerated showcase packed with food. You are usually led to this and told to choose what you want to eat. In the glare of the fluorescent lighting the food looks pallid and untempting, particularly the meat, which has been hacked into unfamiliar-looking cuts. During your meal there is usually a radio playing ancient jazz; occasionally a Turkish or Syrian number comes up. Although the tea is good, it is not good enough to warrant its being served as though it were nectar, in infinitesimal glasses that can be drained at one gulp. (I often order several at once, and this makes for confusion.) When you ask for water, you are brought a tiny bottle capped with tinfoil. Since it is free of charge, I suspect it of being simple tap-water; perhaps I am unjust.

In the evening we went to the very drab red-light district in Beyöglu just behind the British Consulate-General. The street was mobbed with men and boys. In the entrance door of each house was a small square opening, rather like those through which one used to be denied access to American speakeasies, and framed in each opening, against the dull yellow light within, was a girl's head.

The Turks are the only Moslems I have seen who seem to

have got rid of that curious sentiment (apparently held by all followers of the True Faith) of inevitable and hopeless difference between themselves and non-Moslems. Subjectively at least they have managed to bridge the gulf created by their religion, that abyss which isolates Islam from the rest of the world. As a result the visitor feels a specific connection with them which is not the mere one-sided sympathy the well-disposed traveller has for the more basic members of other cultures, but is something desired and felt by them as well. They are touchingly eager to understand and please, so eager, indeed, that they often neglect to listen carefully, and consequently get things all wrong. Their goodwill, however, seldom flags, and in the long run this more than compensates for being given the breakfast you did not order, or being sent in the opposite direction from the one in which you wanted to go. There is, of course, the linguistic barrier. One really needs to know Turkish to live in Istanbul. My ignorance of all Altaic languages is total; in the hotel I suffer. The chances are nineteen in twenty that when I give an order things will go wrong, even when I get hold of the housekeeper who speaks French and who assures me calmly that all the other employees are idiots. The hotel is considered by my guide book to be a 'de luxe' establishment – the highest category. Directly after the 'de luxe' listings come the 'first class' places, which it describes in its own mysterious rhetoric: 'These hotels have somewhat luxury, but are still comfortable with every convenience.' Having seen the lobbies of several of the hostelries thus pigeonholed, complete with disembowelled divans and abandoned perambulators, I am very thankful to be here in my de luxe suite, where the telephone is white so that I can see the cockroaches on the instrument before I lift it to my lips. At least the insects are discreet, and die obligingly under a mild blast of DDT. It is fortunate I came here: my two insecticide bombs would never have lasted out a sojourn in a first-class hotel.

Santa Sophia? Aya Sofya now, not a living mosque but a dead one like those of Kairouan which can no longer be used because they have been profaned by the feet of infidels. Greek newspapers have carried on propaganda campaigns designed to turn the clock back, reinstate Aya Sofya as a tabernacle of the Orthodox Church. The move was obviously foredoomed to failure: after having used it as a mosque for five centuries the Moslems would scarcely relish seeing it put back into the hands of the Christians. And so now it is a museum which contains nothing but its own architecture. Sultan Ahmet, the mosque just across the park, is more to my own taste, but then a corpse does not bear comparison to a living organism. Sultan Ahmet is still a place of worship, the imam is allowed to wear the classical headgear, the heavy final syllable of Allah's name reverberates in the air under the high dome, boys *doven* in distant corners as they memorize *surat* from the Koran. When the tourists stumble over the prostrate forms of men in prayer, or blatantly make use of their light-meters and Rolleiflexes, no one pays any attention. To Abdeslam this incredible invasion of privacy was tantamount to lack of respect for Islam; it fanned the coals of his resentment into flame. (In his country no unbeliever can put even one foot into a mosque.) As he wandered about, his exclamations of indignation became increasingly audible. He started out with the boys by suggesting to them that it was their great misfortune to be living in a country of widespread sin. They looked at him blankly, and went on with their litanies. Then in a louder voice he began to criticize the raiment of the worshippers, because they wore socks and slippers on their feet, and on their heads berets or caps with the visors at the back. He knows that the wearing of the tarbouche is forbidden by law, but his hatred of Kemal Atatürk, which has been growing hourly ever since his arrival, had become too intense, I suppose, for him to be able to repress it any longer. His big moment came when the imam entered. He approached the venerable gentleman with elaborate salaams which were enthusiastically reciprocated. Then the two retired into a private room, where they remained for ten minutes or so. When Abdeslam came out there were tears in his eyes and he wore an expression of triumph. 'Ah, you see?' he cried, as we emerged into the street. 'That poor man is very, *very* unhappy. They have only one day of Ramadan in the year.' (Even I was a little shocked to hear that the traditional month had been whittled down to a day.) 'This is an accursed land,' he went on. 'When we get power we'll soak it in petrol and set it afire, and burn everyone in it. May it for ever be damned! And all these dogs living in it, I pray Allah they may be thrown into the fires of Gehennem. Ah, if we only had our power back for one day, we Moslems! May Allah speed that day when we shall ride into Turkey and smash their government and all their works of Satan!' The imam, it seems, had been delighted beyond measure to see a young man who still had the proper respect for religion; he had complained bitterly that the youth of Turkey was spiritually lost.

Today I had lunch with a woman who has lived here a good many years. As a Westerner, she felt that the important thing to notice about Turkey is the fact that from having been in the grip of a ruthless dictatorship it has slowly evolved into a modern democracy, rather than having followed the more usual reverse process. Even Atatürk was restrained by his associates from going all the way in his iconoclasm, for what he wanted was a Turkish adaptation of what he had seen happen in Russia. Religion was to him just as much of an opiate in one country as in another. He managed to deal it a critical blow here, one which may yet prove to have been fatal. Last year an American, a member of Jehovah's Witnesses, arrived, and as is the custom with members of that sect stood on the street handing out brochures. But not for long. The police came, arrested him, put him in jail, and eventually effected his expulsion from the country. This action, insisted my lunch partner, was not taken because the American was distributing Christian propaganda; had he been distributing leaflets advocating the reading of the Koran, it is likely that his punishment would have been more severe.

– Sirkeci

AT the beginning of the sixteenth century Selim the Grim captured from the Shah of Persia one of the most fantastic pieces of furniture I have ever seen. The trophy was the poor Shah's throne, a simple but massive thing made of chiselled gold, decorated with hundreds of enormous emeralds. I went to see it today at the Topkapi Palace. There was a bed to match, also of emerald-studded gold. After a moment of looking, Abdeslam ran out of the room where these incredible objects stood, into the courtyard, and could not be coaxed back in. 'Too many riches are bad for the eyes,' he explained. I could not agree; I thought them beautiful. I tried to make him tell me the exact reason for his sudden flight, but he found it difficult to give me a rational explanation of his behaviour. 'You know that gold and jewels are sinful,' he began. To get him to go on, I said I knew. 'And if you look at sinful things for very long you can go crazy; you know that. And I don't want to go crazy.' I was willing to take the chance, I replied, and I went back in to see more.

– Sirkeci

THESE last few days I have spent entirely at the covered souks. I discovered the place purely by accident, since I follow no plan in my wanderings about the city. You climb up an endless hill; whichever street you take swarms with buyers and sellers who take up all the room between the shops on either side. It isn't good form to step on the merchandise, but now and then one can't avoid doing it.

The souks are all in one vast ant-hill of a building, a city within a city, whose avenues and streets, some wide, some narrow, are like the twisting hallways one remembers from a dream. There are more than five thousand shops under its roof, so they assure me – I have not wondered whether it seems a likely number or not, nor have I passed through all its forty-two entrance portals, nor explored more than a small number of its tunnelled galleries. Visually the individual shops lack the colour and life of the kissarias of Fez and Marrakech, and there are no painted Carthaginian columns like those which decorate the souks in Tunis. The charm of the edifice lies in its vastness, and in part precisely in its dimness and clutter. In the middle of one open space where two large corridors meet, there is an outlandish construction, in shape and size not unlike one of the old traffic towers on New York's Fifth Avenue in the twenties. On the ground floor is a minute kitchen. If you climb the crooked outside staircase, you find yourself in a tiny restaurant with four miniature tables. Here you sit and eat, looking out along the tunnels over the heads of the passers-by. It is a place out of Kafka's *Amerika.*

The antique shops here in the souks are famous. As one might expect, tourists are considered to be a feeble-minded and nearly defenceless species of prey, and there are never enough of them to go around. Along the sides of the galleries stand whole tribes of merchants waiting for them to appear. These men have brothers, fathers, uncles and cousins, each of whom operates his own shop, and the tourist is passed along from one member of the family to the next with no visible regret on anyone's part. In one shop I heard the bearded proprietor solemnly assuring a credulous American woman that the amber perfume she had just bought was obtained by pressing beads of amber like those in the necklace she was examining. (Not that it would have been much more truthful of him had he told her that it was made of ambergris: the amber I have smelled here never saw a whale, and consists almost entirely, I should say, of benzoin.)

If you stop to look into an antiquary's window you are lost. Suddenly you are aware that hands are clutching your clothing, pulling you gently toward the door, and honeyed voices are experimenting with greetings in all the more common European languages, one after the other. Unless you offer physical resistance you find yourself being propelled forcibly within. Then as you face your captors over arrays of old silver and silk, they begin to work on you in earnest, using all the classic clichés of Eastern sales-patter.

'You have such a fine face that I want my merchandise to go with you.' 'We need money today; you are the first customer to come in all day long.' A fat hand taps the ashes from a cigarette. 'Unless I do business with you, I won't sleep tonight. I am an old man. Will you ruin my health?' 'Just buy one thing, no matter what. Buy the cheapest thing in the store, if you like, but buy something . . .' If you get out of the place without making a purchase, you are entitled to add ten to your score. A knowledge of Turkish is not necessary here in the bazaars. If you prefer not to speak English or French or German, you find that the Moslems love to be spoken to in Arabic, while the Jews speak a corrupt Andalucian version of Spanish.

Today I went out of the covered souks by a back street that I had not found before. It led downward toward the Rustempasa Mosque. The shops gave it a strange air: they all looked alike from the outside. On closer inspection I saw that they were all selling the same wildly varied assortment of unlikely objects. I wanted to get in and examine the merchandise, and since Abdeslam had been talking about buying some rubber-soled shoes, we chose a place at random and went into it. While he tried on sneakers and sandals I made a partial inventory of the objects in the big gloomy room. The shelves and counters exhibited footballs, Moslem rosaries, military belts, reed mouthpieces for native oboes, doorhooks, dice of many sizes and colours, narghiles, watchstraps of false cobra-skin, garden shears, slippers of untanned leather – hard as stone, brass water-taps for kitchen sinks, imitation ivory cigarette-holders ten inches long, suitcases made of pressed paper, tambourines, saddles, assorted medals for the military, and plastic game counters. Hanging from the ceiling were revolver holsters, lutes, and zipper fasteners that looked like strips of flypaper. Ladders were stacked upright against the wall, and on the floor were striped canvas deckchairs, huge tin trunks with scenes of Mecca stamped on their sides, and a great pile of wood-shavings among whose comfortable hills nestled six very bourgeois cats. Abdeslam bought no shoes, and the proprietor began to stare at me and my notebook with unconcealed suspicion, having decided, perhaps, that I was a member of the secret police looking for stolen goods.

Material benefits may be accrued in the process of destroying the meaning of life. Are these benefits worth the inevitable void produced by that destruction? The question is apposite in every case where the traditional beliefs of a people have been systematically modified by its government. Rationalizing words like 'progress', 'modernization', or 'democracy' mean nothing because, even if they are used sincerely, the imposition of such concepts by force from above cancels whatever value they might otherwise have. There is little doubt that by having been made indifferent Moslems the younger generation in Turkey has become more like our idea of what people living in the twentieth century should be. The old helplessness in the face of *mektoub* (it is written) is gone, and in its place is a passionate belief in man's ability to alter his destiny. That is the greatest step of all; once it has been made, anything, unfortunately, can happen.

Abdeslam is not a happy person. He sees his world, which he knows is a good world, being assailed from all sides, slowly crumbling before his eyes. He has no means of understanding me, should I try to explain to him that in this age what he considers to be religion is called superstition, and that religion today has come to be a desperate attempt to integrate metaphysics with science. Something will have to be found to replace the basic wisdom which has been destroyed, but the discovery will not be soon; neither Abdeslam nor I will ever know of it.

PART IV

AUTOBIOGRAPHY

Without Stopping

This extract is Chapter 1 of Bowles's autobiography, Without Stopping *(1972).*

KNEELING on a chair and clutching the gilded top rung of its back, I stared at the objects on the shelves of the cabinet. To the left of the gold clock was an old pewter tankard. When I had looked at it for a while, I said the word 'mug' aloud. It looked like my own silver mug at home, from which I drank my milk. 'Mug,' I said again, and the word sounded so strange that I continued to say it, again and again, until I found myself losing touch with its meaning. This astonished me; it also gave me a vague feeling of unease. How could 'mug' not mean mug?

The room was very quiet. I was alone in that part of the house. Suddenly the gold clock chimed four times. As soon as the last stroke was stilled, I realized that something important was happening. I was four years old, the clock had struck four, and 'mug' meant mug. Therefore I was I, I was there, and it was that precise moment and no other. A satisfying new experience, to be able to say all this with certainty.

This was Uncle Edward's house in Exeter, next door to the Unitarian church, where he was the minister. For me the place already had a legendary aspect, since both Mother and Uncle Fred had spent their secondary school years there, he at Phillips Exeter and she at Robinson Female Seminary. Mysteriously, whenever she mentioned the name of her school, she laughed, yet if she spoke of Phillips Academy, it was almost with reverence. 'I've already entered you,' she told me, and this was disturbing in so far as I gave it any thought.

Now Mother was in the hospital just outside the town;

when Daddy arrived from New York, he took me aside and with more than his usual asperity said, 'Your mother is a very sick woman, and it's all because of you, young man. Remember that.'

I was bewildered and resentful. How could I have had anything to do with her illness? But already I took for granted his constant and unalloyed criticism. His mere presence meant misery; it was one of the inalterables of existence.

I went with Aunt Jen to visit Mother, carrying along two cookies that I had been allowed to shape and bake. They were grimy and inedible, but she laughed and ate them. Later, when we were back in New York, I asked her why it was my fault that she had been sick.

'Oh, my dear! Daddy didn't mean that. You see, you had a very hard time coming into this world. Most babies come in right side up, but you somehow came upside down. And you weighed eight and a half pounds.' This did not explain very much, but it reduced my sense of guilt.

The following year there occurred a phenomenon similar to the one involving the mug, but this time I was forewarned and savoured the sensation voluptuously, letting myself float in total awareness of the moment. It was at the Happy Hollow Farm. I sat on the swing under one of the giant maples, bathing in the smells and sounds of a summer afternoon in Massachusetts. And I let myself fall backward to hang with my head down, almost touching the grass, and stayed that way. Then a clock in the house struck four. It began all over again. I am I, it is now, and I am here. The swing moved a little, and I saw the green depths of maple leaves and, further out, the unbelievably blue sky.

The Happy Hollow Farm was a 165-acre tract of forested hillsides. A meadow perhaps half a mile wide ran through the middle of the land, and there was a cold, deep-running brook that one could hear gurgling in the marsh grass and rushes before one saw it. The house dated from the end of the eighteenth century; it *was* the classical square, two-storey clapboard building, white, with green blinds. It stood back from the road on a rise, partially hidden by four enormous maples. There was an ell at the north end of the house, which contained the kitchen and pantries and the hired man's room. Beyond that came the exciting part of the farm, a series of dark and rustic sheds that extended all the way back to the springhouse. The place smelled of the freshly cut wood that was stacked there, of mildewed burlap, apples, damp earth, and of a whole mysterious gamut of time-encrusted things. Whenever I was found exploring the dim recesses of the sheds, I was told to go outdoors. There in the sunlight I would pretend to be occupied. I could tell by the cadence of the voices coming from inside the house when it was safe to wander back into the sheds.

At the Happy Hollow Farm lived Grampa and Gramma Winnewisser with their two sons. Grampa had bought the property as a kind of retirement project after an accident with a runaway horse had made it difficult for him to walk. Up until that time he had owned the only 'department' store in Bellows Falls, Vermont.

Grampa's first name was August. He was a moody and violent man, subject to sudden surges of temper, when his voice shook the house with bellowed imprecations in German and English. He had no sympathy with anything that required organization, like religions, societies, and governments. According to him, any group claiming to have a common purpose or belief existed only for the mystification and exploitation of its members. Notably exempt from his condemnation were the Freemasons, whom he held in respect, perhaps because he was one himself. I remember his calling my three small cousins and me in from play in order to ask us if we thought there was a god. I, who was under the impression that God was one of the things adults had invented in order to manage children more easily, carefully refrained from answering. But the three little cousins, having been told by their respective mothers that God was real, replied in the affirmative. This was Grampa's signal to explode. 'Pah! There's no god. It's a lot of nonsense. Don't you believe it.'

He was going on in this vein when my Aunt Ulla came in. With the clumsiness typical of the adult who consistently underestimates the intelligence of small children, she remonstrated with him, saying, 'Oh, Father! Not in front of the children, please!'

He's right, I thought, even more firmly convinced. It *is* a lie. They don't believe it. Why should we believe it?

Right or wrong, he was a frightening man. His nose had been disfigured by an inexplicable operation he had suffered as a youth at the hands of his father. He had shattered the bones at the bridge of the nose with a hammer. It was not the strangely shaped and discoloured nose which made him frightening, however, so much as the fact that he himself had performed the same operation on both his sons, so that they both had broken noses like his. This bothered me very much, particularly because my mother often spent twenty minutes or a half-hour at a time rubbing my nose firmly between her thumb and forefinger. Young bones and cartilage, she told me, were malleable, and you had to be very careful what shape they took. I wondered privately if I were slated to be the next victim of the hammer.

Throughout his life Grampa's interest lay in the prices of consumer goods. He knew the exact price of each grade of every object you could name, wholesale and retail, and how much it had varied from the prices of former years. Since he had spent his active life studying price lists, he continued to do it after he sold the store.

On the rare occasions when his sister Fanny came to visit, Grampa seemed really happy. Retreating into the privacy of their own language, which no one else understood, the two would sit until nearly dawn drinking beer and eating rye bread garnished with Limburger cheese and onions. At these times Grampa seemed to have become another, totally different man, transformed by the mysterious language and its accompanying gestures into an urbane stranger.

The choice of names for his three daughters was solely his: he called them Emma, Rena, and Ulla. (They all married men with sissy names, he once remarked, continuing with snide inflection: Guy! Claude! Harold!) But he had a favourite among his sons-in-law, and that was my Uncle Harold Danser, a clever young businessman and, one might almost guess it, the son of a department store owner himself. Neither Uncle Guy nor my father was remotely interested in business; both of them failed wholly to appreciate Grampa's talent for figures. In fact, my father considered him slightly unbalanced, and dismissed the thought of him with a contemptuous shrug, which was easy inasmuch as he arranged his life in such a way as practically never to come into contact with him.

Gramma was the principal counterbalance to the latent emotional violence that often seemed about to engulf her family. I used to look at her and think: What a nice mother she would make. In her presence the world seemed acceptable. Difficulties never made her cynical or despairing, as they did the other members of the family. I had the impression that they, secretly craving disaster, were constantly on the look-out for signs of it. Gramma was strong, calm, and sunny, with no religious convictions, but Grampa's murky blasphemies offended her taste. 'Why do you shout?' she would ask if he began one of his anti-Christian tirades. 'Why can't you just say it?'

Even the sound of Gramma's voice comforted me. When I

heard it, I felt that nothing bad could happen. But the frustration caused by Grampa's tyranny had made her subject to severe headaches. When one of these struck, the house was paralysed. If her daughters were visiting the farm when she was brought low by such an attack, they would sit all day beside her bed, commiserating with her. Grampa was cruel, they said, to have shut her away like this in the country. But Gramma was not sorry for herself. It was not torture for her to live on the farm; it was merely hard work, and she was used to that. Like most New Englanders of her generation, she was very much aware of 'nature' and was happy in proximity to it. When she died, much later, her children all whispered to one another that it was the fact of having been forced to live on the farm that had killed her.

My father had hoped to be a concert violinist, but expectedly his parents, considering this a highly impractical ambition, vetoed it with energy, whereupon he retaliated by having a nervous breakdown. His older brother was already studying dentistry, a fact doubtless instrumental in persuading him, once he was over his tantrum, to follow suit. He married at thirty, and I was born a little more than two years later, his only offspring. Until I was five, he was busy building up his practice; after that he always seemed to have too many patients.

The winters of these early years are largely hidden in the mists that obscure infantile memories. We lived in an old brownstone house of the classical model that had been painted grey, and it had a formidable flight of steps leading from the sidewalk up to the front door. The first floor housed my father's laboratory. I remember the entrance hall as dark and uninviting; there was a smell of gas burners and hot metal in the air. The laboratory was forbidden territory, and its doors were always shut. A long flight of stairs led up to the office and reception room. Still another stairway had to be climbed before we were home, in the four-room apartment on the top floor.

I spent my days playing by myself in the house, except for the occasional hour when I was turned out into the backyard. It was a large flat plot of grass shut in by a very high wooden fence. There was no way of seeing anything beyond the yard. However, on one side there were nine windows, looking out on me like nine eyes, and from any one of them could come a sudden shout of disapproval. If I stood still and watched the clock that was always placed in the window so I would know when the hour was up, I heard taps on a third-storey window and saw my mother making gestures exhorting me to move around and play. But if I began to gallop around the yard, my father would call from the second storey, 'Calm down, young man!' Or his receptionist would wave and cry, 'Your Daddy says to stop making that noise!'

In that house I had a toy chest. By Daddy's edict, everything had to be already in the chest when he came upstairs at six in the evening. Whatever remained outside would be confiscated and I never would see it again. I began the packing-up process at five o'clock; by quarter to six I always had it done and the lid shut. After that I could read until dinner if I liked, since books could be returned to the bookcase quickly. Writing and drawing, however, which were my favourite form of play, could not be resumed until the following day. My mother always claimed that I had taught myself to read, and very likely I did, since I can't remember a period when the printed word did not make its corresponding sound in my head as I looked at it. I still have a little notebook with stories about animals, invented by me and printed in pencil, each one carefully dated at the end, and the year is 1915, which means that I was four years old when I wrote them. My Grandmother Bowles visited us. I overheard her telling my mother, exactly as though

I weren't present, that precocity should not be encouraged; she foresaw disaster unless I were somehow brought into contact with other children, so that I could 'grow in other directions'. I did not know what she meant, but I immediately determined not to accept other directions. 'I warn you, Rena, you'll rue the day,' she said, and I looked across at her and thought: She's trying to break in.

Among the games I kept stacked in the toy chest was one which consisted of several dozen cards, each bearing the likeness of a person one might conceivably have met on the streets of a big city in America in the 1890s. It ought to have been called Civil Status: if you drew a minister or a doctor you took three counters, if a lawyer or a banker, two, if a barber, one, while if your card turned out to bear the picture of a wife beater or an assassin, you were required to pay in three. All this seemed logical enough. But there were other neutral cards which, involving neither payment nor collection, struck me as superfluous and thus suspect. Why had they been included in the deck? They did not look neutral at all; they looked malignant (as indeed did all of the characters, the honoured ones only slightly less than the others). These questionable people included an alderman, a druggist, and a tall formidable creature, wearing eyeglasses and dressed in a black cloak, labelled 'Strong-minded Woman'. I would study the picture of her as she advanced frowning along a street under trees. To me she was the most evil-looking of the whole lot.

'Mother, what's a strong-minded woman?'

'Well, your Grandmother Bowles is a strong-minded woman.'

'Why is it bad?'

'Bad? It's not bad at all. It's very good.'

'But why doesn't she pay anything, then? And why does she look so awful? Look at her!'

I was glad whenever it was Mother who drew the card.

Ostensibly to distinguish my father's parents from Grampa and Gramma, I was taught to call them Daddypapa and Daddymama. As if they had not been for ever separated by the atmospheres of their respective houses! The farm was fully inhabited; the family left no emptinesses. But going into the Bowles house was like stepping inside a forest. There in the dimness and silence Daddymama and Daddypapa were sitting reading their books, he in his den upstairs and she in her study downstairs. The kitchen was cut off from the rest of the house, and I would go there and talk with old Mary, who had been doddering around the kitchen for many years, and her niece Lucy. They paid attention to everything I said, and they never offered suggestions for my improvement. But inevitably I would be sent for. Daddymama, sitting beside the fireplace, would remove her pince-nez and smile at me with an expression both benevolent and disapproving. I knew she loved me; I also understood perfectly that she was not disapproving of me myself, but of my mother in me. This seemed natural: since Mother was not of her family, she would feel hostility toward her. What I resented was the fact that Mother was afraid of Daddymama, dreaded being with her, and occasionally became so ill in her presence that she had to go to bed. But these things were natural phenomena, like the sequence of the seasons, and certainly did not preoccupy me. I could see that the world of grown-ups was one of distrust and intrigue, and I felt fortunate to be a child, so as not to have to take part in it.

Just before the War of 1914 Daddymama had gone to Paris and returned with very impressive clothes. I remember her pleasure in pointing out what she called the 'exquisite workmanship' to the ladies who visited her. When I asked Mother the inevitable question, 'Why don't you go to Paris and get things, too?' she merely laughed. I pressed her for an answer, and she said, 'Mercy, I don't want Paris clothes! Besides, it'll be a long time before your father'll be able to send me to Paris. Daddymama was very fortunate to have gone when she did.'

Daddypapa and Daddymama were like everyone else who lived on West Church Street in Elmira, save for the fact that neither of them had any religious affiliations. Daddypapa said that religion was a very good thing for those who wanted it. For Daddymama it was a private matter; she read Theosophical texts. Undoubtedly her thinking was influenced by her sister Mary and her brother Charles, who were both immersed in what they called the occult sciences.

Aunt Mary lived in Watkins Glen in a big old house known as Holden Hall, and Uncle Charles had a large property at Glenora, nine miles up the shore of Seneca Lake. Thus the three were able to see one another often and compare notes on their respective readings and meditations. Uncle Charles was an exponent of yoga, and at some point he convinced Daddypapa that proper breathing enabled one to inhale prana along with the air. This was surprising inasmuch as Daddypapa was not given to esoteric interpretations; however, he immediately decided that what I needed was more prana. (He even went so far as to suggest that prana could take the place of food when one was hungry.) I was obliged to learn to breathe by stopping and unstopping my nostrils with my fingers. This struck me as arbitrary and wholly absurd, like all the other things invented by the family in order to make my life more unpleasant.

Very early I understood that I would always be kept from doing what I enjoyed and forced to do that which I did not. The Bowles family took it for granted that pleasure was destructive, whereas engaging in an unappealing activity aided in character formation. Thus I became an expert in the practice of deceit, at least in so far as general mien and facial expressions were concerned. I could not make myself lie, inasmuch as for me the word and its literal meaning had supreme importance, but I could feign enthusiasm for what I disliked and, even more essential, hide whatever enjoyment I felt. Obviously this did not always give the desired results, but it often helped to deflect attention from me, and this was already a great victory. For attention meant 'discipline'; each person was eager to try out his own favourite system on me and study the results. Once Daddymama had a woman come and talk with me for two hours. She was a nice woman; I felt at ease with her and conversed as freely as any other child of six. At the end, without waiting for me to go out of the room, she turned to Daddymama and said, 'He has a very old soul, almost too old. You can only wait and see.' It seems there never was a time when the Bowles family were not wont to sit discussing my defects. 'It's not natural', was the commonest introductory phrase. 'It's not natural for a child that age to spend all his time reading.' 'It's not natural for a child to want to be alone.' I even heard Daddymama remark one day to Mother, 'It's not natural for a child of his age to have such thick lips.' (This I resented more deeply than her customary criticisms, since I knew I had my mother's mouth. If I was a monster, then Mother also was a monster, and why didn't Daddymama tell her so outright, instead of using me as the weapon?)

Daddymama had a crooked, sardonic smile, by which she made it clear that she accepted what one said, but with certain strict reservations whose terms she kept to herself. Mother said, 'Your grandmother Bowles is the most *suspicious* woman I've ever seen. And your father is just like her. Don't ever let yourself get to be like them. It's terrible! It poisons everything.'

Of my four grandparents, Daddypapa was the one who most interested me. He had mystery; with his bushy white moustache and his eyeglasses that clipped to the bridge of his nose, he sat alone in his den all day reading. Occasionally he reached for his penknife and cut an article from a magazine or newspaper. He had a filing cabinet full of clippings, most of them about the 'Amerind', which was what he called the natives of the Western Hemisphere. The den was stuffed with books: bookshelves covered the walls up to the ceiling, fully a third of the volumes in French. At some point in his life Daddypapa had decided to learn French so as to be able to read Hugo and Dumas and Balzac in the original. Later, when he was in his seventies, he took up Spanish and continued to study and read that language for the rest of his life. He was a fanatical cat fancier and had decorated his big desk with framed photographs, not of people but of cats he had known.

I would enter the den, he would greet me genially in French and motion to me to sit by his desk, and on the desk I would see a whole collection of pictures and objects which he had brought out of the cupboards and drawers, with the intention of showing them to me the next time I came into the room.

Daddypapa had fought in the Civil War, but he refused to call it that; for him it was either 'the war' or 'the War of the Rebellion'. He was proud of having been in every state of the Union. 'There were some years when I never slept twice in the same town,' he told me. The perfect life, I thought; I too would collect mysterious Indian objects on my way and tales from each part of the country.

We never stayed long in Elmira but continued after a few days to Glenora, on Seneca Lake, where Daddypapa had three separate properties, each with a house ready to live in. It never occurred to me to wonder why he should keep three houses in the same community; I suppose originally he meant to have one for each of his sons and one for himself. About the end of the First World War Uncle Shirley took his family to

Los Angeles, and Daddypapa sold Red Rough, which left Horseshoe Cabin and the Boat House.

Seneca is a long, narrow glacial lake. High shale cliffs edge its southern end. The Boat House had three levels: the boat shed, where the slips for the boats were; the kitchen and servant's room; and finally the living quarters at the top, full of Navajo rugs and blankets and with big Chinese lanterns hanging from the crossbeams. The west wall of each story had been left unbuilt, and the rough shale stuck out into the rooms. Two more flights of stairs had to be climbed before you came to terra firma, and then you were in the woods. It was a dark wood, but one free of undergrowth because its hemlocks had been shedding their needles for many years. A thick blanket of them padded the ground everywhere. Overnight strange things could push up through the blanket: puffballs, Dutchman's-pipes, fungi like slabs of orange flesh, colonies of spotted toadstools, and best of all the deadly *Amanita*, which I was taught early to distinguish. I would seek out an *Amanita* and stand staring down at it in fascination and terror. There at my feet grew death itself, only waiting for the decisive contact.

At night there were skunks and owls abroad, and the unceasing song of the katydids almost covered the patterned murmur of the waves against the cliffs. It was good to wake up in the night and hear that music all around me in the air, while the embers in the fireplace slowly settled and died.

Two boats were moored down in the shed: a large open motor launch and a cabin cruiser with accommodations for eight. This was the *Aloha*, which Uncle Charles had bought in New York and piloted through the Hudson River and the Erie Canal to Geneva, at the foot of the lake. The *Aloha* had a toilet that flushed and a galley with sink and stove, so that real meals, not just picnic fare, could be served aboard. Being good New Englanders, the family felt that it should be taken out only when there were guests to entertain, and accordingly used the open motorboat for everyday rides and picnics. Daddypapa never went on picnics. He called them 'pleasure exertions' and was content to sit reading all day and eat alone at the Boat House. On the beach outside the boat shed there were two rowboats and a canoe, kept under tarpaulin. Eventually I was allowed to go out alone in the flat-bottomed rowboat and finally in the canoe.

One of my pastimes was the invention of lists of place-names; I considered them stations on an imaginary railway, for which I would then draw a map and prepare a timetable. In Glenora the idea occurred to me to carry the fantasy partially into reality: I printed the proper names on small slips of paper and deposited them, each one held down by a slab of shale, at what seemed the proper spot for each, along the paths in the woods. As I had expected, as soon as my father caught sight of them, he came to me and demanded that I go immediately and retrieve every piece of paper. Daddypapa then suggested that they be allowed to remain until the following day. Pulling at his moustache and looking amused, he added that the name I had given the edge of the creek (dry these several weeks owing to a much-discussed drought) was Notninrivo.

Surprisingly, my father chuckled and turned to me. 'So you called the creek Notninrivo, eh? That's pretty good.'

'What's that?' said Mother.

'Nothing in the river,' he explained.

This was their own invention, crass and ridiculous. 'That's not what it means,' I objected.

Now Daddy's face became hostile. 'What do you mean, that's not what it means? What does it mean, then?'

I hung my head. It seemed impossible to explain that Notninrivo was merely the name of the preceding station spelled backward. 'You wouldn't understand,' I said.

'Will you listen to the conceited little rotter?' he cried, beside himself. 'Let's get to the bottom of this! He says the word means something else. I want to know what!'

He seized me and shook me. I hung my head still more.

'For heaven's sake, Claude, let the child alone,' said Daddy-mama. 'He hasn't done anything wrong.'

'It's all affectation!' he snapped. 'It's just a bid for attention.' Even as he said the words, I was aware of the awful irony in the situation. He went on shaking me. 'Come on, what does it mean?'

I shook my head. I wanted to say, 'I'll never tell you.'

Instead, I waited a moment and finally said, 'Nothing.'

He let go of me, disgusted, having proved his point. Shortly afterward I ran up into the woods and gathered all the station signs, starting with the one at the end of the bridge over the creek for Notninrivo and another one by a rotten tree stump a little further along the path, this one for the town of O'Virninton. I had to destroy them in secret, for fear my father might discover the meaning of Notninrivo, which he must definitely never know. I carried the scraps of paper to a hidden cove down the shore and burned them. Then I ground the ashes into the wet shingle and piled several flat rocks on top of the spot.

When I was a baby, Max Eastman and his sister Crystal stayed at Glenora each summer. Mother had always had enormous admiration for Max. 'Handsome as a prince and bright as a whip,' she said of him. 'And knows it,' added Daddy sourly. For more than twenty years the Eastmans stayed away from Glenora. (In 1937 Max came back for a short stay, and I saw him then. At that time I was a Stalinist sympathizer, which, considering the fact that he was the most vocal Trotskyist of the period, made an exchange of opinion inevitable. We got on to the subject of Kautsky, Kamenev, and Zinoviev. It was obvious that I knew nothing save what I had read in party publications. Daddy sat listening, an expression of mingled amusement and disdain on his face. Presently he turned to Max and said, 'Listen to that, will you? You'd think he'd been brought up in the slums of a factory town.' Max laughed. 'No, I wouldn't, Claude. I'd think he was the son of a Long Island dentist.')

Daddymama had a friend named Dorothy Baldwin who often came to Glenora. Dorothy used bay rum as perfume, insisting that she preferred the scent to anything on the market. 'She was always unstable,' said Daddymama, 'but now she's simply degenerated into an out-and-out radical.' 'I feel sorry for the poor girl,' Mother declared. 'She's disappointed in life, that's all.' Dorothy didn't seem disappointed to me; she seemed very sure of herself. One afternoon she asked me if I wanted to take a walk with her. I liked her, and we started out.

We had not gone far up the road before she turned into the waist-high vegetation and began flailing her way through it. 'The path is further on,' I told her. She grinned at me. 'We're going to make our own path,' she said. 'It's no fun to follow somebody else's.' We helped each other get free of brambles every few minutes and made very little progress. At one point I plunged ahead of her and was suddenly attacked by wasps. We got out the way we had gone in. When we returned to the Boat House, I discovered eleven stings.

After Dorothy had left, the family turned to me as one person and expressed the hope that I had learned something from the escapade. Then they formulated the lesson: it was safer to stay on paths, literally and figuratively. The moralizing had its effect on me, albeit in the opposite direction from the one they intended. I knew that Dorothy and I had accepted implicitly the dangers of the walk and that it was not her fault that the wasps had stung me. Vaguely I understood that laws were made to keep you from doing what you wanted to do. Furthermore, I understood that for my family the prohibition itself was the supreme good, because it entailed the sublimation of personal desire. Their attempt to impose this concept was only one of numerous strategies for bolstering their power over me. They had an idea of how they wanted me to be; but in so far as I resembled it, I should remain subjugated to them, or so it seemed to me then. So, secretly I rejected every suggestion while pretending to accept it.

Mother had a thick green book, stuffed with clippings and notes, which she generally kept with her, even when she sat crocheting, and which she consulted several times a day. It was called *Child Psychology*; for some reason I could not fathom, she did not want me to look at it, and so it was not put out with the other books. The author was a Dr Riker, a man for whose opinions Daddy had only contempt. There were passionate arguments between them over the value and application of the doctor's ideas, for their theories on child-rearing were antithetical. Mother believed in showing infinite patience; Daddy was for unremitting firmness. This he called common sense. 'It stands to reason,' he maintained. 'A kid will always go as far as you let him.' Both of them, however, overlooked the fact that at the age of five I had never yet even spoken to another child or seen children playing together. My idea of the world was still that of a place inhabited exclusively by adults.

Paul Bowles's Books Published by Peter Owen

Dates in parentheses are the original dates of publication if not first published by Peter Owen

Novels

Let It Come Down (1952), first published by Peter Owen in hardback 1984

The Sheltering Sky (1949), first published by Peter Owen in hardback 1981

The Spider's House (1955), first published by Peter Owen in hardback 1985

Too Far From Home (novella, with illustrations by Marguerite McBey) (1991), first published by Peter Owen in hardback 1994; paperback edition published 1994

Up Above the World (1966), first published by Peter Owen in hardback 1967; paperback edition published 2000

Stories

Call at Corazón, collection first published by Peter Owen in hardback 1988

Contents: Call at Corazón (1946); At Paso Rojo (1947); Doña Faustina (1949); Under the Sky (1946); The Echo (1946); An Inopportune Visit (1986); Tea on the Mountain (1939); The Successor (1950); The Hours After Noon (1950); The Frozen Fields (1957); Sylvie Ann, the Boogie Man (1958); Monologue, Tangier 1975 (1982); Monologue, New York 1965 (1984); Monologue, Massachusetts 1932 (1983); In Absentia (1985); Hugh Harper (1984); Dinner at Sir Nigel's (1985)

Midnight Mass, collection first published by Peter Owen in hardback 1985; paperback edition 1999

Contents: Midnight Mass; The Little House; Mejdoub; The Dismissal; Here to Learn; Allal; The Husband; Reminders of Bouselham; Afternoon with Antaeus; Madame and Ahmed; The Fqih; The Empty Amulet; The Waters of Isli; Kitty; Bouayad and the Money; Rumour and a Ladder; The Eye; At the Krungthep Plaza; You Have Left Your Lotus Pods on the Bus; In the Red Room

Pages from Cold Point, collection first published by Peter Owen in hardback 1968

Contents: Pages from Cold Point (1949); The Time of Friendship (1968); The Hyena (1962); He of the Assembly (1960); The Garden (1964); The Story of Lahcen and Idir (1960); The Delicate Prey (1949); A Friend of the World (1961); The Wind at Beni Midar (1962)

A Thousand Days for Mokhtar, collection first published by Peter Owen in hardback 1989
Contents: How Many Midnights (1947); You Are Not I (1948); Julian Vreden (1984); If I Should Open My Mouth (1952); Unwelcome Words (1985); The Fourth Day Out from Santa Cruz (1949); Pastor Dowe at Tacaté (1946); The Circular Valley (1948); The Scorpion (1944); Señor Ong and Señor Ha (1947); Tapiama (1957); By the Water (1945); A Thousand Days for Mokhtar (1948); A Distant Episode (1945)

Non-fiction

Points in Time, first published by Peter Owen in hardback 1982; paperback edition 1990

Their Heads Are Green, first published by Peter Owen in hardback 1963; paperback edition 2000
Contents: Fish Traps and Private Business; All Parrots Speak; Notes Mailed at Nagercoil; A Man Must Not Be Very Moslem; Africa Minor; The Rif, to Music; Baptism of Solitude; The Route to Tassemsit

Two Years Beside the Strait: Tangier Journal 1987–9, first published by Peter Owen in hardback 1989; paperback edition 1990

Without Stopping (autobiography) (1972), first published by Peter Owen in hardback 1972

Translations

From the Arabic

For Bread Alone by Mohamed Choukri, first published by Peter Owen in hardback 1973

From the French

The Oblivion Seekers (1972) by Isabelle Eberhardt, first published by Peter Owen in paperback 1988

From the Moghrebi

The Big Mirror by Mohammed Mrabet, first published by Peter Owen in paperback 1989

The Lemon by Mohammed Mrabet, first published by Peter Owen in hardback 1969

Look and Move On (1976) by Mohammed Mrabet, first published by Peter Owen in hardback 1989

Love with a Few Hairs by Mohammed Mrabet, first published by Peter Owen in hardback 1967

M'Hashish (1969) by Mohammed Mrabet, first published by Peter Owen in paperback 1988

From the Spanish

The Beggar's Knife by Rodrigo Rey Rosa, first published by Peter Owen in paperback 1988

Dust on Her Tongue by Rodrigo Rey Rosa, first published by Peter Owen in hardback 1989

The Pelcari Project by Rodrigo Rey Rosa, first published by Peter Owen in hardback 1991

Books by Jane Bowles published by Peter Owen

Two Serious Ladies (novel) (1943), first published by Peter Owen in hardback 1965

Plain Pleasures (stories), first published by Peter Owen in hardback 1966
Contents: Plain Pleasures; Everything Is Nice; A Guatemalan Idyll; Camp Cataract; A Day in the Open; A Quarrelling Pair; A Stick of Green Candy

The Collected Works of Jane Bowles (1970), first published by Peter Owen in hardback 1984
Contents: Two Serious Ladies (novel); In the Summer House (play); Plain Pleasures (collection); Andrew; Emmy Moore's Journal; Going to Massachusetts; From the Notebooks: The Iron Table; Lila and Frank; Friday (stories)

Paul and Jane Bowles titles published in paperback by Penguin Books 1999–2000

Paul Bowles

The Sheltering Sky
Stories (twenty-three stories taken from all four Peter Owen collections)

Jane Bowles

Plain Pleasures
Two Serious Ladies